THE DAY
YOU LEFT

ISBN: 1530335183
ISBN 13: 9781530335183
Library of Congress Control Number: 2016903989
CreateSpace Independent Publishing Platform
North Charleston, South Carolina

For Gary.
I love you, forever.

ACKNOWLEDGEMENTS

I may be more nervous about forgetting to thank someone than I am about finally publishing this book. There are so many people who helped me along the way. First, I want to thank my good friend, Jamie McGough, for encouraging me to do it in the first place and follow a passion that had been forgotten.

To all of my early-draft readers for your input, your encouragement, and your investment in Adam & Ellie: Bridget Campbell, Linda Heller, Cindy Cook, Cathy Perna, Anne Bondi, Lisa Cimmino, Karen Frost, and Debbie Skok Snyder. Thank you to my brother-in-law and fellow writer, Kirby Olson, for plodding through the reading of a women's fiction book, for your insight, and editing advice. Thank you to Melissa Shanley Yetter for advising me on how to write the hospital scenes in this book. If I got it wrong, it wasn't her fault. And to my sister, Stacey Kelly, thank you not only for reading my drafts, but also for being a sister, best friend, and the other half of our dynamic duo.

Thanks to Julie Luongo for her countless edits, advice, encouragement, and just for being an awesome person and writer; and thanks to Tom Shiffer for making the connection between us. Thank you to Chelsea Kuhel for her encouragement and her contributions to editing. To Sarah Hansen, thank you for the most beautiful book cover I could have hoped for.

And at last, thank you to Gary, Mitchell, and Meredith for everything. I'm happy to share my life with you every day.

To Anita,
Enjoy!! ☺
xo Jen

THE DAY
YOU LEFT

a novel

J. Renee Olson

Nearly two months ago, early December

ADAM

A dam fumbled in the dark, then dressed in an old pair of blue jeans and a faded long sleeve t-shirt he found strewn on the bedroom floor. Caitlin, the babysitter he never met who woke him from a deep sleep, claimed Ellie had gone out around eight and, not only had she not returned, but she was entirely MIA.

"I'm sorry to bother you this late, but, uh, Mrs. Thomas was supposed to be back by now, and I only have a junior license. I can't drive after eleven."

He grabbed a coat and his keys and drove to his house—his old house . . . the one he lived in before she kicked him out—and dialed Ellie's cell phone for the fourth time. Again, she didn't answer. His mind clouded, encased in a fog of fear and anger.

He had no choice but to chauffeur Caitlin home, and that meant waking his sleeping children. He opened the door to Lizzie's room and sighed at the sight of her tiny body wrapped in a pink blanket. Blonde curls fell over the soft skin of her chubby cheek. He lifted her from bed, and she cuddled against his chest as he walked toward Tommy's room. Groggy and confused, Tommy protested all the way to the car. Adam's heart sank under an invisible, crushing weight as he strapped them both into car seats and seatbelts.

The winter air had quickly cooled the BMW's interior. He flipped a switch, demanding full heat, and kept the radio off so as not to wake the kids again. Other than warm air blasting through chrome-painted vents, the drive to Caitlin's house was quiet. Adam sat rigid against the seat back, his hands firm on the steering wheel. He tried to remind himself to cut the kid a break, but when Caitlin attempted a conversation he merely responded with a muffled, "yah sure."

He returned to his former home and, after tucking the kids into their beds, spent the next three hours nervously perched on his former couch, unsuccessfully trying to phone his estranged wife, wondering for the millionth time how things between them had become this bad. Buster, their chocolate Labrador retriever, sat staring at him. All Adam could do was stare back.

At three in the morning, panic set in. All things considered, Ellie had never been so irresponsible. Adam phoned the police station, but was told he couldn't file a missing persons report for at least twenty-four hours. Yah sure, he knew the standard, canned response. So did anyone with a television.

He phoned every hospital he could think of, but no, there were no patients named Ellen Thomas, no Jane Doe's matching Ellie's description.

He turned his cell phone over in his hand, again and again, the plastic case rolling and rubbing against the uncalloused skin of his palm and fingers. Then he punched in Sam's number, hoping he'd have a connection, a way to get information that Adam somehow didn't.

Again, no.

Nothing.

Even the bars were closed.

Where could she possibly be? The question, in maddening repetition, skipped in his mind for hours.

A clock on the mantel ticked, cutting through the late-night silence. Every minute was torture, his mind producing one disastrous scenario after another. The mother of his children could be lying somewhere, left for dead. Or, she could've finally become what she claimed to hate most—her own mother. He couldn't stomach either thought.

He was still planted on the oversized beige couch when the first rays of early morning sun fingered their way into the living room. He'd long ago lost track of how many times he'd rung Ellie's phone.

He was tired. He was angry. He was worried. And he felt . . . numb.

As promised, Caitlin and her mother, Judith, returned shortly after dawn to retrieve Caitlin's car.

He opened the door to greet them, and Judith's face lengthened as she took in his haggard appearance. The morning sun at her back cast a halo around her glossy, dark red hair. A gust of wind lifted the scent of her perfume—fresh, like spring rain and flowers—and Adam was overcome by a longing for the sweet jasmine scent of Ellie.

"No word?" she asked.

He shook his head and rubbed at his face, abrasive new stubble scraping against his hands, and they followed him inside.

Judith rested her palm on his forearm and insisted on calling local hospitals and police stations one last time. Adam shoved his hands into his jeans pockets as he watched her dial. He listened as she tried, and failed, to keep an upbeat tone. No doubt, she'd come up empty-handed, just as he had.

He wondered what to tell the kids?

He fell back onto the couch, raked a hand through his dark hair, and released a heavy sigh. Leaning forward, he dropped his elbows onto his knees and hung his head.

"Go look for her," Judith said, kneeling in front of him. "I'll stay with Tommy and Lizzie." Adam's blue eyes roamed her freckled face, masked with worry.

Caitlin slowly paced the floor at the far side of the room, pretending to be interested in book-filled shelves that spanned the length of the wall.

He wanted to cry, and he wanted to scream. He didn't even know where to begin. Before he could decide, the mudroom door opened and slammed shut with a thud. His heart skipped at the familiar sound. *Ellie.*

Her brown hair was a knotted mess, her silk top beyond wrinkled. A knee-length black rayon skirt was twisted sideways at her waist. Her legs and feet were bare. In her right hand, she held a set of full-length, high-heeled, patent leather boots. In a bizarre way, they reminded him of Catwoman.

Adam stood, his blue eyes still staring in disbelief. Through bloodshot vision, he wondered if he was dreaming her return, initially unable to decipher reality from the many circumstances that swam through his wearied mind over the last several hours.

But Ellie's expression quickly transformed from shock to anger—the same anger Adam had become so accustomed to of late. She stepped closer, intently eying both Adam and Judith. Dark makeup was smeared around her brown eyes—eyes that once seemed so familiar, and now seemed so distant.

Judith scrambled to her feet, and she and Caitlin both offered a hurried and awkward goodbye, but Ellie's steely eyes remained on Adam, trained to burn a hole straight through his flesh.

"What are you doing in my house?" Hatred seeped from every pore of her pale white skin.

"*Your* house?" he parroted, struggling to comprehend how quickly his concern for her absence was dismissed, transformed into the scene unraveling before him.

Her eyes narrowed until they were tiny slits. "You never helped before. No need to start now, Adam."

The sarcasm in her voice brought a surge of rage that surprised him. "I might be the one asking questions, Ellie. You're the one who's been out all night doing"—he waved an accusatory hand in her direction—"God knows what. We've been worried—calling hospitals and the police! You left our children for God's sake!"

She rolled her eyes and mumbled something.

"What?" he snapped, taking a step forward, challenging her.

"The kids are just fine," she replied, louder than necessary.

He crossed his arms against his chest and glanced out the window. When he returned his attention to her, he shook his head in disgust. In less than five minutes, relief had been replaced with rapidly mounting anger and hostility normally foreign to his amicable, Midwestern-bred nature.

"You've changed, El. I know that, but I never thought you to be so shallow. I hope your tryst was worth it."

Squaring off her shoulders, she marched toward him. She stabbed her finger into his chest with every abrupt word. "Get. The. Hell. Out." She spat the fragmented sentence with an icy hatred, making him crumple inside.

"Yah, sure." He plucked his coat from the sofa. Cold winter air lashed out and stung his fiery cheeks as he slammed the door behind him and headed toward the car.

PART I

For Better or Worse

CHAPTER 1

Late January

ELLIE

The surface against Ellie's back was cold, and thin paper crunched under her skin as she slid closer to the bottom of the table in Dr. Van Linden's office. She stared at the ceiling, twirled the gold wedding band on her finger, and wondered why she hadn't removed the ring yet. After all, Adam had been gone for two months.

Filled with sadness, she closed her eyes and allowed Adam to pervade her mind. The day they met, his smile and Minnesota accent immediately melted her heart—a memory forever seared into the archives of her brain. She squeezed her eyes tightly, took a deep breath, and tried to relax. But she couldn't focus on Dr. Van Linden's small talk.

What would Adam think now, if he knew she was sick? Would he come back to her? Ellie's hand clenched at her side. She didn't want his pity.

She watched the nurse step away from Dr. Van Linden's side and cross the room. The scent of powder and rose petals lingered in her wake. The smell, familiar from so long ago, was intoxicating and nauseating at the same time. She was instantly flooded with unexpected vivid memories of her mother. Memories she's spent a lifetime trying to forget.

Her chest tightened, and her eyes flew open. She propped herself up on her elbows to face the nurse. "Excuse me, what's that perfume you're wearing?"

The nurse's eyebrows knitted together in confusion. "We don't wear perfume here, dear."

Before Ellie could respond, Dr. Van Linden stood, told her to dress, and left her alone in the room.

She shuddered and rubbed a shaky, sweaty palm against her legs as she walked to retrieve her clothes from a small chair nestled in the corner of the tiny room. It had been more than thirty years . . . long enough to think the memories wouldn't still have the same effect.

Her reflection flashed in a tiny mirror she was sure hung on the wall for the sole purpose of taunting her. She paused and watched her shoulders drop. *Ugh.* Her father, old and tired from years of hard, labor-intensive work, stared back at her from her own round eyes. Gold speckles that used to sprinkle the brown seemed to have faded and gone dim. A wild hair stood at attention at the top of her head. Brown hair that was once a glossy milk chocolate now looked more like dried mud mixed with coarse strands of gray that reminded her of dreary winter sky.

She reached up and yanked the unruly hair from her scalp before she finished dressing, careful to avoid any further interaction with the mirror.

Minutes felt like hours before Dr. Van Linden reentered the room with a warm smile. Fighting the nervous energy filling her like a balloon, Ellie deliberately forced her stiffly held shoulders to relax.

Dr. Van Linden had been her doctor since she became pregnant with her first child, Tommy, now seven years old. Three years ago, he delivered Lizzie. His bald head, hazel eyes, and fair skin were familiar and comforting. She's always trusted him and never questioned his judgment.

Until now.

"Ellie, I know I asked before, but are you *sure* there's no chance you may be pregnant?" Dr. Van Linden asked in his Dutch accent. He raised a single brow, his face set with the determination and certainty of someone who knew the end of a story he hadn't read yet.

Ellie huffed and shifted her weight. "No way."

I'm forty-one years old for Christ's sake.

She fought to suppress the fear coursing through her veins. She was just here two weeks ago, surely she was driving Dr. Van Linden crazy, but she *knew* there was something wrong—something far worse than menopause, or perimenopause, or whatever he suggested was wrong the last time. Pregnant would be bad, but she was definitely not pregnant. Pregnant wasn't even possible at the moment.

"Ellie?" Dr. Van Linden asked.

She looked up to meet Dr. Van Linden's inquisitive eyes and defensively wrapped her arms around her chest.

"I think we should do a test, just to be sure." He flipped through her chart, reminding her that she was exhibiting the common signs of pregnancy: intermittent menstrual cycle, mood swings, trouble sleeping . . .

His voice faded in the background. Her pulse quickened, and she found herself nervously running two fingers against her soft, cotton sweater. She was exhausted in every possible way. The nightmares didn't help. They started after Adam left. She considered telling Dr. Van Linden she couldn't sleep because of them, but the thought was fleeting.

" . . . and lastly, weight gain." Dr. Van Linden tossed her file onto the counter with a loud thump, and Ellie jumped, startled.

"You weighed in five pounds heavier today than you did two weeks ago," he said. "You've been nauseous, too. And vomiting, yes?"

Ellie looked down, recalling the gradually increasing ring of flab across her middle section. She struggled to control the mixture of anger and tears bubbling inside her core.

"I just feel . . . sick . . . most of the time. Something *else* has to be wrong." She pushed a section of brown hair behind her ear and shook her head. "There's *no* way I can be pregnant! I've . . . I've bled! I've had periods, even though they're not regular." She fixed her eyes on Dr. Van Linden with the defiance of a young child. "How do you explain *that?*"

Dr. Van Linden laughed. "Pappekak," he said with unnerving nonchalance.

"What?" Ellie asked, confused.

"Nonsense. Rubbish." Dr. Van Linden waved his hand dismissively. "These things are tricky, but there's always a chance, and some bleeding is perfectly normal during pregnancy. Let's just do the test and see."

Ellie's jaw tightened. How do you tell your doctor—the one who stood at the end of your bed and delivered your babies—that you now have a failed marriage, that your life has been void of sex since your husband moved out three months ago—especially since you have a hard time admitting it to yourself?

"Ellie?" Dr. Van Linden peered at her over gold-rimmed eyeglasses. "But—"

The palm of his hand shot up, stopping her. "It'll make *me* feel better." The firmness of his tone was final.

Ellie huffed and dropped her shoulders dramatically. "Fine. I'll pee in a cup," she mumbled, tired of arguing, aggravated at the irritable impatience rising in her chest.

Dr. Van Linden nodded. "Good. I'll send the nurse in." Ellie wanted to scream at the way he said *good*—the o's, accentuated with his Dutch accent.

Not güd, she thought as she watched him leave the room.

She usually considered his Dutchy-kind-of-way to be charming and maybe even soothing—the way vowels were often emphasized and w's that sound like v's—but not now. No. No. No!

Not güd. Not güd. Not güd!

Fifteen minutes later, when the doctor returned, Ellie was standing impatiently at the edge of the exam table, purse on her arm, glancing at the clock on the wall.

Dr. Van Linden peered at the chart in his hand and shook his head, and Ellie's heart leapt into her throat.

Oh God . . .

She grabbed onto the edge of the table in an effort to steady herself.

My kids are going to grow up without a mom.

Just like me.

Dr. Van Linden looked up, and his face filled with sudden alarm.

"Ellie, you're white as a sheet."

"Do I have . . . " It was hard to swallow. Hard to breathe. Hard to force the word through her vocal chords. She finally managed a whisper, " . . . Cancer?"

"Wha—? Why would you think *that?*" Dr. Van Linden laughed, and Ellie wondered what could be so funny in a moment in which she found no humor.

"Ellie," he said, a smile stretched across his face, "as I suspected, you're having a baby. The test was positive. Let's see," he said, glancing at some papers, "it's January twenty-fourth. We aren't sure exactly when conception took place, but I think the baby should come somewhere around August . . . "

The rest of Dr. Van Linden's words were muffled, and Ellie could see two of him, but she was unable to talk. Her legs were weak and unstable, her head was heavy, and her body tingled. Everything was decelerating. Even her breathing seemed to be entering a state of slow motion. Despite her best efforts, each inhale and exhale was shallower than the one before.

It was a feeling . . .

. . . she couldn't . . .

. . . quite . . .

. . . place . . .

CHAPTER 2

ADAM

Adam pulled a frozen dinner from the microwave, and steam escaping through the thin plastic film singed his fingertips. Instinctively, his hand flinched, and a string of uncharacteristic curse words escaped his lips as he watched the paper dish fall to the floor. He raked his uninjured hand through his dark brown hair and sighed.

Perfect—no dinner and now a mess.

He yanked a spoon out of a drawer and ladled the spilled green beans—and whatever that meat was supposed to be—back onto the plastic tray and tossed it into the garbage. The less than appetizing smell in his kitchen reminded him of a high school cafeteria. Certainly not like Ellie's hotdishes.

With a handful of paper towels, he mopped up the gooey mess and tossed it into the trash before yanking open the refrigerator. Eight bottles of beer, a moldy block of cheese, and a chunk of bread that could be used as a hockey puck. No choice necessary.

Effortlessly, he popped the top on a pale ale and watched it spin on the counter until it settled. He replaced the magnetic bottle opener on the freezer door. It came with the furnished apartment. It was the only thing hanging on the white door then, and it remained the only thing hanging there now. No cheerful pictures of a bright yellow sunshine above pink and purple flowers colored by Lizzie were hung. There were no happy memories captured by family photos. He took a long swig and wondered what Ellie and the kids were doing for dinner.

Ellie.

He missed her food. Her laugh. Her humor.

And her warmth beside him in bed at night.

The old Ellie, that was.

He closed his eyes, and the smiling, chubby faces of his children appeared in the darkness as vividly as if they were standing in front of him. His shoulders slumped forward, and his chest tightened.

He missed seeing Tommy at the kitchen counter in the morning with his unruly, thick, dirty blond hair, as he attempted to eat cereal and proceeded to spill half of it on the counter. His heart ached when he recalled the way Lizzie ran for the front door to greet him when he arrived home each night, screeching with joy, her golden curls bouncing up and down.

Again, he pushed a hand through his own dark hair. Staring at nothing in particular, he wondered if Tommy and Lizzie's hair would darken with time as his did.

He even missed the endless chatter at the dinner table, the negotiations with Tommy to finish his vegetables that would sometimes last more than an hour.

He had seen the kids, of course, although it wasn't the same. They'd gone for ice cream, for dinner, for walks in the park. Lucky for him, neither Tommy nor Lizzie had asked for an explanation. If he had to guess, he'd bet they were happy enough just to see him and have fun while they were at it. To some extent he was too, and he was glad not to be faced with their questions because, frankly, he didn't like the answers. So he'd allowed the topic to go unaddressed. But the intimacy of not being with them at home, of not seeing them sleep in their beds and wake in the morning, had left another hole in his heart. He hadn't brought them to the apartment. Bringing them into a physical space that represented his life without Ellie—without their family unit—would make the reality of it all too concrete. He'd rather go on hoping it was all just a nightmare that would end when he finally woke up.

He walked a few steps to the living room and flopped his body onto the couch. Surrendering to fatigue, he allowed his head to fall back and his blue eyes to close. They instantly burned against his eyelids. The cushions under his broad, tall frame were soft, but his stiff muscles struggled to relax.

The fight had completely left him, not that he'd ever been much of a fighter. When he was a child, his aunt would tell him over and over, *'Adam, you need to confront things head on.'* But she didn't understand the Minnesota-nice with which he was bred. Confrontation was something he had never been comfortable with, and maybe that was the problem. Perhaps, he should've fought harder, yelled a little more, found a way to *make* Ellie see how much he loved her.

But he failed. And now it was too late.

Unfortunately for him, he was still in love with her. And that was the biggest problem of all.

He pressed a finger into his temple in response to his throbbing head. The thought that she didn't feel the same way made his eyes tighten and his chest constrict.

Her voice echoed inside his head, *"Just leave, Adam."*

He knew it was his fault, at least partially. A dreadful silence existed between them for far too long, but he couldn't recall when it started. In truth, he never saw it coming. He tried, over and over, to pinpoint exactly when things fell apart, but all he knew for sure was that now, at the age of forty-three, after seventeen years of marriage, he'd lost the most important thing in his life: his family.

Truth be told though, he wasn't even sure he knew Ellie anymore. She'd been volatile. A sweet nurturing nature, previously her calling card, seemed to have disappeared. Recent conversations had left him anxiously wondering which of her personalities he'd meet on any particular day. None of them seem friendly.

The day after he had to chaperone sixteen-year-old Caitlin home was the day a theoretical line in the sand had been clearly drawn between them. Any sense of the unity they'd shared for almost two decades seemed to have been severed in a single conversation that lasted only minutes.

Well, other than the day she kicked him out and he packed his bags.

For better or for worse, isn't that what they said? He thought he knew Ellie better than anyone. He thought she knew him. Yet he couldn't help but wonder what had happened to his wife. The question haunted him, robbed him of sleep, made it okay that he often went to bed hungry, for it was hard to tolerate the thought of food and the cold, empty bed that waited for him on the other side of the wall.

CHAPTER 3
ELLIE

Ellie stepped cautiously around boxes filling her cluttered attic in search of her scone pan. After emptying every item from every kitchen cabinet, she was sure it was there somewhere, in the midst of the bits and pieces collected over her adult lifetime with Adam.

Adam.

Unlike her, Adam was always a packrat. Now, here she was, in this large house with all of these *things*. And without him.

They were supposed to have four kids, enough to fill all five bedrooms. Adam could never understand how dreadful her experience with pregnancy was. He thought the joy and excitement of feeling the baby move should have made up for any discomfort.

Complications with Lizzie put them both in the hospital for nearly a week. Adam sat at the edge of Ellie's bed and stared at the bruises on her arm where they had to reinsert an IV under her skin. Antibiotics dripped through the tube, and a machine beeped in tandem with her pulse in the thick silence of the sterile room.

She couldn't look at him, so instead she focused her eyes on Lizzie who was finally asleep in the hospital bassinet a few feet away.

"I can't do it again," she said, her voice breaking. "Please don't ask me to."

Adam sighed, and she thought she heard tears interfering with his ability to speak. "I won't," he said.

He lied.

Within months, he seemed to have forgotten all about her complications. Over the next year, he brought up a third child often. Ellie stood her ground; she was done at two. She decided to stop getting frustrated with him, figuring that since he'd never have a uterus, he would never understand.

She was right; he would never understand.

She was wrong; she still got frustrated.

Wind hissed outside of the exposed rafters, and more cold air seeped into the unheated space. She pulled her sweater tighter against her body and continued to weave her way through the jumbled mess. She could only imagine the depth of Adam's disappointment once he learned she would now be filling another bedroom with a third child. One that didn't belong to him.

She lifted the dusty lid from a box to her right and stared at the contents in surprise. Invisible sharp needles pricked at her skin. They raced along her scalp, up her arms, down her back, even all the way to her feet, tucked into warm winter slippers.

She hadn't seen them in such a long time. She didn't care to now.

Leftover save the date cards from their wedding, neatly nestled in stacks tied with white satin ribbon, mocked her. The contrast between these beautifully printed cards and their relationship today hit her like a wall of thick fog, and she struggled to catch her breath. Blinking back a growing sense of melancholy, she reached out for the small ivory cardstock.

Save the date!
Ellen Anderson
and
Adam Thomas
Saturday, September 16 . . .

It was a lifetime ago, yet the memory was vivid. She could almost feel the smooth white calla lily petals under her fingers, the silk gown against her skin. She could smell the fragrant, flower-lined aisle as if she were walking toward Adam that very moment.

Adam, who had a smile wider than the Grand Canyon plastered to his face.

Adam, who left you.

She shook her head and pushed the box closed. Anger and regret boiled within her tiny frame.

She last visited the attic during the holidays when she pulled out decorations, all the while feeling angry and resentful rather than cheerful and festive at Christmastime. This year was even tougher than the first year without her mother—when she was still shell-shocked and grieving—before the resentment had set in.

＊＊＊

Even though he'd already moved out, and even after their ugly spat earlier that month—the night Caitlin babysat—Adam came and spent Christmas week in the spare room.

"For the kids," he had said.

"Okay, for the kids," she agreed.

Each day, he rose before the kids and went through the motions in an attempt to make things appear ordinary.

On Christmas morning, Ellie woke to the smell of coffee and pancakes wafting up the steps. She padded into the kitchen and found Tommy and Lizzie eating breakfast.

"It was the only way I could bribe them to wait for presents," Adam said, watching her eye their plates that perhaps should have been bowls, based on the amount of syrup their pancakes were swimming in. "We were waiting for you."

"I guess I was tired," she said in a defensive tone she didn't have time to consider.

"I know. That's why I told them not to wake you." He smiled and handed her a cup of coffee, made just the way she liked it.

She cradled the warm mug in her hand and felt herself relax. For an instant, she expected Adam to pull her toward him and hold her there, pressed against his chest for a few moments, like he used to. But instead, he winked and walked past her. He clapped his hands together, an echo booming through the kitchen. "Who wants to open presents?"

Tommy and Lizzie jumped from their stools and scrambled into the living room, Adam close behind. She fell into pace with them, but only after shaking off the nostalgia that crept up on her like a shadow at sunset.

The kids tore through their presents with fervor as they always did, until only one package remained. Tommy and Lizzie both ran to see who was lucky enough to still have something left.

"Oohhh!" Lizzie said, as they both turned to face Ellie. Within seconds, they were at her feet. "This one's for you Mommy," she said, as Tommy handed her the small box.

She turned to Adam, surprise etched in the lines of her face. It hadn't escaped her—the reminder that she and Adam had no gifts under the tree for one another—but she hadn't expected anything different, either.

"The kids were with me and, well . . . " He shrugged. "Open it."

She looked back down at the gold ribbon and tugged on it until it fell to the side. From inside the box, she pulled a scarf, swirled in her favorite shades of blues and tans that reminded her of the ocean, the material soft as a newborn baby's skin.

"I love it." She wrapped it around her neck to hide the lump that had grown in her throat. Her eyes trailed off into the distance, beyond where Adam was sitting. "I'm sorry, I didn't get you—"

"Don't worry about it." Adam shook his head and turned away. "Lizzie, how about some batteries in that dolly of yours?"

Lizzie shrieked, and they headed for the kitchen.

Ellie slid the scarf from her neck and sucked in a jagged breath before following them to prepare the turkey for the oven. She sliced carrots as Adam continued to fill one toy after another with batteries, struggling to open each compartment with various screwdrivers.

The kids played with their toys until they were exhausted, until Adam and Ellie were exhausted from the endless unpackaging, assembly-required, and directions that seemed to come with every gift. They ate dinner, made cinnamon buns, and watched *Rudolph the Red-Nosed Reindeer*, and Ellie found herself smiling. It didn't matter that wrapping paper was still strewn throughout the living room when the kids went to bed or that none of them had gotten out of their pajamas or even that one of Tommy's favorite toys was broken and would need to be exchanged. Nothing could dampen the happiness wrapped around her like a warm blanket. She kissed Lizzie goodnight and slipped into the bathroom, wondering if this was her very own Christmas miracle. She sniffed her pajama top, wondering if she should change. Or shower. Maybe things were going to be okay after all.

But then Adam knocked lightly at the door. Her smile faded as soon as she opened it. Adam had changed into a pair of jeans, and his duffle bag was packed, slung over his arm.

"You're going?" she asked in disbelief, trying to catch up to the swinging pendulum carrying her emotions.

Adam shrugged. "I have to sooner or later."

"But . . . " A million things she wanted to say coursed through her mind—that she didn't want him to go, that she should have bought him a present, that she *really* loved her scarf, maybe even that she wanted to wear it now, with nothing else, because she missed the warmth of his skin against hers, but she couldn't force any of those words to meet her lips. Instead, she shifted her weight and asked, "what will I tell the kids?"

Adam's body seemed to deflate as he exhaled. "Tell them I had to work." She watched him turn away and listened as the sound of his footsteps disappeared in the darkened hallway.

──┼ ┼──

The pendulum swung again, anger resurfacing at the memory. She had been naïve enough to think his intentions were more than just for show, but when Christmas was over, so was the charade. She shook her head at the thought, slammed the attic door closed, and took a moment to lean against it. Her pulse raced with anger, and she focused on breathing. Slowly. Calmly.

But Adam was stuck in her head.

She started toward the kitchen again, her mind scattered.

They were, after all, supposed to be one of the 'lucky couples.' She could hear the echo of friends' voices, even now. *How do you stay in love? How do you keep the spark? You still seem like newlyweds, even after all of these years. When we get married, we want to be just like you!*

──┼ ┼──

They met in an economics class at college. The first time Professor Roberts called on Adam, and he spoke, Ellie melted at the sound of his warm Minnesota accent. She immediately noticed the way he raked his hands through his thick hair when he was nervous.

A month into the first semester, Ellie arrived at class late on a Monday morning. Professor Roberts' students quickly came to expect that he would be late every Monday. Although he was usually gruff and intense, he often rushed in, disheveled and wincing like he had a bit of a headache. Rumors often placed him at popular local bars on the weekends, and there had even been insinuations that he started dating an undergraduate. Ellie looked at this as an opportunity to sleep in. Her classmates, it seemed, saw it as an opportunity for financial gain.

Arriving early for once, Ellie found several classmates gathered in charged silence. At the center was Jason Ford—classic cocky, spoiled rich kid—holding a crumpled piece of paper, his eyes focused on lining it up with a wastebasket in the corner of the room. There were two stacks of dollar bills on a desk in front of a girl with long blonde hair who was biting her nails. Jason flicked his wrist and shot. It landed in the basket. Kids all around the room yelled and hollered and raised their hands to high-five Jason.

Next, Adam stood where Jason had been, crumpled paper in hand. Again, the room fell silent. He shot, just as Ellie sneezed. His arm jolted unnaturally, as if she'd interrupted his concentration. The paper hit the edge of the basket and bounced onto the floor. Everyone turned to look at her and she felt a rush of heat prickle up her neck, all the way to her ears.

Jason went straight to the desk and scooped up the money. "Better luck next time," he said, clapping Adam on the shoulder.

Adam glanced at Ellie, passing right by her on the way to his seat. She couldn't help but notice how he smelled—like warm spice and a crisp winter breeze all bundled together.

She was wishing she could disappear when Professor Roberts rushed into the room, papers haphazardly sticking out of the top of his bag. Ellie sat through class, not hearing a single word of what was being said, wondering if she should request a transfer. She went home that night and continued to contemplate her unusual stroke of luck while she made dinner for her father and cleaned up the kitchen afterward. She went to bed thinking about it. And then she realized what she needed to do.

The next morning, she passed a note to Adam: *How much did you lose?*

He unfolded it. After a moments pause, he scribbled something and passed it back.

She opened it: *$40*

Forty dollars! It was a lot of money for someone working to put herself through college, someone whose father already worked two jobs just to pay the bills at home. Eighty was even more. But she did it anyway.

She took out a new piece of paper, tried to stop her hand from shaking, and wrote another message: *I want in on the game. Double or nothing. Monday morning.* She passed it to Jason.

He read it and arched an eyebrow at her. She watched a smile creep across his face, and he nodded. She returned her gaze to Professor Roberts, but not her attention. She would have to go home and study up. It had been a long time.

Monday morning came following a night of restless sleep. Her entire week had been consumed with thoughts of that morning. She had hit the basketball hoop every night, like she used to do with her dad before things got too hard. Like she continued to do for many years, alone, to take her mind off of her mother's absence. Then, after she retired to her room each night, she practiced with a balled up piece of paper and a wastebasket.

She strode into the classroom with her shoulders pushed back, and even to her surprise, she winked at Adam as she passed him, standing as a spectator this time, arms crossed over his chest.

She slapped forty dollars down on the desk in front of the blonde, right next to Jason's forty. No doubt, Jason's cash came from Daddy-big-bucks.

"Ladies first?" Jason said, crumpling the paper and offering it to her.

"Be my guest." She gestured for him to take his turn.

Their audience laughed.

Jason pointed a finger at her, as if they'd shared an inside joke, as if he thought she was being endearing, but she knew she had already rattled him a bit. He stepped up, aimed, and shot. It went straight in the center.

Ellie took her turn, matching his success.

They shot three more rounds, standing a foot further from the basket each time.

On the fourth attempt, Jason's shot was a quarter inch short. The paper hit the top rim, and everyone gasped to see which way it would go. It fell over the edge and onto the floor. Instantly, classmates surrounded Ellie, congratulating her, even slightly lifting her off of her feet.

She could see Adam, still where he had been, arms still over his chest. But he was smiling. He met her eyes, uncrossed his arms, and clapped a few times, as if to say *well done*.

She made her way to the blonde and collected her winnings. Then she walked straight to Adam and pressed it into the palm of his hand.

"For sneezing," she said.

His expression twisted into confusion. "You—you don't have to—"

"Figured I owe you." She shrugged, already turning away from him.

He looked down at the money in his hand, and she saw the realization on his face. It was more than he had lost. He peeled back two twenties. "At least take your share," he said in protest.

"Keep it," she said. And then, convinced it was now or never, the next four words came tangled in a rush of courage. "You can take me to dinner."

The slight flush on his cheeks only intensified her interest. Then, his fingers swept through his hair. She was amused and intrigued. His blue eyes reminded her of the sea on a hot summer day. She wanted to challenge them and melt into a heap on the floor all at the same time.

She winked at him. "I'm a cheap date," she said, "promise."

His mouth curled up into a smile she knew she'd never get tired of seeing.

It was only a burger and fries, but it may have been the best meal she'd ever had. Later, over coffee and a shared piece of apple pie at an all-night diner, he told her it was the best money he'd ever lost.

She pointed her fork at him. "Not true. I told you, I'm a cheap date. I don't think I've cost you eighty dollars yet."

"Well," he said, scooping another piece of pie onto his fork, "we might have to do something about that." She smiled, and then they were both laughing, and it seemed neither of them wanted the night to end. Ever.

Adam was endearing and genuine. A keeper. He was different than the guys she was used to, gentle and mild-mannered, but with a confidence and determination at his core. For the first time in Ellie's life, someone was eager and able to take care of her.

At Adam's insistence, they moved in together as soon as Ellie graduated. The apartment was small and simple. They had spent their savings on first and last months' rent and furniture, and they made pasta nearly every day because they couldn't afford much else. Still, they slept against the warmth of each other every night, and Ellie was happier than she had ever hoped she could be.

A few weeks after moving in, they were watching a movie. The characters were dining on caviar and expensive champagne at some ritzy hotel. Adam snapped his fingers in front of Ellie's face.

"What?" She turned to face him.

"You look forlorn."

She shrugged and turned back to the movie. "No."

"Do you like caviar?"

Her eyes slid back to him. "What?"

"Caviar. Do you like it?"

"Never had it."

"Me either."

Adam bolted from the couch and grabbed an old pair of sneakers that had been discarded by the front door. He shoved his feet into them and laced them up.

"Where are you going?" Ellie asked, pushing herself upright on the cushions.

Adam kissed her on the top of the head. "To get some caviar."

"We can't afford caviar." Her eyes were wide.

"Don't you want to try it?"

Before she could respond, he winked and went out the door.

In the twenty minutes she waited for him to return, she continued to watch the movie without hearing a word of what was said, worried and wondering what had gotten into Adam.

When he finally busted through the door, she jumped to her feet. A plastic bag dangled from his right hand.

"Sit down," he said.

She remained standing. "What's in the bag?"

"I told you: caviar."

She crossed her arms. "What's in the bag?" she asked again.

He pointed at her. "Don't make me blindfold you."

Her eyebrows shot up, and Adam mimicked her expression. She couldn't help but laugh.

"I mean it," he said, still pointing for her to sit. "And don't look."

She huffed in mock disapproval and stood still.

"Will you sit down if I say please?"

The lines around her mouth hurt from how deeply she was smiling.

His blue eyes smiled back.

"Fine." She raised her palms in surrender and plopped onto the couch. "But it's pretty lonely over here."

"Not for long," he called over his shoulder as he headed into the kitchen behind her—which was really just the other side of the living room.

"You'd better hope I don't find myself a stand-in."

"You wouldn't dare."

She heard glasses clinking and the tearing of plastic. She turned to see what he was doing, but Adam's eyes were on her immediately. He stopped.

"I. Will. Blindfold. You."

"Ugh!" Still laughing, she dropped her head into her hands.

The microwave door slammed shut, and she sniffed the air. "Did you get . . . popcorn?"

"Nope."

A minute later, he was handing her a bowl.

"That's popcorn," she said, peering into it.

The warmth of his finger fell across her lips. "It's caviar."

"But I don't even know if I like caviar."

He rolled his eyes. "God, you're difficult. It can be whatever we want it to be. We can pretend."

"And here I thought I got myself hooked up with a wealthy hero that was going to whisk me away and fulfill all my dreams.

"And I thought I had avoided getting tangled up with a difficult woman." He lifted one of the glasses and offered it to her. "You're champagne, dear."

Ellie watched bubbles float up through the liquid.

Adam took the other glass for himself. "To us," he said, as he clinked his glass to hers.

The sweetness of sparkling white grape juice swam down Ellie's throat, and she smiled, certain that, wealthy or not, Adam *was* the hero that would fulfill all of her dreams.

CHAPTER 4

ADAM

Adam had a board meeting scheduled for seven the next morning, but sleep didn't look promising. He punched the pillow, wondering again if the insomnia would ever end. Finally, he dropped an arm over his eyes and gave in, allowing nostalgia to weave itself into the corners of his mind, the connecting tissues of his his heart, as Ellie filled the darkness.

He was two years ahead of her, and by the time they had moved in together after she graduated from college, he was already two years into his career at Exactitude Accounting, a small but prestigious audit firm. They spent their first weekend as official roommates lounging in bed, rather than unpacking boxes. She made pasta for dinner, and they ate propped up on pillows. They watched old movies in black and white, the only thing that would broadcast over a flimsy antenna he'd rigged up. It didn't matter much; they weren't that interested in the television.

Ellie's hair left a damp spot on her pillowcase after she showered, and the sweet smell of jasmine floated through the air from her side of bed. He traced circles over her smooth legs with his fingertips and watched her nipples respond through the thin, white sheet. Even asleep, their skin never lost contact.

The early morning light was still gray on Monday when he untangled himself from her and slid out of bed.

"Where are you going?" she asked, bolting upright as she rubbed her eyes.

"To work." He kissed the top of her head. "We can't stay in bed forever."

When he came out of the bathroom thirty minutes later, she yanked him back onto the mattress by his tie.

"Ellie—" he started to protest, but her lips were already locked on his, her hands working to unlatch his belt.

And for the first time in two years, he arrived at work late.

Charles Henry, the company's president and CEO, wasn't just a terrific boss, he was the father Adam wished he still had. Charlie immediately took Adam under his wing, and like the transformation of a nestling to a fledgling, Adam quickly flew up the corporate ladder.

Over the course of the next three years, Adam was late a handful of times, but Charlie never said much. He only winked and complemented Adam on the sweet scent of jasmine that clung to his clothes. Adam interpreted the gesture as a testament to Charlie's fondness for Ellie more than a sense of loyalty to his mentee.

On his fifth anniversary with Exactitude, Charlie made him a VP.

He called Ellie the second he got back into the chair at his desk.

"I'm getting a corner office," he said, stretching a rubber band between his fingers. "Even better, we can buy a house."

She insisted they celebrate, and when he got home he found his present seductively wrapped in a new piece of white lingerie.

"I may have already spent part of your new raise." Ellie fingered the lace border that settled at the top of her tanned thigh.

After nine years with the company, at age thirty-one, Adam was promoted to Chief Operations Officer, second in command to Charlie.

By then, they were settled into their new house in Emerald Glen. Ellie was self-employed, a CPA in a small office they purchased five years before. She had a fast-growing list of clients and a small support staff. But they hadn't yet had kids, and freedom was something they took for granted. They had lazy weekends, holidays abroad, and ate leisure dinners out.

To celebrate Adam's promotion, they dressed to the nines and went out for a four-course dinner. Adam found himself more interested in Ellie's low-cut, floor-length dress than in his fifty-dollar meal.

He lifted another piece of steak and offered it to Ellie.

"I can't wait to take that tie off." She ate the steak from his fork.

"Well," he said, pulling at his collar, feeling as if someone had just pushed the thermostat up, "at least I know you don't just love me for my money."

He worked in tandem with Charlie for nearly four years after that, until one day his wings were clipped, and he found himself diving toward the cold, hard surface of earth.

After a light tap on the door, Adam looked up to see Charlie walking into his office. He had been out sick for four days, which was unusual enough, but he looked as if someone had wrapped his skin in rawhide and then covered it with a layer of white chalk. That was when Charlie told him about the brain cancer.

"How long have you known?" he asked.

"Not long."

"But there must be something they can do, right? They must have—"

Charlie reached out and placed his palm over Adam's hand where it rested on the desk to silence him. His eyes said all there was to say.

Six weeks later later, Adam was called into a meeting with Exactitude's board of directors. Charlie was unable to return to work, but he had made a recommendation to promote Adam to CEO.

His hands were still shaking when he called Ellie.

"What if I . . . can't do it?"

"You already have been," she said, her voice so soft he could barely hear her over the pounding in his chest. "Charlie hasn't been in the office much for nearly a month. You've already been making most of the decisions. You said so yourself."

Adam shook his head and fought to shrink the lump growing at the back of his throat. "I can't do it without him."

"You can, and you will," she said. "You just don't want to, and that's okay."

"It's not right. It's not his time."

"I know."

Fifteen days after that, Charlie passed away at the age of sixty-one.

Later that night, Adam reached under the sheets and found Ellie's hand. "El?" he said. "Let's not wait anymore."

"For what?" she asked, her voice thick with sleep.

"Let's make a baby."

CHAPTER 5
ELLIE

Ellie broke an egg above the metal bowl on the countertop in front of her, watched the yellow yolk seep into the grayish egg white, and considered the fragility of life. She wondered if Charlie were still here today, if he would have set Adam straight, if he would have been able to talk some sense into him on her behalf.

The first time she met Charlie, at a cocktail party hosted by Exactitude, he took her into a hug as if she were his long lost daughter, and she knew right away she would come to love him.

"He's a fine catch little lady. Hang on to him," Charlie said, playfully raising a brow and winking an eye as he released her. She looked up at Adam and smiled, all the while thinking, *yes, he is.*

Her hands tightened around the spoon. Fueled by frustration, she whipped the batter faster and faster, watching the ingredients blend together, wishing it were this easy to repair her marriage. Her family. Her life. Finally, she returned the bowl to the counter with a clank and released the air she didn't realize she was holding in her lungs.

"Let's have a dinner to celebrate," she said, rubbing Adam's shoulders. "I'll cook." Adam had folded himself into a living room chair as soon as he'd arrived home. It was the end of his first official week as CEO.

"While Charlie's dying?" he asked, yanking at his tie. He shrugged away from her touch, stood, and left the room.

Later that night, he took Ellie in his arms and apologized. He made love to her, handling her so gently that it seemed he was afraid he might break her. She kissed his eyelids repeatedly, trying to erase the pain settled in his beautiful blue eyes.

Two months after Charlie died, and after she had made the suggestion three more times, they hosted a dinner. Adam started the night with a moment of silence, a somber reminder of a bittersweet celebration.

Close friends and colleagues crowded around their dining room table filled with food Ellie had made—eggplant parmesan, chicken breast stuffed with crabmeat, Devil's food cake—it was an elaborate spread. Sam pumped Adam's arm, clapped him on the back, and said something near Adam's ear that Ellie couldn't hear. She circulated through the room with bottle after bottle of wine, refilling glasses more times than she could count.

At the end of the night, she leaned against the dining room archway, sipping from a glass of lemonade—one of the few things she could drink that didn't make her retch since she found out she was pregnant a few weeks before—and watched Adam. He was slightly off-balance, the tips of his cheeks flushed from too much alcohol.

Kathy hugged and congratulated him before she and Tom stepped out into the night air. Only Sam and Suzanne remained. As Suzanne went to leave, she cradled Adam's face in her hands and told him he needed a shave. Ellie smiled.

Adam closed the door, leaned up against it, and sighed. He swayed slightly as he sauntered across the room toward Ellie. His hot hands came to rest on her hips.

"I love you," he said, the words a little too soft around the edges. "But I suppose I need to go to bed now."

He kissed her forehead, his lips damp and without form, and headed toward the steps. Ellie watched him until he disappeared, then she turned toward the aftermath. Leftover scents of Italian sauces, chocolate cake, perfume, and snuffed out candles lingered in the air. Her stomach floated into her chest again and soured. Even without the nausea, she was exhausted. She decided to do something she wasn't sure she'd done since she and Adam had first moved in together. She turned out the light and decided to leave the mess for later. Tomorrow, Adam would help.

The next morning she woke to find Adam's side of the bed empty. She ate a few crackers she'd been trained to keep on the nightstand before padding into the kitchen. The house was quiet. And the dining room was still a mess. She stepped outside and curled up with the newspaper on a patio chair next to a clay pot that exploded with pink and purple pansies. An expansive, well-manicured yard was tucked in between the house, elaborate landscaping, and a huge barn that stood at the edge of their property.

An hour later, her eyes fluttered open. She fought to bring the world back into focus.

"Where are you going?" she asked, realizing that Adam was standing beside her chair, a set of car keys dangling from his hand.

"To the office. Marc called, and there's a problem. A big client's being audited, and we need to do some research."

"But it's Sunday," she said, sitting up. "Where were you earlier? I woke up and you were gone."

"I went for a run." He kissed the top of her head, warm from the sun, and began down the landscaped path toward the front of the house. Toward his car. Away from her.

"How long will it take?" she asked, sliding the newspaper from her lap, swinging her legs off of the chair.

"I dunno. A couple of hours at least," Adam called over his shoulder.

Frustration poked at her chest. "Is Marc showing up at work, too? On a *Sunday?*"

Adam stopped and turned to face her. "Yah, he is," he said, cocking his head. "I'll see you later, okay?"

A wave of heat flashed through her body, but she couldn't tell if she was angry or embarrassed. Mostly she was confused. She forced a smile and wondered what had gotten into her. "Okay," she said.

A few seconds later, the sound of Adam's BMW roared to life and then faded away. As she walked back into the house, the left-over scent of last night's celebration brought her to a seated position on the kitchen floor. She fought to control the waves of nausea and glanced up at the mess in the dining room. She would have to open all of the windows and work quickly. Today, she would be on clean-up duty alone.

Ellie peeked through the oven window at the rising cake. It had become natural for her plans to shift without warning along with her cravings. In the middle of looking for her scone pan, she decided she wanted chocolate cake instead. Besides, she never did find her pan.

Cooking and baking were always sure to take her mind off her daily troubles. She loved getting lost in the process—in the aroma and texture of the ingredients and the amazing experience of a finished product teasing your taste buds and filling your insides with comfort. But most of all, food was nurturing, and Ellie loved to nurture. The best reward was the effect her food had on others—when they were happy, content, and yearning for more even after they were stuffed full. That was what filled her inside.

But tonight her mind would not rest, and there was no one to feed.

She crept upstairs and quietly pushed Tommy's door open. Slipping into his room, she peered down at his round face. Curly, disheveled hair hung over his eyelids and spilled around his red cheeks. Even with the ceiling fan whirling above, he had kicked off his covers. At seven years old he was already beginning to lose some of his childish features—his fingers long and slim instead of short and chubby, his face now softly chiseled with features of the man he would someday be. But when he slept, Ellie could still see the innocence and vulnerability that made her heart melt.

These were the times when she loved motherhood most—when she could stand over her children in awe, when she wasn't running ragged and her name wasn't being screeched by a needy small person every other minute. She dropped a soft kiss on her son's cheek.

Tommy hadn't always this peaceful—born a colicky baby, he made his inexperienced parents fraught with worry and exhausted from countless sleepless hours. In those early days they were up from dusk till dawn with an infant who never stopped screaming. They tried rides in the car. They bought drops and gadgets. They sat him in his car seat and propped it on top of the clothes dryer. It seemed that for every two ounces he drank, one came back up. They were spent.

Nothing seemed to help, and two weeks into what was supposed to be new parental bliss, Ellie sat on the edge of the bed, bouncing and rocking Tommy in her arms.

"Can't you take another week off?" she asked, standing and shifting her weight, desperate to make Tommy stop crying. Her breasts were filling with milk, aching beneath her bra, but he'd just finished eating a few minutes before.

"I run the company, El, I kinda have to be there. It's already been two weeks."

She watched him pull ties out of the closet. He moved over to a drawer, picked out some socks, and dumped them onto the bed.

"What's with all the clothes?" she asked.

"I figured it'd be better if I slept in the spare room for a while."

"You're *leaving* me?" Her eyes widened in surprise.

Adam added a few suits to the growing mound that now completely covered the area where he normally slept. "Don't be ridiculous," he said without turning to face her. "I can't exactly sleep in here. You've seen how well that's worked out."

"So I just get to handle it all by myself? It's okay for *me* to be tired? For *me* not to sleep?" Her eyes had shifted from wide to wild.

Adam yanked a duffle bag from the bottom of the closet and threw it onto the bed. He raked his fingers through his hair and sighed. "You're not working, Ellie, and I'm in charge of running a company. What do you want me to do?"

There it was: she had given up her job, and she was expendable. Adam, on the other hand, was not.

That night, she called Suzanne and cried. She hung up and stared down at the tiny alien, bundled in a bassinet, who had suddenly invaded their lives and disrupted everything. Her marriage seemed to be derailing as a result. And she cried again.

Hell together was hard enough; now she was in hell alone.

The next afternoon, Suzanne barreled into their kitchen, her thin arms laden with groceries, brown silky hair pulled into a ponytail. Ellie was at the sink washing dishes when she heard the door slam shut. She stared at her best friend in surprise as Suzanne shooed her away and ordered her to take a nap.

When she woke, the sweetness of tomato sauce and fresh, hot bread hung thick in the air. Her stomach growled, and she smiled, thankful that the smell of the things she loved no longer made her insides clench with agony. She looked around the room, shadows indicating the sun was low the sky. She wondered how long she'd slept, and realized she didn't even remember what time Suzanne had arrived in the first place.

In the kitchen, she found her friend placing a salad on the table. Tommy was propped up on her shoulder, cooing quietly and rubbing his face against a cloth draped under his tiny body in a jerky motion specific only to babies. Adam was already shoveling a fork full of lasagna into his mouth, smiling as if he hadn't had a meal in months.

"Ellie! Come and sit." Suzanne pulled out the empty chair in between her and Adam. Tentatively, Ellie slid into it. Suzanne was already piling food onto a plate in front of Ellie, and Ellie stared at her, wondering if this was what it felt like to be Adam. She glanced from Suzanne to the baby, still content on her shoulder.

"How did you do all of this?" Ellie asked.

Suzanne furrowed her brow. "What do you mean?"

Ellie opened her mouth then closed it again. "Thank you," she finally said, unsure of what else to say, feeling somewhat inadequate but grateful at the same time.

Suzanne smiled and rubbed a few quick circles around Ellie's back. Then she stood and went to the fridge to pour Ellie a drink.

Ellie took a bite of lasagna and blinked back the tears stinging the edges of her eyes. She glanced at Adam, who was solely focused on his food. He hadn't acknowledged her presence at all.

They went on like this for weeks. Suzanne, like an angel that didn't seem quite real, appeared every day, took the baby, and cooked a meal in their kitchen while Ellie slept. Adam chatted about the news and the weather and gave praise for the wonderful dinners placed in front of him each night. But Ellie could feel the distance between them, the coolness emitted from his skin. He stopped pulling her into his arms for an embrace. He didn't kiss her hello in the morning, and he went to sleep in the spare room without saying goodnight.

Still, as the days ticked by, Ellie could feel strength return to her body one inch at a time. She began to cook beside Suzanne while her friend filled her in on the latest gossip. One night, she picked up Tommy and realized she was smiling even though he was crying. That was when she knew the stars had shifted.

Two weeks after Suzanne had stopped visiting every day, Tommy had a particularly bad night. Ellie scooped him up from the bassinet at eight in the morning and fought to open her eyes. Again. She hadn't had more than two hours sleep, and probably no more than thirty minutes at a time. Her pulse throbbed against her temple. She walked through the house and realized Adam had already left for work.

Tommy continued to scream, his face crimson red. She set her hand on his forehead, unsure whether he was hot from fussing or something else. She found her cell phone, and twenty minutes later they were on their way to the pediatrician's office.

"Nothing to worry about," the doctor said. "Just some bad gas. Sometimes that happens." He gave her a list of foods and told her to watch what she eats since she was breastfeeding. She was already doing that. "You may want to consider supplementing with a gentle formula too, at least for a while. See if it makes a difference." He handed her a sample-sized can of formula powder.

When Adam got home, just before six, she and Tommy were finally asleep. Startled to see him standing above the bed when she opened her eyes, a tiny screech escaped from the back of her throat.

"Jesus," she whispered, bolting upright. It was strange to see him in the bedroom he hadn't stepped foot in for nearly two months.

Adam pulled the tie from his neck and loosened the buttons at the top of his shirt. "We eating anytime soon?" he asked. "I'm starved."

Ellie stared at him and felt something close to hatred rise from her toes all the way to her chest. Once the fervor hit her arms, she wasn't sure she could stop herself from strangling him. Before she could fully consider it, Tommy began to wail. Exhaustion sucked the air from her lungs, and she closed her eyes and sighed.

"I'd better go change." Adam glanced at Tommy on his way out of the room.

Instead of picking the baby up, she pulled a bag from the closet and began to stuff clothes inside. Her mind raced in time with the pounding in her chest. She threw in a razor and at the last minute remembered her breast pump. Then she found Adam in the living room, TV remote in hand. He didn't even look up until she tore it from his grasp and flicked it off.

"Where are you going?" he asked, eyeing the bag on her shoulder. The twisted expression of confusion on his face would have led a stranger to believe he had never seen her before.

"I'm leaving. And Tommy's still crying, so I suggest you go get him."

She was already halfway across the room when she heard Adam scramble out of the chair, the remote crashing to the floor.

"Wh—what do you mean you're leaving?" he asked. "Where are you going?"

"Anywhere but here," she mumbled, not bothering to turn around.

"Ellie, wait!" He was nearly shouting, his voice laced with panic. "I don't know what to *do* with him."

"Figure it out," she said over her shoulder. She grabbed her car keys from the shelf and slammed the door behind her.

Her heart pounded as she pointed her car away from home, and she was flooded with a gray and black rainbow of emotions. She considered turning around to save Tommy from the incompetence of his father, but she forced herself to keep going. She knew he would survive. They would both survive. Then she realized she wasn't sure *where* she was going. She thought of Suzanne and Sam, but she didn't want to see anyone, not even for the company of her best friend.

Suzanne.

She pulled the car over and punched out a quick text message.

Adam's on his own with the baby.
If he calls you, do NOT save him. Please!
Will explain later.

She woke from a deep sleep at three in the morning, her breasts sore, droplets of milk seeping into her bra. It took her a minute to remember where she was, in a conservatively wallpapered hotel room. She had checked in and glanced at the multiple missed calls from Adam. Then she switched off her phone and climbed between a set of white sheets that felt like a cloud against her tired body.

She had to get up and relieve the pressure bursting in her chest three times, but she slept until noon. When she returned home the next day, she found Adam sitting in a living room wingchair. Lines of exhaustion creased his face, and Tommy was curled up against his chest. They were both asleep. Despite her anger, she couldn't help but smile. She was unpacking her bag when Adam appeared at the bedroom door.

"You're back."

"Yep."

He crossed the room and pressed his chest against her back. "I'm sorry." He wrapped his arms around her from behind. She could feel his breath whisper against her ear. "I've been a jerk."

After that, Ellie felt marginally better. Adam took to saying "I love you" a lot more, and she knew she still loved him with her whole heart. He wanted to be the husband she desired—she could see that in his eyes—but she found that he had no inclination that she needed help until she asked. Often, she just resigned herself to the fact that she was on her own and tried to accept that it would be okay.

Four years later, Lizzie was born. She was a more agreeable baby, and she slept for hours at a clip.

But Exactitude had gone public.

"I can't run a company and answer to stockholders without proper sleep." Adam stopped pulling suits from the closet and turned to face her. His shoulders dropped, and he sighed. "It won't be like last time, I promise."

And it wasn't, not exactly. But he moved to the spare room all the same, and the loneliness anchored itself into her bones.

⊷⊶

Ellie moved down the hallway and cringed at the loud squeak of the hinges on Lizzie's bedroom door as she pushed it open. She approached the bed and knelt down alongside her sleeping daughter. Her fingers moved affectionately across Lizzie's silky, golden hair. The faint smell of nail polish still lingered in the air hours after Lizzie scrunched her red lips into a pout and begged, "Mommy make my fingers beautiful." At just three years old, she was a princess indeed. Ellie kissed the top of Lizzie's head. On her way out, the door hinges protested again as she pulled it closed. She made a mental note to lubricate them tomorrow—a job that used to belong to Adam.

Lizzie had been delivered cesarean, and when Ellie stood after the surgery, she felt as if her insides would fall straight to the floor. Steps were challenging, and staples pulled at her healing abdomen whenever she lifted the baby. Her inability to drive for two weeks had isolated her from the outside world.

Just as she'd started to physically heal, Adam's schedule got busier. In addition to running Exactitude, he had accepted board member positions with both the hospital and the local college.

Community and charity events they were expected to attend—
something she didn't mind before kids—crowded their calendars.
She was exhausted and agitated at the expectation that she take
on the role of middle-class socialite. Besides, she no longer had a
place in the business world—a world everyone at such functions
seemed to share but her—and she began to send Adam alone.

Perhaps Adam's at one of those events tonight.

She pulled a pajama top over her head, stricken by the thought
that she no longer had any idea how her husband of seventeen
years spent his days and nights.

It was pure poppycock. That was probably what she should have
told Adam from the very beginning, but she didn't. And now, here
she was.

Poppycock, poppycock, poppycock. The word stuck with her after her visit with Dr. Van Linden, so she arrived home and searched
it on the Internet . . .

"POPPYCOCK: Word Origin: Dutch. Dutch dialect *pappekak.*
Synonyms: nonsense, bullshit, hogwash, rubbish, foolishness . . . "

She took an instant liking to this new piece of vocabulary. But
then, who wouldn't appreciate a nice way to say bullshit? It fully en-
compassed her view on life lately—probably because it accurately
summed up her marriage.

Now, she couldn't get it out of her mind.

The priest tried to warn them during their pre-wedding classes
of what he referred to as "matrimonial turbulence." Back then, the
thought of it just seemed so . . . well, silly. But she and Adam had
long surpassed a bumpy ride; they were in a full-fledged nosedive.

Overwhelmed by sadness, she moved to the bathroom, mind-
lessly going through the motions of tasks she'd completed thou-
sands of times before. But her mind was hazy. She began to cleanse
her face before she realized all of her makeup had already been
washed away. The toothbrush in her hand moved up and down
methodically as if it were robotic. She spit and watched toothpaste

slither down the drain, and a disturbing truth settled in her mind: figuratively, her marriage had done the same.

She placed a hand on her stomach and looked in the mirror.

She'd passed out in the doctor's office, for God's sake.

How could this be happening?

And how could she bring another child into this world?

Alone again.

A tear ran down her cheek.

Only this time, the baby won't even share Adam's DNA.

CHAPTER 6

ADAM

Adam silenced the engine of his BMW and sighed, realizing he didn't remember his drive to the hospital.

He walked into the boardroom of Center Valley Medical Center ten minutes late, sending a sheepish nod toward Sam Predmore, the hospital's CEO. Sam made eye contact, a silent acknowledgement, and continued to update the board on progress of the hospital's east wing renovations. His tall, broad frame, thick eyebrows, and serious expression commanded attention. Adam slipped into his assigned high back leather seat without a word. The room smelled of coffee, and Adam's stomach responded with a growl. Still, he decided getting up would be disruptive, bad enough he was late.

"Psst." It was Marie, Sam's secretary. She slid the agenda for to-day's meeting—February 1—and a stack full of papers across the table toward Adam. Sunlight shining through a wall of windows behind him reflected off of the white paper and stung his tired eyes.

Sam concluded while Marie passed another stack of papers to each board member. Bonnie Singleton took the brief interruption as an opportunity to speak out of turn. "Sure is good to see our Treasurer could join us," she said, staring directly at Adam.

Bonnie, a local boutique owner and fellow board member, was also the town bitch, and everyone knew it. Still, her comment cut into Adam's nerves more than usual. His eyes moved across the faces of board members on the opposite side of the long polished maple table, and he caught a couple of them rolling their eyes before he settled on her round, chubby face. In customary Bonnie fashion, she looked colorful. Bright red lipstick was smeared across thick lips that curled up in sarcasm, and her eyelids were painted with an excessive amount of eye shadow. In an attempt to ignore her, he forced a tight smile and turned his attention back to the agenda.

"Let's just continue, shall we?" Tom Spleck, Chairman of the board, peered over his glasses and sent a look of warning in Bonnie's direction. Florescent lights above illuminated his silver hair. "Adam, you're up next with the Treasurer's report."

Adam delivered the numbers, focusing strictly on the facts, going through a motion he could easily repeat in his sleep.

Emotionless.

Until Tom called on Pamela.

Pamela, a VP at the hospital, had the duty of keeping the board informed of patient situations that were unusually problematic— unfortunate circumstances politely referred to as "challenges" in the boardroom.

Some challenges involved clients who couldn't or refused to pay. Sometimes there was a threat of the hospital being sued, and on occasion they would see a unique situation. Their ultimate goal was to do what they could to help the members of a community they strived to serve.

Pamela rose from her chair, wearing a tailored red suit coat, matching skirt, and taupe-colored high heels. A string of pearls hung neatly at her neckline.

"Nice outfit, Pamela. Nothin' like keepin' it professional," Bonnie said. A smirk inched its way across her face.

Sam looked toward the ceiling in frustration, and Adam narrowed his eyes at Bonnie. Pamela's attire was blatantly professional in comparison to Bonnie's blubbering gossip. Evidently, the red suit wasn't purchased at her store.

Pamela cleared her throat but didn't falter. "Today I want to plead for your assistance with Bobby Fleich," Pamela said. "Seven-year-old Bobby and his parents were brought to the hospital by ambulance two days ago after their car was struck by a tractor-trailer. Mr. and Mrs. Fleich were both pronounced dead shortly after they arrived. Bobby sustained multiple injuries. He's showing some improvement, and we expect to see him come out of ICU soon, but the insurance company is refusing to pay further medical costs since the policy owner, Mr. Fleich, is now deceased. They claim they can deny coverage because the policy had recently lapsed."

Goosebumps raced over Adam's skin, and the hair on the back of his neck stiffened before she had even completed her sentence.

"Lapsed?" Jim, another board member, asked while he methodically rotated a pen between his lanky fingers.

"Apparently the father was self-employed with a family policy, and the policy premium wasn't paid the last two months. The boy is now an orphan. No immediate family members have come forward yet. The debate of whether or not he's medically ready to be released is ambiguous at this point, and I'd appreciate your consideration in having him stay here on our dime for a while."

Pamela's tone was calm and matter-of-fact, and Adam wondered how she could maintain such cool composure. He flattened his shaky hands against the stack of papers in front of him, an attempt to still the panic rising in his chest.

"How long's a while?" Bonnie asked.

"The police are working on finding next of kin, and we're nursing him back to health as quickly as possible. It's the social worker's opinion that foster care could bring grave repercussions at this critical point in his life, considering the combined traumas of his medical condition and the loss of his parents," Pamela said.

Adam hated these "challenges." These meetings. This scenario was the worst he'd ever sat through.

Breathe. In. Out.

Voices around the table became nothing more than muffled sounds. Bonnie looked angry, and Jim's face flushed red as he argued a point. A fuzzy gold halo formed around Pamela's blonde hair, her movement somehow distorted.

Adam put a finger to his pounding head and touched a thin line of sweat above his brow. His stomach turned inside out.

"Let's bring some order to this meeting." Tom hit the edge of his coffee mug with a spoon. "Would anyone like to make a motion?"

"I move we let the boy stay for a maximum of one week before we reassess the situation," Sam said.

"I second," Jim said.

"Further discussion?" Tom asked.

Adam stood and leaned on the table, an attempt to steady his jellied legs. His vision was blurred, the room spinning like a kaleidoscope.

"Excuse me. Please … proceed without me." Adam managed to mumble the words on his way out, although he wasn't sure how with a sizable lump growing in his throat that threatened his air supply.

Relieved to find the bathroom empty, he entered the first stall, locked the door, and sat on the edge of the toilet seat. The cold bathroom smelled of antiseptic. He wondered if he should make himself vomit.

Before he could decide, the bathroom door swung open and then closed with a bang. Adam stiffened, wondering how long he'd been staring at the white tiled floor.

"Adam?"

Sam.

"Yah." Adam cleared his throat and tensed further at the cracking of his own voice.

"You okay? You were white as a ghost in there." Sam asked, audibly concerned.

"Yah, sure. Just some bad breakfast or something."

"You've been gone for nearly fifteen minutes. The meeting's over."

"I'm good. I just need a second."

Sam sighed on the other side of the door. "Adam, we're friends. Talk to me." Sam paused. "I know it's been tough with Ellie and all . . ."

Adam hesitated, then stood and opened the stall door. Sam, at six-foot-two, hovered slightly over Adam's five-foot-eleven frame. Adam's line of sight was even with Sam's long arms, hanging like small tree trunks against his broad body.

He forced himself to look up and found Sam studying him from head to toe. His baby-blue dress shirt was stuck to his sweaty chest, and his tie felt like a noose around his neck. A furrowed brow of concern sat below Sam's wheat-colored hair that had always reminded Adam of farming fields in the Midwest.

Adam tried to breathe again, but the guilt filling his chest left little room for oxygen. More than business associates, he and Sam had developed deep mutual respect and a strong friendship over the years. But Ellie remained the only person in Adam's world who knew about his past, about the most painful years of his life.

Adam pulled at his tie and found his way to the sink. He splashed water on his face, trying to force thoughts of Bobby from his mind. So young. So innocent. He was the same age as Tommy, for God's sake.

The same age I was.

"Tell you what," Sam said, "meet me in my office in ten minutes and we'll talk."

"I'm okay, really," Adam said. But the anxiety shone through, slick on his skin. He licked his lips and raked a few fingers through his hair. He attempted a laugh, but even he realized it sounded more like a bitter taste spat from his lips.

"I won't take no for an answer," Sam said as he walked toward the door.

"Sam—"

Sam raised his palm and paused at the exit with a reassuring smile. "See you in ten."

PART II

For Richer or For Poorer

CHAPTER 7
ELLIE

Ellie drove slowly down the perfect, tree-lined streets of Emerald Glen, Pennsylvania, and gazed at the giant homes that passed outside her window. One after another, each of them showcased impeccable, manicured landscapes, even in the dead of winter, every one tucked behind a tall iron gate like a treasured jewel. As she examined them one at a time she felt . . . nauseous.

She considered the baby and swallowed hard, forcing herself to think about a new life she could barely acknowledge as real. She stopped in her driveway to drink in the sight of the large stone home she and Adam bought years ago. Like the others, it was pristine on the outside. But charm and grace didn't dwell inside its walls. She wondered how many of her neighbors were pretending perfection like she and Adam had been.

Still paused in the middle of the driveway, she slid the transmission to park and rested her head against the cold leather steering wheel. She summoned a mental picture of the least pretentious place she knew, which also immediately brought her thoughts to the least pretentious person.

Her father.

And her hometown.

Allentown, a mere few miles away, was a stark contrast to the wealthy country club lifestyle of Emerald Glen.

Yes, Allentown from the Billy Joel song, she'd told people over and over. And Billy described it perfectly—hard workers, coal, and factories. The salt of the earth, the working middle-class—that was her dad, Bill Anderson. He had been a blue-collar worker for the once great Bethlehem Steel, and they had lived a simple life in a half-double row home in Center City.

At a young age she came to understand two things through personal lesson: be careful in whom you place your trust, and things are not always what they seem to be.

Ellie's mother, Joyce, didn't work. She always made pancakes on the weekends, cooked big dinners, and kept a clean house, even though it was small. She often curled up with Ellie on the couch and read books while she stroked her fingers through Ellie's long brown hair.

Each night, when her father came home at the end of his workday he'd change out of his blue work pants and shirt and spend time carrying his little girl around on his shoulders. Once Ellie was too big to ride so high, he'd bounce her around the house on his strong, broad back.

Afterward, Ellie would sit at the kitchen table completing her homework while her parents stood at the stove chatting.

Her parents had a nightly ritual—Joyce would cook while Bill dipped his fingers in her sauce or popped pieces of whatever else was on the menu into his mouth. Then Joyce would scold him and shoo him off with her kitchen towel. Her lecture was always followed by a swat on the butt and a kiss from Bill. Smiles and laughter were plenty, and Ellie never missed the exchange. She'd glance at them sideways, relishing the love she saw between them.

Then, a week after Ellie's eighth birthday, something changed.

That Monday morning, Ellie woke, dressed for school, and descended the steps as she always did. Her mother usually met her in the kitchen, waiting with Ellie's breakfast, but Ellie found her standing on a concrete step, just outside the backdoor. Ellie pushed the screen door open, and her mother spun around. Smoke curled from a cigarette in between two fingers of her right hand.

Ellie's forehead wrinkled. Joyce didn't smoke. She wanted to ask . . . why . . . or something . . . anything . . . she was so startled by the image she wasn't sure . . . but the silent message stamped on Joyce's face stopped her—like a forbiddance to speak.

Joyce threw the cigarette to the ground, stomped it with her left shoe, and then rushed past Ellie into the kitchen. She pulled a muffin from a package and handed it to her daughter.

"Eat it on your way to school." She placed her hand on the center of Ellie's back and led her out the front door onto the sidewalk. Then, she turned and retreated back into the house.

Ellie stood shell-shocked, wondering what had just happened. Usually her mother cooked oatmeal or heated waffles, and they sat together every morning. Never before had she sent Ellie off to school without a hug and a kiss on the cheek. Ellie walked to school—only two blocks from their red brick row home—and contemplated the muffin. Finally, she shoved it into her backpack untouched.

That night, Joyce was on edge. Bill stood at the stove, but his visit only lasted a few minutes before she sent him away. Ellie found it hard to focus on her homework and skipped half of the assignment.

The next morning, her mother set a box of cereal and a bowl on the kitchen counter in front of Ellie. Then, without a word, she went upstairs and started the shower, leaving Ellie to fend for herself and get off to school. Ellie stared at the bowl. She crossed the room and pulled a milk carton from the refrigerator, her hands shaky.

That night when Bill arrived home, Ellie noticed the smile that usually sat on his face was missing. He didn't stand at the stove, and the house was so silent it made Ellie's ears hurt. The air was thick, and it was hard to breathe in the kitchen, so Ellie gathered her homework and took it to her room.

She wanted to ask them what was wrong, but she was too scared. Later, she went to bed hoping she'd wake up and things would return to normal. But Joyce stayed on the back porch Wednesday morning. This time, she didn't extinguish the cigarette. She merely glanced at Ellie before she turned her back again, sucking in another drag of smoke.

That was the last time Ellie saw her mother.

She arrived home Wednesday to an empty house. She searched each room, but Joyce was nowhere. The backdoor stood open, crisp October air seeping in through the screen door. Ellie went to shut it and caught sight of countless cigarette butts scattered across the concrete step. She closed it with a bang, her heart thumping against her chest. She returned to her parent's room and sat at her mother's dressing table. Several glass bottles filled with perfume were nestled on top of a shiny silver tray. Everything seemed in its place, exactly as it should be. She hopped onto the queen size bed and buried her face in Joyce's pillow. She half expected to inhale traces of cigarette smoke, but the scent was of powder and rose petals, exactly like her mother was supposed to smell. She stared at the ceiling for a long time before she fell asleep, curled up around the pillow. When she woke, her father was standing above her looking as confused as she felt.

They phoned friends and neighbors and finally the police. They posted flyers on telephone poles and trees. Days stretched into weeks and months, and eventually they realized Joyce wasn't coming back, although no one could ever determine what had happened or why she'd left. She was never seen or heard from again.

A few months after her mother's desertion, Ellie woke in the night and noticed a light on downstairs. She tiptoed down the steps and through the hall and peeked around the corner. Bill sat at the kitchen table, bent over stacks of envelopes and papers strewn across its surface. His head rested in his hand, his arm propped up by an elbow on the table. His fingers were pushed deep into his dark hair, and moisture from a tear lined his cheek. His face was fraught with worry, covered in stubble, and the wrinkles on his forehead and around his eyes seemed deeper and darker than ever before.

After that, the phone rang often, but Ellie was instructed not to answer. Bill worked longer hours. He volunteered to take overtime shifts when they were offered, and took side jobs whenever he could.

When she got older, Ellie learned that her mother had accrued substantial gambling debts without her father's knowledge before she left. Bill spent the rest of his working years paying them off.

Ellie was forced to learn, as a child, to be an adult. There was no happy playtime at the end of Bill's workday. Her father was kind, his love toward her generous, but when he was home, he was tired, and *she* took on the role of caring for *him*. While he was at work, she looked after herself. She cooked, cleaned, and did the laundry. No one ever made her pancakes, or even cereal, again for breakfast. Even when she got older, she didn't have friends, and she didn't go out.

Although Joyce Anderson took only a suitcase full of clothes from their family home, she robbed her daughter of innocence and tainted Ellie with doubt about everything in life from that point forward. Most of all, she struggled with trust and the ability to love openly.

At least, that was what the therapist said.

Ellie sat in the driveway, staring at the large oak door on the front of her home, and wondered how she would die and whether she'd be alone.

Without love.

Without Adam.

Her father died at the young age of fifty-eight. He never retired, and he never met his grandchildren, even though both were privileges he earned tenfold.

She decided early that she would stake her claim in life one day, and that she'd find a profession that would be kinder than her father's was to him. Mindful of her goals, she maintained honor-roll-worthy grades. Instead of going to college in places she'd always dreamed of, she took a full academic scholarship at a local university because it was close to home, where she could continue to work and help her father.

She was determined to marry for love and only if she could trust without reservation. She thought Adam was all of the above, but in the last few months she often wondered how she could have been so wrong.

━◁┼ ┼▷━

She forced her shoulders back and pulled the car around to the garage. As the door rose, a red sign, partially stuck behind some winter sleds, caught her attention. On it, *Ellen Anderson, C.P.A.* was inscribed in gold. She must have seen this sign every day, perhaps several times a day, but it had been a while since she'd actually noticed it. She cut the engine, stepped out of the car, and crisp, cold air caught in her throat. She moved the sleds, pulled it out, and propped it up so she could see it better. She sat beside it, and cold from the cement floor seeped into her warm body. She ran her fingers over the letters that once represented such a big piece of her life, and she shivered.

An independent certified public accountant, Ellie ran a successful private business for ten years, but when they decided to start a family, she and Adam agreed she should stay home with the kids. After all, they both felt the pain . . . the emotional scars from growing up without a mother. How could she do anything but stay at home and take care of her own children? So, she sold her practice.

And gave up my independence.

Adam, Tommy, and Lizzie: they were her family.

How could we not be enough together?

She thought they were strong.

Now we're not even together.

She stood up, sighed, and pushed the sign back against the gray concrete brick wall. After a moment's hesitation, she pulled her coat tighter around her chest and walked outside. Grass, brittle from months of cold, crunched under her feet with every step as she made her way through the lawn, toward the back edge of their property. Her body warmed, and her pulse quickened, until finally it was in front of her.

She squinted against bright light bouncing off of the metal roof and shielded her eyes with her hands. The winter sun was brilliant, shining down from a blue, cloudless sky. The red brick barn was still one of the most beautiful buildings she had ever seen—old, glorious, and charming. When she and Adam decided to buy this house, it was the barn that cinched the deal for Ellie.

She lifted the metal latch and pushed at the large door. Loud creaking echoed off of the walls as it swung open. An abundance of light filtered in through the windows they added years ago and warmed the cement floor that was poured just after that. As she stepped in, a whiff of dust hit her nose, and she sneezed. An unexpected wave of sadness made her want to cry. Then again, she almost always felt the urge to cry lately. She took a few more steps, to the center of the empty space.

What a shame, not to use something so beautiful. They had planned to refurbish the barn into an office for Ellie. They acquired permits and began construction, but then came the kids. And that was that.

Even more depressed than when she left the garage, Ellie started back toward the house. When she opened the back door and stepped into the mudroom, a bundle of brown fur disguised as the largest chocolate Labrador retriever most people have ever seen barreled around the corner. Buster jumped and ran around once in a tight circle, almost as if he was chasing his tail. His enthusiasm made her laugh, even if only for a moment.

"Hey'ya Buster, how ya doin', buddy?" She allowed him to lick her face as she bent down to scratch the soft fur on his back and tousle his floppy ears.

The phone shrilled from the kitchen, interrupting their play, and her smile turned into a frown. She patted Buster one more time on the stomach. Frustration filled her head as she walked down the hall and around the corner. Lizzie was only at preschool three hours a day, and she needed that precious span of quiet to maintain the tiniest sense of calm. But someone was always demanding her time and with that, another small piece of her sanity disappeared.

She answered, trying not to sound as annoyed as she felt.

"Oh, hi Ellie! It's Bonnie Singleton. How are you doin' dear?"

The familiar voice, chock-full of hollow sincerity, made Ellie cringe, and she silently scolded herself for not having caller-ID. Bonnie was one of the most ostentatious people Ellie had met since she and Adam became part of Emerald Glen's who's-who community. And unfortunately, she was in attendance at *every* event. Owner of a local women's clothing store, she catered to TV personalities, doctor's wives, wealthy widows, and essentially anyone rich with lots of time to gossip. Everyone knew Bonnie, and most of them were sorry because of it. This was particularly true when they were the focus of her attention, and Ellie squirmed at the apparent and unfortunate reality that Bonnie's attention was momentarily directed toward her.

"I'm fine, Bonnie. What can I do for you?" Ellie asked, struggling to be polite.

"Well," she paused (there was always a dramatic pause with Bonnie), "as you may know, I am again the committee chairperson for the hospital ball this year. It's their biggest fundraiser, you know, and this year we're goin' to incorporate an auction to spice things up."

Ellie rolled her eyes at Bonnie's phony singsong voice. "Who else would they call on for such an important job, Bonnie? I'm not surprised; you always make the event so fantastic!" Ellie said, mocking Bonnie's false sincerity.

Ellie had always hated the hospital ball.

"Thank you, darlin'. I do need some help from all you little people out there, though, and this is where you come in, Ellie dear! I wondered if you'd do us all a teensy favor and donate somethin' for the auction?"

Ellie held the phone away from her ear and silently mouthed Bonnie's words with sarcasm. *Little people?*

My God, could the woman get more conceited? She shook her head and returned the phone to her ear.

"I could look around the house, but I'm not sure exactly what we could give that'd be all that—"

"Oh no, dear . . . I don't want any of your personal belongings. You see, I've heard from people round town that your cookin' is just to *die* for, and I thought it'd be fantastic if you could offer to prepare a dinner for eight people in someone's home," Bonnie said. "Wouldn't that be just the best thing you ever did hear of? It'll be a hoot!" Bonnie chuckled, amused at herself.

"You want me to cook dinner? For eight people?" Ellie wrinkled her forehead and massaged her temples.

This was absurd, even for Bonnie.

"That's what I said, darlin'. We like to keep our auction items fresh and interesting. Think about how unique this'd be!"

"Bonnie . . . " Ellie leaned against the kitchen counter and twirled a napkin between her fingers, trying to figure out how to get out of this and off of the phone. "It's true that I love to cook, but I don't think I'm qualified to do something like this. I have no formal training or . . . *anything* even close—"

"If you feel you can't *handle* it, then I'll just relay that information back to the committee. It's no problem, really. I guess I was wrong about you Ellie, you have yourself a good day now, sweetie." Bonnie's voice was slow and sarcastic.

And her tactics worked.

Irritation and contempt took over, and words began to spill from Ellie's mouth before her brain had time to process them.

"I didn't say I *couldn't handle* it. Tell you what, sign me up."

When she hung up, it dawned on her that she may be just as insane as Bonnie.

CHAPTER 8

ADAM

A square-patterned blue carpet squished under Adam's feet and workplace cubicles blurred in his peripheral vision as Adam walked toward Sam's office with purpose. He was determined to make this brief and then get to work.

"Adam?" Marie called, as he walked by her desk on his way toward Sam's door.

Adam stopped, annoyed at the interruption of his single-mindedness. "Morning again, Marie." He forced a tight smile.

"Sam had to run downstairs for just a minute. He said to have a seat in his office, and he'd be right with you." She secured a paperclip at the top of a stack of documents in her hand with a cheery smile.

"Yah sure . . . " he stammered, " . . . actually, it's okay . . . " *Best possible scenario!* "It can wait," Adam said. He raised his palms, and his smile curled upward. "Do me a favor and just tell him I'll catch up with him later, okay?" He turned back toward the hall that would take him to the shiny metal elevator, grateful for the unexpected get-out-of-jail-free card.

"Oh no you don't," Marie called out.

He froze.

"Sam told me that it *is* important, and that I should *not* let you leave this building under any circumstances unless he talks to you first."

Adam's shoulders fell. He turned to face Marie. Like him, her smile was gone.

"You wouldn't want me to get in trouble, now would you?" She folded her arms across her ample chest. "Because he was adamant, and I have no problem calling security to save my own tail." She smiled at him above her double chin with a look that suggested she was teasing but perhaps crazy enough to actually go through with it.

Adam managed another tense smile. Barely. "You betcha, I'll just wait in his office."

He sunk into one of the oversized leather chairs opposite Sam's desk. The office smelled like a newly smoked pipe, although Sam didn't smoke. The scent was usually soothing, but that day Adam wasn't sure anything could calm his nerves. He propped his arms onto his legs and hung a heavy head in his hands.

As promised, Sam didn't take long. "You look a little better." He pat Adam on the back as he walked to the other side of his desk.

"I *am* better. See?" Adam sat up straight and forced a smile. "Everything's fine."

Sam peered at him, unconvinced.

"You know, Sam . . . " He paused, trying to choose his words carefully. "I apologize for this morning, but I really do have to get to work."

"Have you talked to anyone other than me about what's happening with Ellie?" Sam question was tentative, but he wasn't one to mince words.

"No." Adam lowered his eyes to the floor before they snapped back up to Sam again. "You didn't tell Suzanne, did you?"

Anxiety flooded Adam's stomach at the consideration that the entire town might be aware of his separation from Ellie, temporarily overriding his thoughts of little Bobby Fleich.

Sam shook his head and sighed. "It's the only thing I've ever kept from my wife. Frankly, I can't believe Ellie hasn't told her. They're best friends."

"You know how Emerald Glen is . . . "

Where everyone's perfect.

Sam raised his eyebrows.

"Ellie and I have talked about it. We just . . . thought it was best to keep it quiet for now," Adam said.

Sam leaned back against his chair and looked out the window. "I don't like it. If you aren't careful you're going to be a patient in this hospital, rather than just a board member."

"If it weren't for the apartment, I probably wouldn't even have told you."

"We're friends." Sam's expression was a mixture of hurt and surprise. "And you're not going to win this argument with reasoning like that."

"I appreciate you renting me the apartment, and I hate to put you in this position with Suzanne, but I'm just not comfortable with the gossip that you know will come when people find out." Adam returned his head to his hands.

"Eventually, though . . . "

Sam paused, and they both remained silent for a long moment.

"What are you going to do long term?" Sam asked, rephrasing.

"I was kind of hoping we might reconcile."

"Oh." Sam held his hands in front of him, his elbows resting on the arms of his chair. He paused for a moment and lightly tapped his fingertips together. "Have you discussed that with Ellie?"

"No." Adam raked his fingers through his hair. *I wish.* He thought they would have been through this by now. He thought things would be back to normal.

Sam leaned forward in his chair. "I won't tell Suzanne anything, *for now*. But if I see you like this again"—Sam shook his head—"I won't stand by and watch you fall apart."

"Fair enough," Adam said. *Thank God I'm excused.* Adam shook Sam's hand. He had just made it to the door when Sam spoke again.

"Oh, and by the way, we voted to keep that boy here for a week and then revisit the situation."

The words brought Adam to an abrupt halt. His body ran cold, preventing him from turning to face Sam. He fought hard to mutter a reply through the lump that had returned to his throat. "That's great, Sam. Thanks for the update." He made it down the hall as fast as his legs could carry him without actually running.

CHAPTER 9

ELLIE

Ellie repeatedly slammed her cordless phone on the granite kitchen countertop while mentally cursing the day she met Bonnie Singleton.

She walked to the laundry room, pulled a duster, polish, and paper towels from the shelf and tossed them into a bucket with cleansers and disinfectants. Her frustration fueled a burst of energy that had to be acknowledged.

Now.

She scoured the kitchen sink and wiped down the counters. Without pausing, she marched to the powder room, where she scrubbed the toilet, diligently avoiding her reflection in the mirror as she slid a paper towel over the surface until it sparkled. Once the living room furniture was polished, she found herself standing in the foyer, red-faced and breathless.

She stood near the banister at the foot of a grand staircase, the entryway's showpiece. Gliding her hand over the smooth surface of the wooden railing, she thought about how much she loved this house—the house she and Adam chose. *The home we made together.* Although the house was big, it had never seemed empty.

Until now.

They had furnished it for real living with soft, practical furniture in colors that reflected the brown, gray, and blue earth tones they were both so fond of. The walls were filled with artwork; some were paintings by up-and-coming local artists, some framed creations made by their children.

Shoes, boots, hats, sunglasses, and coats overflowed from hooks and a shelf above a bench inside the mudroom door at the garage entrance. Adam's things used to add to the clutter, but not anymore. It was one of the things that annoyed her most—his messy disposition—and she often accused him of teaching the kids to follow suit.

After all, he was a grown man, why couldn't he just pick up after himself? Must I do everything? Must I be the only one to keep things tidy? I'm not the maid! She'd yell the words, but no one ever seemed to hear them. Adam would merely look at her as if she'd lost her mind, and that only fueled her anger.

She was tired. Tired of the mundane routine of dishes and laundry and sweeping the floor, of school lunches and homework, of changing sheets and hearing small voices yell "Mom!" all day, all evening, during every waking moment, and then some. She was annoyed with Adam who would come home from work and sit to watch television or play with the kids while she started dinner after already finishing a full day with no breaks.

And now, she found herself in an empty house, without Adam's clutter, without Adam's company at dinner, without the laughter of her children as he played with them and tossed them into the air. She slept in a bed without the comfort of his warmth.

And she was still tired.

And unhappier than ever. The thought hit her in the chest, nearly taking her breath away.

Her eyes drifted back to the living room, and she wandered through it. She dragged her fingers across the oversized beige couch where she and Adam used to sit and read during lazy

Saturday afternoons when she was pregnant with Tommy. A sturdy wooden rocker rested in a corner at the far side of the room, a cream colored blanket draped over its arm. She picked through a stack of books nestled in a basket beside the curved base of the chair, and toward the bottom found several children's stories. The familiarity of these tales she had read countless times brought stinging to her eyes.

Built-in oak bookcases spanned the entire length of the east wall. She studied groups of framed pictures interspersed between books that filled the shelves. They told a story: about her kids, about their family, about her life. Her eyes moved across them slowly, one by one . . . Lizzie in the bath with bubbles on her chubby cheeks . . . Tommy on a swing, his knee scraped from a fall off his bike the week before . . . Adam and her on their wedding day.

All the way at the top, a black wooden frame was pushed toward the back, just far enough to be out of view. She stretched and strained to reach it. Finally, she pulled it down and blew the dust off its surface. The photo was a black and white of her and Adam in the early days of their relationship, taken at their old apartment before they were married, the memory as clear as if it'd been yesterday.

The night of the picture, they had met in the bedroom after work, as they often did. Adam unknotted his tie, slid it from his neck, and loosened the buttons of his dress shirt. Just as she kicked off her heels and began to peel the nylons from her legs, he appeared at her back and pressed against her, his fingers moving to the zipper at the back of her skirt.

"Allow me." He bent down and dropped a kiss on the side of her neck. His hands slid over her hips, and moments later they were where they often ended up.

As their pulses slowed, they lounged under a sheet, carelessly draped over their bodies. With flushed cheeks, they stared and smiled at each other until he reached out to pull her closer. For the next hour, they shared stories about their day, laughed together, and talked about the future, all while Adam gently traced invisible figure eights on the bare skin of her arm with his finger.

Their nightly ritual didn't always include sex. Sometimes they would change into something comfortable and just lounge together. Either way, the intimacy remained. Communication, spoken and unspoken, always there.

"Let's never stop doing this," Adam said.

"What, having sex?" Ellie laughed.

He raised his eyes to the ceiling and jabbed her in the ribs. "Yah, that too." He smiled, and then his face turned serious. "But, I mean *this*—talking like this." His fingertips slid softly over the skin on her shoulder. "I've never been this close to anyone, El. I've never been able to talk to anyone the way I can talk to you."

She rolled over to face him, ready to agree, but Adam's eyes were cast downward, and she found herself uncomfortable with his pensive expression. Gripped by anxiety, she summoned her most enthusiastic voice.

"I know!" she said. She leapt out of bed and returned with an old 35mm film camera they had purchased the month before. It was used, from a thrift store, but to them it was still a new treasure. "Let's take a picture," she said. "That way we can always remember to never stop doing this." She threw sweatpants and a t-shirt at Adam and then dressed herself.

"What are these for?" he asked, his brow creased.

She rolled her eyes. "I'm not taking the picture while we're naked."

"We're covered up," he said, grabbing a section of the sheet and bunching it in his hand.

"Just put them on."

He remained still for a moment, as if he expected Ellie to change her mind. "Crazy woman," Adam finally said. When she didn't respond, he shook his head and did as he was told. They fell back onto the bed and held the camera at arm's length above them. Although they attempted the shot several times, this was the only one on the roll that came out. The others cut off his head or hers, or his left side or hers. Ellie was ecstatic when they picked up the pictures, and she framed this one the moment they got home.

She ran her finger over the glass.

She was right—it would forever be a reminder.

How could we forget not to stop talking?

Their evening routine continued for years, even through her pregnancy with Tommy. It was after he was born, when they were pacing the floors with a crying infant, that things changed. She never even thought about it, never even noticed it *had* changed, until now. Not really. Not seriously. She was too tired and too busy.

And now it's too late.

Holding the picture frame against her chest, she slid to a seated position on the floor. Memories flooded her mind, and she realized communication between them might be the only thing that ever did change. Adam was always messy, she just never minded cleaning up after him until two messes became four. Even with busy careers, things were easy before the kids came.

She rested her head against the wall at her back. A nanny was never on her wish list. She never wanted someone to mother her children. She just needed a little help. Why couldn't Adam see that?

Then again, she couldn't remember if she had ever told him.

"Oh Adam, why did we stop?"

The sound of her own desperate whisper made her wince. She rose to her feet and replaced the frame, but this time she positioned it toward the front of the shelf.

Guilt washed over her. Not talking was one thing. Keeping secrets was another.

And the most unbearable part was her ultimate betrayal.

She placed a hand over her stomach and considered terminating the pregnancy—she'd thought about it several times since her visit with Dr. Van Linden, of course she had—but then she thought of her kids. And then, how could she?

Her heart heavy in her chest, she returned to the kitchen. Time to assess the damage to her house phone.

She could no longer bear the burden of a life that has become a train wreck.

Not without talking to someone.

Not without going insane.

She picked up the phone and, with a shaky hand, dialed one of the few numbers permanently etched into her brain.

CHAPTER 10

ADAM

A dam arrived at work and paused outside of his office. He took a moment to examine the words displayed in block print, etched into a silver plate and bolted onto the sleek maple door.

Adam J. Thomas
President and CEO
Exactitude Accounting Firm

The years had gone by so quickly, and sometimes he wondered how he had gotten here: forty-three years old, president of a company, two kids. And now, separated from his wife.

He knew the demands of his career put stress on their relationship. He sometimes attended meetings late into the evening, and although he always managed to stay on topic, the nagging voice in the back of his head repeatedly reminded him that he was missing a night with his family—the only place he *really* wanted to be.

Their vows were for richer or poorer, but financially he felt pressured to work harder, to be successful, and to bring home enough money to give them anything they desired.

Well, almost anything.

Not that Ellie ever said she needed or wanted anything they didn't already have. The only thing she ever seemed excited about was the barn, and well . . .

He recalled the look on her face when they found out she was pregnant with Tommy, when they decided to scrap the idea of turning the barn into her office, and he cringed.

Now he can only think of one thing *he* wants that he doesn't have.

What are you left with when you lose the thing you treasure most? The question swirled in his mind. Reluctantly, he pushed the door open and took a seat at his desk, answered emails, and visited on-line news sites, but he found it hard to focus.

"Knock, knock." Marc Walsh, Adam's COO, entered without an invitation and walked past Adam's desk quickly enough to send a few papers flying into the air. Marc was a wrestler, and even in his forties it still showed. With a stocky build, he was a force of nature.

Marc stopped in front of the television and clicked it on.

"Another one!" Marc motioned toward the screen, where a reporter was jabbering about yet another bank that had entered receivership with the FDIC. His dark, thick eyebrows closed together in concern, and he frowned.

Adam tapped his pen against the desk. "This far beyond the financial meltdown, you'd think we wouldn't still be seeing this." Adam shook his head. "I don't remember them being a client." His eyes met Marc's. "Tell me they weren't?"

"They weren't," Marc said.

Adam allowed his shoulders to relax.

"As I understand it, there are rumors of another acquisition, and I'm told it's mostly due to insolvency issues."

"Who?" Adam asked.

"ABT Bank and Trust."

"Oh, fun."

"Yep, get ready." Marc clicked off the television and stormed out the door at the same pace in which he entered.

Adam tossed the pen onto the stack of papers in front of him. He didn't doubt that all reports from his company were fair, accurate, and unbiased, but he despised being connected in any way to another business that may have been anything less than one hundred percent forthright or could have performed something unethical under his nose.

Of course there was always a possibility, but he wanted no part of it. He loathed potential inquisition by the FDIC or any other agency looking to point fingers and place blame. The thought alone made him sit straighter, caused his cheeks to flush, and gave him a headache.

He has always stressed the importance of ethics with his employees. During the financial boom, other accounting firms were winning bids for larger Fortune 500 companies. They were dominating the marketplace, while Exactitude kept its revenues and sales goals at a slow, steady pace. "Persistence and integrity," he would tell his team, "is what will make us the best we can be."

And he was right.

Executives were arrested and hauled off to jail when companies like Enron and WorldCom fell from their perch as the twentieth century ended and the twenty-first began—a result of shady accounting practices like cooking the books. In 2008, he watched the television in fear when dismal consequences and massive economic destruction rippled with fury around the globe, created by banks and financial institutions that failed to be prudent.

Because Exactitude continued on a patient path, they managed to keep their stock price stable—a huge accomplishment considering the substantial declines experienced by many other financial organizations.

Adam studied the printed words displayed in a picture frame at the corner of his desk:

Exactitude Accounting Firm

It is our mission, as a Certified Public Accounting Firm, to provide an honest examination of financial records. We will act with the highest of ethical standards and integrity and ensure that conflicts of interest do not exist in our client relationships. Our reports will be factual and free of personal opinion.

He considered the meaning of this statement—a statement he had read every day for the last twenty-one years—a statement that has served him, his company, and his employees, well. The message was created by principles formulated under Charlie's guidance, a wise man, someone he missed every day.

He was proud of his accomplishments at Exactitude, but he suddenly wondered if the company he loved so much had somehow become a conflict of interest with his marriage. Over the years, people had advised him to hire more help and not to take on so many roles. They had warned that one or two people could not do so much alone. Currently, Marc held responsibility as both the company's Chief Operating Officer and Chief Financial Officer, leaving Adam to pick up some of Marc's responsibilities.

He drummed his fingers against the wooden desk and wrinkled his forehead. Adam cringed at the thought—one he never stopped to consider before—that not only hadn't he thought of how the stress of being understaffed had affected his own marriage, he hadn't thought of how it may have affected Marc's personal life, either. Marc was a good employee and a friend. He put in long hours without complaint, but if Adam was honest, he knew it couldn't be easy. Marc must also be sacrificing time with his wife, Toni, and his son, John.

Of course, he knew why they did it—it was all about the revenue. He would never do anything without total integrity, but he had pushed himself and the person he relied on most in business to save the company money and make the stockholders happier.

He shook his head. *Sometimes life has got to be more important than money.*

Adam pushed away from his desk and started toward Marc's office, knowing what he needed to do. On the way, he checked his watch and noticed the lunch hour was already upon them—12:17 p.m.

For more years than he could remember, he went home for lunch to decompress whenever he had the opportunity. Since he'd moved out of the house, he has stayed at the office and buried himself in work. Perhaps, he considered, it was time to reconsider old habits. After all, most of the fundamentals he learned from Charlie and came to follow over the years had served him well. That was, when he had actually followed them.

PART III

From This Day Forward

CHAPTER 11

ELLIE

While Suzanne made a cup of tea for each of them, Ellie sat at the table in the breakfast nook and wondered how to start a conversation she knew she needed to have. She fidgeted with her fingers, bit her nails, and finally shoved her hands under her legs in frustration. Her eyes moved to the white farm sink in search of dishes to clean, but she had already done that. Even the granite countertops were scoured and shining.

She watched Suzanne with envy. Her brown hair shone with bronze highlights that always seem perfectly placed, her brown eyes without a trace of the exhaustion Ellie felt. In a black pencil skirt, white silk tank top, and matching suit jacket, Suzanne was the ideal model for classic businesswomen's fashion. Without the fingerprints that normally covered the tall stainless steel refrigerator, even her reflection was perfect.

Not that Ellie was jealous of her friend. She's wasn't, really. But she longed for the days of old, when she felt perfectly put together and well-rested.

"Suzanne, I can do that," Ellie said for the third time.

"I'm perfectly capable." Suzanne pulled a carton of cream from the refrigerator.

"But it's my kitchen. I invited you here, and now you're waiting on me. I feel bad." The moment the words were spoken, Ellie realized she didn't mean them. It was nice to have someone wait on her for a change. She didn't feel bad. She just felt … nervous.

"By the looks of those gray bags under your eyes, I think *I* need to be making the tea for *you*. And what's wrong with your hair, El? It looks like it hasn't been washed for days, much less combed."

Ellie absently touched her hair and wondered if things were even worse than she had thought. She pulled an elastic hair tie from her wrist and collected her hair into a ponytail.

Suzanne gave Ellie a sideways glance while dropping sugar into the warm liquid. "When are you going to tell me what's going on here?"

"I was . . . cleaning."

Suzanne raised one eyebrow, her silent *'I know better than that'* gesture, and Ellie blushed at the feeble excuse. Suzanne slid a hot mug in front of Ellie. "We only have … what?" she asked, checking her watch. "Maybe an hour before Lizzie wakes from her nap? You can do better than that."

Ellie breathed into the steam rising from the sweet smelling tea and hoped for a calming effect. She stammered and stuttered and tried to decide where to begin until she finally blurted out the words, "I'm pregnant."

Suzanne's eyes widened in surprise before she smiled and dismissed the news as nothing more than a blip on life's radar. She actually said that.

Ellie stared at her with a blank expression.

Suzanne's smile slowly faded. "What?"

The clock ticked in the silence between them.

Ellie told her that Adam moved out almost three months ago.

Suzanne's face lengthened, and she set her mug on the table with a loud clang. The wounded expression in Suzanne's eyes questioned how Ellie could keep such a big secret and for so long. Ellie hung her head and apologized, fighting back the tears, trying to explain.

"If Adam finds out I told you, he'll be really . . . well, pissed wouldn't begin to cover it."

Suzanne softened and placed a hand over Ellie's arm with a reassuring squeeze.

"And that's not all. The baby"—Ellie looked at the floor—"it's not Adam's." A fresh set of tears burned against her eyelids. She didn't think it possible to cry so much, but hearing the words aloud was even worse than the silent thought.

Suzanne sat shell-shocked for what felt like an eternity, but in reality was only maybe a minute, while Ellie wondered what to say next. Unable to say anything, she waited for a response. Finally, Suzanne walked to the sink, dumped her remaining tea, and deposited her mug in the dishwasher.

Oh my God, she's leaving! You've ruined your marriage and *lost your best friend.* But her fears were replaced with relief when Suzanne crossed the kitchen to the mini-bar and poured a tall glass of white wine. She returned to the table, sat down, and looked at Ellie.

"Well, my friend, you may not be able to have any of this, but I sure as hell need a glass," she said. "Tell me everything."

Ellie listed the problems between her and Adam—she felt lonely and taken for granted, she was tired of the mundane job of being a mom and a wife, they stopped talking and drifted apart, and the distance between them grew until the silence and resentment was unbearable. "So, finally, one day I told him to get out."

"And?"

Ellie shrugged her shoulders. "He left. And I couldn't believe he did it. I'm not even sure if I meant it when I said it, but he left." Her hand began to tremble, and she moved it from the table to her lap. "How could he do that? How could he leave me when he knows? He knows how hard it was for me when I was a child. *He knows!*" Her voice escalated in frustration with every sentence.

Suzanne sat pensive for a minute while Ellie moped and stared at the floor.

"Well, honey, not to defend Adam—it sounds like he's been a bit of a jerk—but you did tell him to leave." Suzanne twirled the stem of her wine glass on the surface of the table. "Did you want him to stay or did you want him to go?"

The question stung, but Ellie didn't expect polite agreement from Suzanne. That was why she called her.

Ellie released her shoulder-length, mousy brown hair from the ponytail that was now beginning to give her a headache. "You know, I envy you." Ellie twisted the hairband between her fingers.

"Why, because I say what I mean?" Suzanne asked with a chuckle.

"No. I miss my job."

Suzanne smiled and nodded. "I remember those days. It's easier now that the kids are teenagers. Well, at least in some ways. But when they were young I wanted to pull my hair out." She ran her finger over condensation that clung to the outer edge of her wine glass and looked into the distance. "Going back to work when I bought your practice was good timing for me. I felt better. I get it." She looked at Ellie with a smile that quickly turned into a frown. "Tell me you don't regret selling it to me?"

"You're joking?" Ellie flashed a look that said *'don't be stupid,'* and Suzanne smiled.

Ellie thought about how easy it was to bond with Suzanne when she first moved to Emerald Glen—a friendship that solidified quicker than the time it took her to bake the first cake they would share over afternoon tea. They were both CPAs, and they understood each other's language—a language that most people didn't comprehend.

Suzanne's kids were younger then. She was a stay-at-home mom, while Ellie was building a career and growing a clientele.

Charlie tried to convince Ellie to work at his firm when she finished school, but she didn't want to work with Adam. She preferred to keep their personal and business relationships separate. Besides, she always felt more comfortable in the intimate space of her office, just her and her clients, versus the corporate world that Adam and Charlie lived in.

When Ellie and Adam started a family, selling her thriving practice was the logical thing to do. But her clients had become friends, people who appeared at her desk year after year, sometimes month after month, sharing intimate pieces of their lives with her. She went to their retirement parties, visited them in the hospital when their children and grandchildren were born, attended funerals when their love ones passed away.

Handing them over to a stranger who wouldn't care as much as she did was unfathomable. When Suzanne approached her with the proposition of purchasing the business, it was an offer Ellie couldn't refuse, the ideal situation for both of them.

She didn't regret giving it all up to stay at home with her kids. To the contrary, she felt obligated to stay with them, since she'd lost her own mother at just eight years old. But still . . .

"Ellie?" Suzanne asked. "Is there something else? Not that I need any more surprises, but you seem to have checked out over there."

"It's just that . . . " Ellie lowered her eyes. "I hate myself, for missing it." Shame for saying aloud what she had been feeling for so long threatened to swallow her whole. "How can I feel that way after living through my mom leaving us?"

Suzanne gave Ellie's hand a gentle squeeze. "You can't beat yourself up this way. You're a good mom. It's not the same." Suzanne reclined in her chair and pointed at Ellie's stomach. "We still haven't discussed the father of that baby." Her words were tentative and came without judgment, but the truth behind them—the fact that this child was not Adam's—sliced through Ellie's heart. She could literally feel a pain in her chest.

"Remember when you and I were supposed to get together for dinner a couple of months ago? I showed up at your office, but you weren't there because you forgot? I think you were out at a client meeting or something?"

Suzanne nodded. "What does that have to do with this?"

"I was feeling really bad about things with Adam that day, and I got to talking to Katie."

"My secretary?"

Ellie nodded and explained that Katie was on her way out and invited Ellie to have dinner with her and a friend. She didn't know them well. Actually, she hardly knew them at all, but for the first time in forever she felt like more than a mom who never left the house except to run errands. But her excitement quickly diminished. Dinner was dreadful, full of phrases she didn't understand like hashtag and retweet, and she carelessly consumed more martinis than her five-foot-five frame could handle.

"That's where I met Ryan." Ellie recoiled at the sound of his name.

"Ryan who?"

"The UPS guy that comes into your office every day." Ellie offered a timid look.

"You mean the Ryan that looks to be about twenty-three-years-old with body-builder muscles? *That* Ryan?" Her mouth was gaping in shock. "You slept with *Ryan*?" A broad smile spread across her face, and she made a tisk-tisk sound. "Oh my God, Ellie! You bad, bad girl."

"It's not funny," Ellie said with a tight-lipped expression. "This is the biggest crisis of my life."

"I know, I know." Suzanne waved her hand and shook her head. "But Ryan?" She looked dazed. "How did you ever end up . . . you know, *with* him?"

Ellie rested a weary head in her hands. She ran her fingers deep into her hair and pulled at the roots, wondering why this all couldn't just be a nightmare.

"I don't remember," Ellie said.

"What do you mean you *don't remember?*"

"I told you. I drank. A lot." Ellie took a deep breath. "And the next morning I was at Ryan's. Magic. Poof." Ellie released an invisible burst with her fingertips. "I didn't even know where I was at first. I woke up lying in this bed that smelled like body odor. I was dressed. Well, I was mostly dressed."

Suzanne probed Ellie to continue with an impatient hand gesture.

"My skirt was on, but my top was unbuttoned. And then I went to use the bathroom and found"—Ellie closed her eyes and tried to suppress the lump forming in her throat—"my panties on the floor." Her body swelled with shame, and beads of sweat formed on her back. "I put myself together and got out of there."

"What about Ryan?" Suzanne was still wide-eyed.

"He was snoring like a train on the other side of the bed. He didn't wake up, though—thank God—and I haven't talked to him since."

"Wow." Suzanne let out a breath.

"That's all you have for me? 'Wow'?"

"What do you want me to say? You just laid something pretty close to the sins of Adam and Eve on me, and all before one o'clock in the afternoon."

"Suzanne!"

"Sorry," Suzanne said, shaking her head and blinking her eyes with exaggeration.

She emptied the remainder of wine in the bottle that had since made its way from the bar area to the table, swallowed it in one gulp, and swiftly returned her glass to the table. She straightened her posture and focused her eyes, tight on Ellie.

Ellie braced herself, recognizing this behavior. This was the let's-get-down-to-business-Suzanne.

"So, Ryan doesn't know right?" Suzanne asked.

Ellie shook her head and cringed at the thought.

"Do you still love Adam?"

Ellie frowned, sadness washing over her. "I've messed it all up." She pushed her fingers deeper into her hair and held her head, propped up again by her elbows on the table.

"You have to talk to him and tell him about the baby."

"Because that would be such a wonderful conversation. Let's see. Adam, I still love you and I want you to move back in with me because I'm having someone else's baby! How's that?" Ellie rolled her eyes and gave Suzanne a tight smile.

"You want him to move back in with you because you still love him, regardless of whose baby you're carrying."

"Okaaay . . . but I can't just pass this child off as being his." Ellie's eyes widened. "Is that what you're suggesting?"

It was Suzanne's turn to flash the '*don't be stupid*' glare. "I think your biggest mistake all along is that you haven't been honest. Not with yourself *or* with Adam *or* with Ryan. Or me, for that matter, until now."

Ellie looked at the floor. She wondered if she should start counting the floorboards. It seemed to be the most suitable place for her to look these days—downward in shame.

"I'm telling you this as your friend," Suzanne said. "A marriage does not work without communication. I'm close enough to you and Adam to know that your love is real. That tiny fact alone makes you one of the lucky ones. But you can't keep that going if you don't talk and listen to one another. Don't let this go on any longer. If Adam loves you, he'll come back. But whatever happens, he's Tommy and Lizzie's father, not to mention the man you love. From this day forward, Ellie, you need to be honest with yourself and with your husband."

Ellie stomach lurched. She could no longer tell if it was the baby making her sick or her nerves.

"And I think you need to work."

Ellie's head snapped up. "What?'

"You need a job."

Ellie shook her head. "You know I can't—"

"You. Need. To. Work." Suzanne tapped a French-manicured fingernail on the table with every word and leaned forward, peering at Ellie like a teacher scolding a student. "Even if Adam comes back, you aren't going to be happy unless you reclaim some sense of yourself outside of these four walls."

"I can't."

"You can. You must. You are a good mother, Ellie. You need to do this for your kids as much as for yourself, and you'll be a better mother for it, trust me."

Ellie wanted to believe her.

I can't . . . leave them.

The door in the mudroom opened and then slammed closed, interrupting their conversation and causing Ellie to jump. This was only supposed to be a party for two, and when Suzanne glanced at her inquisitively, Ellie looked toward the hallway with unease.

"Ellie?" Adam called, as he headed around the corner and into the kitchen.

Her shoulders fell in relief at his familiarity, and she relaxed. Until she saw his expression.

"Suzanne," Adam said, looking confused. He glanced at the wine bottle on the counter and then studied Ellie's face. "What a surprise," he added.

Again, she looked down. Her eyes were still burning, her tear-stained cheeks hot and undoubtedly red.

"Hey, Adam," Suzanne said. Ellie's stomach leapt again at the telltale caution in her voice. "How've you been?" Suzanne's lips spread into a smile as she walked to the other side of the counter. She reached out and gave Adam a friendly hug.

A rigid form extended from his head to his legs as he reciprocated hesitantly.

"Ellie and I were just finishing lunch." She turned away from Adam and toward Ellie. "Is it okay if I run, sweetie? I have some errands before my next client." The expression on Suzanne's face was filled with alarm and consolation all at the same time.

Ellie forced a smile and gave a permissible nod, but she was unable to pretend that the space between the three of them was anything but awkward.

CHAPTER 12

MR. & MRS.

Adam tossed his keys onto the counter, and Ellie braced herself for what she knew was coming.

"I suppose you told her even though you promised you wouldn't. And don't even try to deny it, El, I think I know you well enough to see what's going on here." Adam motioned to the empty wine bottle on the counter and her disheveled appearance.

Oh, if only he knew how much she wished she *had* drunk that wine. As if the kids weren't enough to deal with, as if she wasn't already stressed to the brim about the pregnancy, now she had to listen to a lecture from Adam.

"I'm sorry, okay." She rose to clear the counter and tidy the kitchen—something she did when she was nervous. "I couldn't do it anymore without talking to *someone*. I mean really," she huffed, "it's been three months. How long are we going to play out this charade?" She rinsed her mug and set it in the dishwasher. It clanked against a glass, the sound loud enough to make her wonder if it had shattered. Her pulse began to pound as she tossed the empty wine bottle into the recycle bin.

Adam looked at her, but he didn't answer. This wasn't what he came here for, and he didn't want to fight. She looked worn-out and distraught—which was exactly how he felt.

"What do you want, Adam?" she asked, her voice still escalated in defense. She crossed her arms over her chest and wondered why he wasn't responding and what possibly could've brought him here now, in the middle of a workday. "Did you come to pick a fight with me? Do you *need* something? What is it?"

Adam took a moment to consider the sarcasm in her voice and what to say next. So many of their recent conversations seemed to have gone this way. Fleetingly, he wondered when that started. What he *really* wanted to do was put his arms around his wife and never let go. What he *really* wanted to do was tell her how much he loved her. But he couldn't tell her because she was always so cold and distant. And what if she didn't still love him back? Those were the doubts that always seemed to win in the end, forcing him into a corner, causing him to either stand and fight or flee and run for safer, calmer ground.

"Well?" she persisted.

"I just . . . " He couldn't decide.

The phone rang, interrupting their conversation. The shrill noise seemed louder than normal, somehow magnified in the silence and tension between them.

"Are you going to get that?" He was unsure of whether he was happy or annoyed at the intrusion.

Ellie rolled her eyes and walked toward the phone with an attitude Adam had seen Lizzie take more than once. She answered in a voice that indicated her lack of patience.

"Well hello, Ellie dear! How are you? It's Bonnie Singleton." The sappy, thick tone of Bonnie's voice threatened to push Ellie to the edge of sanity.

Ellie gritted her teeth. "What can I do for you, Bonnie?"

"Well," Bonnie said, sighing and pausing dramatically, "we had a committee meetin' for the hospital ball, and you know, they were all just *sooo* pleased that you were willin' to cook a dinner, but they had one teeny tiny request, if you could be so gracious, darlin'."

Now what does this wretched woman want? Ellie felt like she was about to be eaten by a shark.

"Okaayy?" Ellie said slowly.

"They didn't think eight people was as practical as ten. You know how it is, people have so many friends, and ten is just a round, double-digit number. And you know, since we're approachin' the middle of February, we really need to get this wrapped up, dear. We only have a little more than a month to go!"

Ellie leaned up against the wall and massaged her forehead.

"So, honey, do you think you can make dinner for ten people instead of eight?"

"Sure, Bonnie. Ten it is." *Twelve if I can get off the phone with you.*

"Oh how wonderful!" Bonnie exclaimed.

As soon as Ellie opened her mouth to say goodbye, Bonnie started up again.

"Oh, and by the way, how's that husband of yours? He gave us all quite a scare at the hospital board meetin' you know."

"Excuse me?" Ellie asked. She turned to look at Adam.

"Didn't you hear? He got up in the middle of a nomination to vote and ran straight out of the room, white as a sheet and all wobbly kneed. I hope he isn't gettin' that nasty bug that's goin' round." Bonnie made a tisk-tisk sound. "Oh, and that poor boy, Bobby."

Bewildered, Ellie watched Adam take inventory of the refrigerator from across the room, only half listening to Bonnie. The circumstances under which he walked into the kitchen hadn't allowed her to process the tired expression on his unusually pale face.

"Poor, poor boy. I just don't know what in heaven's name they're goin' to do with him since they still haven't found next of kin," Bonnie said.

Ellie caught the end of Bonnie's sentence, and her heart skipped, bringing her full attention back to their conversation.

"What did you just say?" Ellie asked.

"I *said* I just don't know what we're goin' to do with that little Bobby. It's so sad," she said, "that poor boy, losin' his parents in a car crash like that. I just hope they find the next of kin soon because you know, my goodness, we just can't keep him in the hospital forever."

"Oh, *that*." Ellie glanced at Adam again. Fragments of information began to fit together like pieces of a puzzle, and a horrible clarity settled over Ellie, along with whole lot of guilt for being so mean only a few minutes before.

"Yes, that's a problem. Well, Bonnie, I really do have to run, okay? Ta-ta." Ellie quickly hit the off button, before Bonnie had an opportunity to reply.

She looked down at her shoes for a moment and then held the cordless phone against her forehead, contemplating how to best approach Adam, but she knew there was no good way. Finally, her eyes settled on him.

"What was that all about?" Adam asked, pulling a large plastic bottle of lemonade from the refrigerator and pouring himself a glass. "Want some?"

Ellie shook her head and waved a hand dismissively. She replaced the phone and leaned against the wall behind her. "Adam?" she said in the gentlest tone she could muster.

"Yah?" He picked up his glass, took a long drink, and returned it to the counter.

"Did you go to see him?"

"Who?

"Bobby."

Adam froze, his body straight as a rod, his hand still on the lemonade glass in front of him. For a moment, Ellie wondered if he was even breathing, but sad eyes that began to swim behind glossy tears broke his motionless pose.

Anger and frustration disappeared from the kitchen as quickly as they entered. Ellie crossed the room and reached up to Adam, softly touching his cheeks and wiping away a tear. She transferred her hands to the back of his neck and pulled his head down toward her shoulder. He allowed himself to fall into her, his back heaving with each heavy, painful sob as she stood for a long time, shushing him and telling him she understood.

CHAPTER 13

ELLIE

Ellie added a touch of sugar and cream to the coffee in front of her and stirred methodically while she debated the irony so often present in her life. That morning, she was the one who needed a shoulder to cry on; but in a span of less than two hours, she *was* the shoulder being cried on.

She walked into the living room and found Adam sitting on the couch, his body a reflection of utter exhaustion.

"Coffee," she said, handing him the warm mug.

He took it from her and smiled as she sat down beside him. "You know," he said, his voice raspy, "I thought maybe we should go to the hospital ball together?" He placed his free hand over her knee.

She stared at him, her expression blank, stupefied at his sudden change of topic, especially one so trite.

"Why? So people don't talk?" Resentment crept into her blood again, ever so slightly.

"No, because I *want* to go with you."

"Poppycock," she said.

"What?" Adam asked.

"It means bullshit. I don't believe you."

"Yah, I know what it means," Adam said, clearly frustrated.

"Oh." Now she felt stupid.

"But nobody uses that word," he continued.

Dr. Van Linden does, she wanted to say. She bit her tongue.

"I'm serious, El. I really want us to go together. No hidden agenda."

She examined his face, a face she knew well after seventeen years of marriage. The lines etched into his fair skin seemed to have multiplied, the gray hair sprinkled into dark brown above his ears filling in a larger space now. She searched his blue eyes, trying to decide whether to trust him, whether to believe his objective wasn't to save face in the eyes of their upper-middle class community.

This was the problem with Adam—he had never been much for talking or openly expressing emotion, and often she was left feeling doubtful and confused.

His hand moved on top of hers and covered her skin with warmth. "I miss you, El."

Ellie's heart jumped in her chest, her throat constricting at his words—words she has wanted to say to him, words she has longed to hear him say. But the summersaults in her stomach pulled her back to reality—back to the baby.

Oh Adam . . .

She swallowed hard. The afternoon sky was already darker outside. Clouds had rolled in, light filtering through the windows gloomy compared to the brilliant sun of this morning. Normally, this would depress Ellie, but now she was almost thankful. Perhaps the partial darkness could aid in hiding the doom she felt inside.

"Daddyyyy!" a voice screeched with joy from the steps as Lizzie came barreling down them, around the corner. She jumped into her father's lap, her joy unbridled.

"There's my girl!" He hugged her tight before tickling her. She squealed with delight.

"Daddy, I miss you so much." She snuggled up against Adam's chest, visibly unaware of his haggard appearance.

Ellie's heart melted as she watched Adam rest his head on Lizzie's and close his eyes, holding her close as he stroked her hair.

What had she accomplished by asking Adam to leave? She wondered if she made the right choices, if there was something else she could've done. The space and distance between them—not just their marriage, but among their family unit of four—had grown larger than ever. How could she hope to reconcile and resume any version of their once happy life together now, when she knew the discomfort in her stomach wasn't caused only by the sadness she felt in her heart?

Suzanne's voice echoed in her mind: *From this day forward, Ellie, you need to be honest with yourself and with Adam.* But she couldn't possibly tell Adam about the baby now.

Not now.

She took in his blue eyes—red-rimmed and swollen—and envisioned the board meeting where they debated Bobby's fate. She could almost feel Adam's pain as if it were her own.

I can't tell him now. But I'll tell him soon.

Lizzie turned her cheek against Adam's chest and looked at Ellie. "I'm hungry Mommy, can I have a snack?" she asked, interrupting Ellie's thoughts.

"Sure, honey."

Ellie blindly headed for the kitchen. Small feet padded behind her, and Lizzie jumped up onto a barstool while Ellie pulled a tub of yogurt from the refrigerator.

Adam followed behind Lizzie and entered the room struggling to fix his tie.

"I don't know why you're bothering with that," Ellie said, pointing at his tie.

Adam looked down and frowned at the blue and gold silky material, crumpled from the weight of a thirty-two-pound little girl.

"You aren't really going back to work, are you? I mean, don't take this the wrong way, but you look like crap." Ellie poured Lizzie some apple juice.

Lizzie looked at Adam and giggled. "Yeah Daddy, you look like crap!" she exclaimed, a broad smile across her lips.

Ellie shot Lizzie a look of surprise.

"You have to watch what you say around this one now," Adam said, shaking his head and chuckling.

Ellie couldn't help but smile at him.

"I'd watch out if I were you." He swung his tie back and forth, using it as a pointer between Ellie and Lizzie, his lips curled up in a boyish smile. "Before long you might not be the only two women in my life you know, at least not if Bonnie Singleton has anything to say about it."

Despite his playful tone, a surge of jealousy surprised Ellie. She had never considered anyone other than herself and Lizzie as the 'women in Adam's life.'

"Bonnie Singleton?" she asked, cautiously maintaining a nonchalant expression.

"Oh, you know, she gets her mind set." Adam shook his head. "She called me the other day and said they've decided to auction off a group of Emerald Glen's most accomplished men at the hospital ball this year, and she wants me to be a part of it. I suppose she just wants to make fools out of us."

What?

"You mean some random person will pay money to spend time with you?"

Adam shrugged.

"And you said *yes?*" Ellie's eyes widened.

"Did I have a choice?"

"Isn't that called . . . I don't know, prostitution?" The word was out before she could sensor herself. So much for nonchalant.

"What's prostisushun?" Lizzie asked, wrinkling her forehead.

Adam raised his brow at Ellie and flashed a cautionary glance. "You're an adult, you could've said no."

"Sam's doing it. And Tom. And Anthony." Adam shrugged. "I'm a board member. I couldn't say no."

Ellie's head filled with fury toward Bonnie for suggesting something so inappropriate. Tom Spleck was the President and CEO of the Chamber of Commerce, Anthony Mostello a politician—their very own born and bred State Representative—and then of course, there was Sam from the Medical Center. Every one of them was happily married.

Well, except for Adam. Panicked, she wondered if that was what scared and upset her most.

Her eyes narrowed, and a smile crept across Adam's face.

"Oh okay . . . you're *jealous!*" he said with observable delight at her disapproval.

"I am not jealous." She huffed dismissively.

"I can see it in your face. I know you, Ellen Thomas, and you are *sooo* jealous."

Lizzie released another giggle and turned a yogurt-covered mouth toward Ellie. Ellie wrinkled her nose at Adam and reached for a napkin to wipe Lizzie's face.

"I don't know what you're getting yourself so riled up over, you did after all, kick me out." Adam shrugged. "Just sayin'."

"Mommy, you kicked Daddy out?" Lizzie asked, her voice muffled through the napkin, her young eyes wide and accusatory.

Ellie shot Adam a look of warning and turned back to Lizzie, bewildered. She wondered exactly how this innocent three-year-old had interpreted her father's absence over the last three months.

"Bonnie called and asked me to participate with a donation of my own this year," Ellie said, anxious to change the subject, especially in the presence of Lizzie's tiny ears.

"Oh? What for?"

"She wants me to make dinner for eight—no—ten people, in someone's home. Can you imagine?" As soon as the words were said, she felt stupid. Her contribution, not nearly as risqué as Adam's, sounded ridiculous in comparison.

Adam looked surprised, then proud. "I think it's great."

"You're just saying that because I'm your wife and you have to." She let out a laugh that came out sounding more like a resentful snort.

Ellie's head was still swirling. *Big, nasty Bonnie with her chubby painted face. Why doesn't she ask women to be auctioned off? What a double standard. Probably because she wants to take the entire male roster home herself.*

Adam walked toward her, stopping once they were nearly toe-to-toe. "I'm saying it because I mean it. I think you're the best cook in the world, and I'm reminded of it now, more than ever. I miss your cooking."

His eyes pierced her skin. She felt raw and exposed, but comfortable at exactly the same time. The intensity of the electricity between them caught her off guard, even after seventeen years and two children, even with unresolved issues still lurking in the background.

Breathe, Ellie, breathe.

"Oh man . . . are you guys going to kiss now?" Lizzie sighed dramatically and giggled from her seat at the kitchen counter.

And the spell was broken.

Adam and Ellie both turned toward their frizzy-haired daughter. With a theatrical roll of her eyes, Lizzie slapped a pudgy hand to her forehead, but the smile spread across her tiny lips remained.

"We couldn't do that without you, Lizard," Adam said, scooping up her small body.

"Don't call me Lizard!" Lizzie screeched and squirmed as Adam pulled her into the fold.

Ellie played along, and the three of them embraced in a family hug while she and Adam showered Lizzie's rosy cheeks with kisses, causing her to shriek with delight.

These are the times, Ellie thought, that she missed most.

If only life could be as simple as it is perceived through the eyes of a three-year-old.

CHAPTER 14

ADAM

It had been more than a month since Adam decided to visit Ellie for lunch. The last few times he had Lizzie and Tommy, Ellie invited him to stay at the house and eat rather than take them out for dinner. Last weekend they took the kids to a park—together— it had been Ellie's suggestion to tag along. There was a moment, when Lizzie was swinging, and Tommy was dangling from the monkey bars, when Adam looked at Ellie and felt his breath catch in his throat. The sun was glistening off of her brown hair, and the broad smile on her face reminded him of the old Ellie—the one he fell in love with, the happy Ellie; her endearing expression was one he hadn't seen in so long.

Things between them seemed better, and he longed to tell her he wanted to try again, but he could still sense something holding her back, keeping her distant, just far enough away that she was out of his reach. But he couldn't figure out exactly what it was.

The last couple of weeks had brought vivid dreams. Him at home with Ellie, in their bed. Everything as it should be. Tommy and Lizzie piled on top of them on a lazy Sunday morning. But he always woke at dawn to his harsh reality—alone, the sheets next to him vacant and cold. Occasionally he was even soaked with sweat.

Adam squinted at the bedside clock, trying hard to bring the numbers into focus—1:24 a.m. He stared at the phone resting in the palm of his hand and struggled to shake the grogginess from his body. For a moment, he wondered if he was having another dream.

A muffled sound came from its speaker, and he raked his fingers through his hair. He lifted the phone to his ear.

"I'm sorry, who is this?" he asked.

"My name is Linda Stratton. I think we've met a couple of times. I'm Marc Walsh's sister."

At the mention of Marc's name, Adam sat up in bed, rubbed his eyes, and glanced again at the alarm clock—1:25 a.m.

"Okay Linda, what can I do for you?" he asked, still struggling to wake up enough to make sense of her call.

"I'm so sorry to call you at this hour, but I've sort of been nominated as the calm one . . . to make some important phone calls. I'm not sure how to tell everyone this, so I'll just come out and say it . . . " Her shaky voice broke off.

"Linda?" Adam asked. His pulse quickened.

Linda drew in a deep breath before she continued, her tone anxious. "Marc and Toni's son, John, was killed in a car accident a couple of hours ago."

A sharp intake of breath caught in Adam's throat. He glanced again at the clock—1:26 a.m.—and pushed at the quilted blanket pooled around his waist. He stepped out of bed to look in the mirror, willing this to be a nightmare, waiting to wake up. The faint sound of Linda's muffled sobs brought his attention back to the phone. Feeling dizzy, he walked to the bed again and sat on the edge of it.

"What happened?" he asked, struggling to make his voice audible.

"He was late getting home. Probably afraid he was going to miss curfew. You know how kids are. The police said he was driving too fast, and when he took the sharp corner on Pine Street he . . . well, he didn't make the turn, and his car struck a tree. They said he was," her voice broke and became a low whisper, "dead on impact."

"And Marc and Toni?" He wasn't sure what he expected her to say and instantly regretted asking. What *could* they be other than devastated?

"A lot of family and friends are still arriving here at the house," she said, edging his question.

"I'll be there in a little while," he said. "And Linda?"

"Yes?" she asked, her voice jerky with tears.

"Thanks for calling. They gave you a hard job."

Adam hung up, stared at the phone, and forced the oxygen through his lungs.

In.

Then out.

Slowly.

A conscious effort to avoid a panic attack.

First Bobby. Now this. All within two months.

He wasn't sure how much more he could take. He wanted to go see Bobby again in the hospital—talk to him after he was awake. He knew what that boy was going through. He just couldn't bring himself to do it. He was a coward.

He was still a coward. But Marc he could not avoid.

Must go.

Breathe.

In.

Out.

But he couldn't face it alone.

He picked up the phone and called the only person he could turn to. She answered in a sleepy voice so familiar it made him want to cry and smile all at once.

"El, I need you."

━━━

Parked cars from Marc and Toni's driveway spilled into the street, facing different directions, making an already surreal experience seem even more chaotic. Adam parked behind a white truck and silenced the engine. Ellie squeezed his knee before lifting her hand from the place it had been resting since he picked her up.

"You going to be okay?" she asked.

Words eluded him, but he nodded an acknowledgement that he knew they both understood. He had no choice.

They walked up the dark hill toward the house, passing by people talking in hushed voices. Some were sobbing. Others were puffing cigarettes in an attempt to calm their nerves. Smoke swirled around in the air, making it even more difficult to breathe.

The house buzzed with a somber vibe that transported Adam back to his childhood. He was sitting in the corner of his family's living room, watching shadows move around him. He could still smell the perfume from the many ladies who came to tell him his mommy and daddy would always love him. They all said they were sorry, and he wondered, at the age of seven, what they did wrong. They squeezed his cheeks and gave him hugs that nearly smothered him to death while he kept wondering what it all meant.

He asked repeatedly when they were coming home. A lady with white hair and plump cheeks said his parents were asleep and couldn't wake up, but that didn't make sense. People couldn't sleep forever. Sometimes his mom would say she wanted to, but she never could.

A group of older ladies stood in a corner and whispered a lot while they glanced at him from across the room. The next day, one of them took him to town, where they visited a pretty woman with long shiny hair the same auburn color as his mom's. They called her a counselor, and she was super friendly. She let him sit on a really soft couch, gave him crayons, and asked him to draw some pictures. Then she told him his parents had died and that no matter how much they loved him, no matter how much he loved them, they couldn't come back.

For weeks, different people slept in his parent's bed, made him dinner, and got him off to school. Each of those mornings, he woke and returned to his parent's bedroom once it was empty. He'd climb into their bed and pretend they were there, cuddling beside him like they used to do on lazy Sunday mornings.

They said it was a drunk driver, but at seven years old, he didn't understand what that meant.

His Aunt Bev finally flew in from Texas. It was only the second time he'd met her. She spent a lot of time meeting with men in fancy suits and ties. They called them attorneys and "business people." She was his appointed guardian, his only living relative, left to manage the trust his parents had set aside for him. A couple of months after their death, she announced she just wasn't "cut from a cloth capable of raising a child" and sent him off to a year-round, all boys' boarding school.

It wasn't until he approached graduation and applied for colleges that he learned she had squandered the remaining money in his trust account. At eighteen years old, he didn't have the business sense to make it a legal issue. As an adult, he didn't have the stomach for it.

About four years ago he received a call from one of her Texas friends, informing him his aunt had passed away. While he felt obligated somehow to mourn her death, he couldn't. He merely felt indifferent.

Ellie squeezed Adam's hand—hard. He looked at her, dazed and somewhat disoriented. His body was numb and tingly at exactly the same time.

"You okay?" she asked.

He shook his head no, but what could he do?

They continued past crowded rooms and navigated their way through a sea of people until they arrived at the dining room. Toni sat at the table with two other women who bore a strong resemblance to her, presumably sisters, one on each side. Her face was puffy, her eyes bloodshot, but instead of crying she was staring far into the distance at nothing in particular, her expression blank and absent.

Ellie tugged at Adam's arm and pulled him toward Toni. When they arrived in front of her, Toni looked up. Confusion crossed her face, almost as if she didn't recognize them at all.

Adam couldn't speak. He turned to Ellie, trying to communicate his inability to find his voice through his eyes. She gave an understanding nod.

"Toni," Ellie said, kneeling in front of her and taking Toni's hand in hers. "We're so sorry. What can we do?"

Toni's blue eyes searched Ellie's face. The light that naturally shone in them had gone dim; her expression was empty and lost. "Can you bring my son back to me?" she asked in a low, cold tone.

A tear fell from Ellie's cheek, and she bowed her head, squeezing Toni's hand tighter.

Adam stared at them both while tears pricked at the backs of his eyelids. The pain was almost too much to bear. His chest felt as if it may break apart into a million pieces. He knew they couldn't go, and he felt guilty, but he wanted to flee, to run as far from this scene as he could, as quickly as possible.

A hand rested on Adam's arm, pulling him from solitude. He turned to face Marc, whose dark unkempt hair and scruffy beard framed dim eyes that were sunken into a ghostlike face. He looked ten, maybe twenty years older, a shocking transformation compared to the man Adam saw at work only yesterday.

"Marc," Adam said, shaking his head and struggling to speak in spite of the lump in his throat.

Marc's body crumpled. He fell into Adam's arms, sobbing like the seven-year-old boy Adam had fought for so many years to leave in his past.

CHAPTER 15

ELLIE

E llie watched the purple triangular flag on the hood of their car flap in the wind as they drove out of the funeral home toward the cemetery. It reminded her of how quickly time passed, whisking life away at Mach speed without consent.

It had been more than a month since she and Adam started speaking on a regular basis again—since little Bobby Fleich landed in the hospital—and she still hadn't told him about the baby.

She'd had a plan. She was going to tell him once he had time to get past the shock of Bobby. But a couple of weeks later, Valentine's Day came around, and Adam brought her roses. He was sweet, nervous, and excited—a combination she hadn't seen in him for so long. He even surprised her with dinner from their favorite Thai restaurant and insisted on cleaning up the kitchen. She couldn't bear to bring him down from the cloud they both seemed to have landed on.

The following week, she found herself overwhelmed with a very sick Lizzie and multiple trips to the pediatrician. Not to mention the attention she had to give Tommy and the fatigue that had set in due to a progressing pregnancy. She simply had no energy to try to explain her shortcomings to Adam.

And now, with the passing of Marc and Toni's son creating yet another blanket of emotional grief, how could she tell him about the baby? Not now.

Adam followed the other cars in the funeral procession and turned left onto Main Street. People everywhere were dressed in green, holding plastic cups of beer in celebration of St. Patrick's Day. They passed by her car window in a blur. It was only 11:45 a.m., but the festivities downtown would no doubt last until the early hours of the next morning. It reminded her of when they were young and carefree, when she and Adam used to frequent bars and dance at clubs until dawn.

But that was a lifetime ago.

Now, at forty-one, her heart felt heavy, her body old and tired, and she wondered how she could possibly muster enough physical energy to grow another human being.

The cemetery was crowded, as was the funeral home—as were most funerals of those who passed at a young age, far before their years should have been finished. Adam laced his fingers through hers as they walked to the gravesite in silence amidst a flock of mourners. Her black, knee-length dress slid against her skin as she moved, and her legs felt heavier with every step. She breathed in the somber air that surrounded them, filled with anguish about more than just the coffin resting on the lawn.

Her tears were genuine, but came from an assortment of grief— sadness for Marc and Toni's loss, disappointment for the life that could've been lived by young John Walsh, anger and shame toward her indiscretions, and a love for Adam that seemed destined to slip away.

The reverend finished with a prayer, and Adam squeezed her hand before pulling her into his shoulder and holding her there.

Normally the gesture would make her feel safe. Instead, it left her terrified and frightened of losing forever the one thing that always made her feel most secure—her husband.

Ellie stepped out of the shower and pulled a towel from the wall. She applied jasmine lotion to her legs and took notice of the heaviness in the muscles beneath her skin. Recollection of the way her body struggled to maintain any sort of efficient circulation when she had Tommy and Lizzie made her wince at the absolute panic that she figured must be transpiring inside this time around, at forty-one.

She examined her reflection in the mirror. She was slightly heavier overall, but unlike her other two pregnancies, she could barely see a difference in her stomach so far.

She slid a nightgown over her head, walked to the bedroom, folded the sheets down, and climbed in between them. Just as her head hit the pillow, the bedroom door creaked open and Adam stepped into the room.

"Lizzie's finally asleep," he said.

"Did she say what was wrong?" Ellie asked.

He shrugged his shoulders. "I don't think she knows."

"I hope she's not getting sick again." The last thing Ellie wanted was another trip to the pediatrician.

Adam combed his fingers through his hair, and Ellie smiled at the familiarity of his nervous habit.

"Honestly? I suppose she can sense the stress that you and I are under, and she's just reacting," he said. "She'll be fine in the morning."

Stress. Her stomach flipped at the thought of her secret. A secret she knew would eventually come out and cause even more stress. For all of them.

"It's been a long day. I'm gonna head to the shower," Adam said. Barefooted, he turned toward the bathroom and padded across the old, wood-plank floor.

The bathroom door stood half opened, and Ellie watched the muscles in Adam's back flex as he peeled off his t-shirt. When he stepped under the water, an unexpected shiver moved up her spine.

Three days ago, when they left Marc and Toni's house on the night of John's death, Ellie knew Adam couldn't be alone. *Stay,* she had said. And he did. They walked to their old bedroom, curled up together under the white duvet on their four-poster bed, and held each other for comfort. They both remained silent, too exhausted to speak. When Ellie rose the next morning she was surprised at the realization that, even though she only slept a few hours, she slept better than she had for months.

Since then, they'd walked around in a mournful daze, helped take care of arrangements when they could, and tried their best to muddle though a normal routine with Tommy and Lizzie. Adam spent some time at work and maintained frequent correspondence with the office. After all, he and Marc couldn't both be out at the same time, at least not for long.

They spent the last three nights sleeping beside one another, comfortable yet awkward at the same time. Coping with the tragedy at hand was all they had energy for, and neither of them had spoken a word about the changes unfolding between them.

The mattress bounced slightly as Adam slipped in between the sheets beside her. In an instant, she was aware of his scent, a reminder that pregnancy had a strange way of heightening your senses. She considered how distinct it was—the smell of Adam. He still smelled like warm spice and a crisp winter breeze all bundled together. He smelled that way three hundred and sixty five days a year. She hadn't realized she'd missed it so much. Until now.

Warmth from his body filled the space between them. She turned toward him and found he was facing the other direction. She watched his back move up and down with each inhale and exhale and fought an overwhelming urge to reach out and touch his bare skin.

As if he could feel her study him, he rolled over. He reached out and ran his thumb across her cheek. She closed her eyes and contemplated revealing her secret, but when she opened them, he was above her. He moved closer, placed a gentle kiss on her cheek, then her neck, and finally his lips brushed softly against hers. Every inch of her body was buzzing.

"Adam," she whispered. "I have to tell you something."

She didn't want to stop, but . . .

You have to tell him!

"Shhhh." He held a gentle finger over her lips. "Don't talk."

His hands moved up her nightgown, and his blue eyes sliced through her with an intensity that made every nerve tingle.

He was swift but gentle, their contact intense, her emotions raw. She dug her nails into his back, trying to forget that she was with anyone other than him, wanting to pretend the baby she held was Adam's, that they were happy, that John was alive, that Bobby's parents were okay, that all of their pain could disappear.

Later, Ellie lay in silence, savoring the feeling of Adam's arms wrapped around her as her pulse slowed to a normal pace. She pushed her back against his chest, anxious to be closer to him, to feel safe forever.

"El?" he whispered from behind her ear.

"Yeah?"

"Let's try again. I love you, I miss you, and I can't live without you. No one understands me like you, Ellie. Not really, not the way you do. Please don't tell me to go again."

He pulled her tight and buried his head in the back of her hair. Pain pierced through Ellie's chest.

How can I tell him?

"I don't want you to go," she said. A tear dropped onto her pillow, and she closed her eyes, trying to pretend.

PART IV

Forsaking All Others

CHAPTER 16

ADAM

Adam stood in the foyer waiting for Ellie, reflecting on the last couple of months. When he suggested they go to the hospital ball together, his intentions were sincere, but he had only dreamed they would be lucky enough to be back in a place where the company they shared was so genuine.

Finally, I have my wife back.

Exhilaration at the thought that everything in his world had been set right filled him from within, and a smile spread wide across his face.

Well, almost everything.

Two weeks had passed since John's funeral, the wreckage left behind difficult to deal with. The aftermath was still the elephant in the room, both at home and at work, never really leaving Adam's thoughts. But slowly, everyone was healing, and in a strange way Adam felt that he might even be conquering some of the oldest demons buried deep within his soul.

The tragedy reminded him that life was for living, and he intended to live the rest of his with the woman he loved, wasting no further amount of time. He told her so a couple of days after the funeral, and found a speechless Ellie staring back at him—a rare event in their long history together.

"All ready," Ellie said from the top of the stairs.

Adam turned to look at her and found himself dumbstruck. A silky red gown draped slightly off the edge of her ivory shoulders and fell over each feminine curve with grace, until it dropped to the ground around her feet. Her breasts, fuller than usual, peeked out from a scooped neckline and threatened to make them late. Adam had noticed that she'd put on some weight—although he'd never say it—but he didn't mind. She looked sexy and radiant, practically glowing. He was speechless.

"What's the matter, do I look okay?" she asked, as she reached the bottom step. She examined her dress, self-consciously smoothing it against her body.

Adam let out a long, low whistle and flashed a broad smile.

"Are you kidding me, Mrs. Thomas? You look amazing! Actually," he said, reaching out and pulling her into him with force, "I'm afraid we might not make it to the ball tonight."

"Stop it." She swung her purse at him, her smile cracking wider.

Adam bent down and kissed her, relishing the sensuality of her lips against his.

"Adam, be serious." Ellie grabbed onto his tuxedo jacket as if to steady herself. "We really need to go now." Her raspy voice told Adam he was getting the better of her. He pulled her in tighter, but she quickly pecked him on the cheek and squirmed free before heading for the door. He frowned and fell into step behind her.

"I'm just glad it isn't raining," she said. "You know how wet the weather can be in April."

"Yah sure, and you're changing the subject," he said, patting her on the butt as she exited the house in front of him.

The lounge was already teeming with ladies in ball gowns and men in tuxedos when they arrived, a wall of people surrounding a bar at the far end of the room. Adam and Ellie bumped elbows and dodged drinks that threatened to spill onto the next person passing by while they greeted familiar faces on their way through the crowd.

"Finally," Adam said, resting his elbow on the edge of the bar. He turned toward Ellie. "What do you want? Wine?"

"You know . . . " she paused, "I think I'll just stick with cranberry and seltzer."

"Cranberry and seltzer?" Adam asked. In all of their years together, Ellie had never ordered a cranberry and seltzer. Ever.

"My stomach feels a little funny, and I just want to play it safe, okay?" she said, raising an eyebrow.

He continued to stare at her quizzically for a beat before a large man bumped into his left arm and apologized while hurrying away. Adam tossed one more questionable glance in Ellie's direction but gave their order to the bartender without probing any further. While they waited, he scanned the room. There was a fire roaring in an ancient stone fireplace, a harpist strumming in the far corner, and every familiar face seemed to be in attendance—it was your typical Emerald Glen soiree.

Once their drinks were served, they made their way to the hors d'oeuvres station at the opposite end of the room. They were making a plate of cheese and crackers when Bonnie Singleton materialized at their sides.

"Well hello darlings! Aren't you both just lookin' like the cat's meow tonight? 'Specially you, handsome Adam," she said, pulling on his bowtie. "One of Emerald Glen's most accomplished men!"

"Bonnie, you look lovely as always," he said, glancing at Ellie, who finished rolling her eyes just before Bonnie turned to her.

"Beautiful dress, Ellie dear. Too bad you didn't get it at my shop," Bonnie said with a hint of arrogance. She leaned in toward Ellie and in a brisk, sweeping motion, looked up and down her figure. "Might want to lay off the cookies and ice cream though, darlin'," she whispered a little louder than necessary.

Adam raised his eyebrows in surprise and braced himself for Ellie's response, but Bonnie stepped to the side and positioned herself between him and Ellie while pulling another woman closer to her side. Adam wondered how he didn't notice her before. She was tall, thin, and outfitted in a tight, floor-length dress that matched her golden blonde hair. Her lips shimmered, and soft light from the room bounced off of every inch of her smooth, tanned skin.

"Adam, you just *have* to meet my friend Jacqueline!" Bonnie said, pushing her forward an inch.

"Call me Jackie," she said, in a voice dripping with seduction. She held out her hand in a manner that suggested he kiss it.

"Pleasure," Adam said, clearing his throat. He smiled politely, took her hand, and gave it an awkward, light shake. His eyes moved to the small space between Bonnie and Jackie in search of Ellie, but the room was tight with guests standing shoulder to shoulder, and he could only see a thin slice of red silk through the narrow gap. He wondered if someone else had caught his wife's attention.

Jackie's face reflected her disappointment at his disinterest, but only for a moment, before she leaned forward and spilled her glass of wine on Adam's pants.

Astonished, he stared at her.

"Oh, I'm *so* sorry!" Jackie exclaimed with a tiny smile.

Was that an accident?

It had been a long time since a woman was this forward with him, and he found himself stunned. And immobile. He watched her grab some napkins from a waiter passing by and tried to decide how to respond to her bold behavior.

"Let me get that for you," Jackie said, blotting at the crotch of Adam's pants.

The embarrassment and surprise of her advance sent blood rushing to his cheeks, shading them the color of Ellie's dress. Adam looked down and took a step back, but before he could speak, a hand appeared from nowhere and grabbed Jackie's wrist, stopping her arm in midair.

"That'll be good enough," Ellie said, looking at Jackie with a face that screamed *I dare you!*

"Jackie's very interested in bidding on Adam in tonight's auction," Bonnie said. Her insensitivity to the events unfolding in front of her was exasperating.

"I can only imagine," Ellie said, her steady, narrowed eyes still glued to Jackie.

Adam, increasingly uncomfortable, shifted his weight.

"Jackie, I'd like you to meet my *wife*, Ellie." He cleared his throat. "Let's take a walk honey, so I can clean up." He motioned toward the hall leading to the bathrooms and forced a smile.

"I'm looking forward to seeing you on stage, Adam," Jackie said. Her voice practically purred as she glanced at Ellie, her blue eyes shimmering with challenge.

Adam grabbed onto Ellie's arm and pulled her away for fear the two of them might actually end up on the floor pulling each other's hair out.

"The nerve of that woman!" Ellie huffed as they walked away. "And what's so funny?" she asked, punching Adam in the arm as he stifled a laugh.

"You're cute when you're mad." He smiled and planted a kiss on her forehead. "Let me run in and try to get this stuff off my pants."

"I'm waiting here to make sure she doesn't try to follow you in," she called as he turned toward the men's room.

He circled back and bent down near her ear. "And you're jealous again," he whispered. He pecked her on the cheek and smiled before disappearing through the door.

Adam blotted the wine from his pants as best he could and grimaced at the wet spot, in the worst possible place. He moved to the automatic dryer and tried to angle his body under the hot air, forcing a smile at each man who walked in and flashed him a look of question. Finally, when the stain was less noticeable, he headed to the sink and washed his hands. He glanced in the mirror, raked his fingers through his hair.

At least it was white wine.

As he exited the men's room and rounded the corner, he saw Ellie talking to Dr. Van Linden—someone he hadn't seen in quite some time, a man who was always a pleasure.

"It's the good doctor!" he said, approaching them with a smile. "So good to see you, doc. How've you been?"

He extended his arm for a handshake and caught a glimpse of Ellie, who looked fidgety.

"Adam! Good to see you, too. I was just asking Ellie how she was feeling."

"Are you okay, honey? You do look a little pale." Adam studied her with concern.

"I'm fine," she said, her smile tight. She waived her hand dismissively, and her eyes fell to the ground.

"I don't mean how she's feeling now." Dr. Van Linden chuckled. "I was referring to the pregnancy. Congratulations by the way," he said, clapping Adam on the shoulder. "How does it feel knowing you're going to be a father again?"

Bewildered, Adam's eyes moved between Dr. Van Linden and Ellie. Ellie was still staring at the ground, looking as if she was about to faint. Dr. Van Linden was beaming, seemingly oblivious to any oddity.

Just then, an older woman approached them from the end of the hallway, waving her arms in the air and calling Dr. Van Linden's name in a voice louder than necessary. Her heels clicked against the stone floor as she rushed to his side. Once she reached him, she bent forward and greeted the doctor with a hug.

During the exchange, Adam remained disoriented. He continued to glance between the woman, Dr. Van Linden, and Ellie, but he had no idea what to say. Or think.

The woman breathlessly apologized for interrupting, said that she must borrow the doctor for a moment, and scurried away with him into the crowded room.

As Adam watched them disappear into a mob of people, the room around him moved in slow motion. The smile slowly disappeared from his face, and Dr. Van Linden's words echoed in his head.

"... *pregnant* ... "

"... *a father again* ... "

Adam looked at Ellie, and puzzle pieces latched together in his mind: *Ellie's emotional state* ... *her weight gain* ... His eyes stopped on the cranberry and seltzer in her hand.

Suddenly, without saying a word, Ellie turned and walked quickly toward the exit. He followed her, almost breaking into a full-fledged sprint in an effort to catch up. Once outside, he found Ellie vomiting at the edge of the building. It was dark and secluded, but the faint sound of music wafted toward them from the entrance.

"I'm sorry, Adam, I'm so sorry." She wiped her mouth with the cocktail napkin from her drink.

"Why didn't you tell me?" He was baffled.

She stood as if in a trance, silently shaking her head, seemingly unaware of the speck of vomit stuck at the corner of her mouth.

"Ellie?"

She didn't move, except to shake her head.

Adam searched his mind for any rationalization. *Maybe she was scared because she was getting older, worried about starting over ... what?*

Another baby. Another baby!

An overwhelming sense of nostalgia washed over him. In spite of the nerves filling his stomach, and the confusion clouding his mind, things seemed clearer than ever.

He walked toward her and grabbed her hand, pulling her in.

"You know I love you, El. And we're going to have another baby. I couldn't be happier." He took the napkin and blotted her face before bending down and deeply inhaling the scent of her hair.

She grabbed the napkin, pushed him away, and looked up with forlorn eyes he was unable to read.

"I can't do this," she said. Her head continued to shake back and forth, methodically, over and over, even as she spoke. "I can't do this anymore, Adam. Not anymore. I can't."

"We can fix things. I know—"

"It's not yours."

"What?"

"The baby. The baby isn't yours."

Adam took a step back and studied her face.

"Why do you keep pushing me away?"

Her eyes welled up with tears, her expression still dazed.

"It's true. We were separated. I'm sorry. I can't do it anymore. I can't lie anymore."

Tears streamed down her face, and Adam thought it strange that she looked almost as shell-shocked as he felt. A devastating realization of truth and reality slowly settled in his mind. His body felt heavier with each passing second, as if concrete were filling every vein, replacing every ounce of blood. Dizzy, he reached out to lean against the stone building beside him. His brain raced for answers, and finally, his thoughts rewound to the night he chauffeured Caitlin home—the morning she came in at dawn with no explanation—and he felt sick. He had forgotten all about it. He was angry, but he never really thought she was with someone else—with another man. And she hadn't told him otherwise.

"How . . . could you?" He could barely manage the words, his ridged body frozen in place.

She hung her head, pathetically blubbering through tears. "There was always a reason I couldn't tell you. First, it was Bobby. Then there was John. And now—"

"And now? Now *what* Ellie? You leave it up to *Dr. Van Linden?* We've been living together again for weeks and you couldn't even tell me yourself? You had to let me find out like"—anger throbbed in head, his voice escalating—"like *this?*"

"It meant nothing."

"Please Ellie, that's so cliché."

"Really. I don't even remember. I didn't realize. I drank too much and—"

He huffed, disgusted. His eyes drilled through her. "So now you're a slut *and* a drunk then?"

"Adam—"

"No!" he shouted, raising the palm of his hand to shut her down. "I can't talk to you right now."

He turned and started for the car, but halfway through the parking lot he remembered he couldn't leave. He was part of to-night's featured events.

Lucky me, he thought.

CHAPTER 17

ELLIE

E llie looked up at the moonlit trees, then at the grass beneath her feet, but she saw nothing at all. Voices and laugher echoed through the night air as people strolled through the parking lot, inching closer to the building, but the sounds were muffled, her brain incapable of deciphering specific words.

A paralyzing fear surged through every inch of her body, numbing her legs and feet. She shook her head, an effort to escape the trance that had captured her.

Her hand was wet. She looked down at the soiled cocktail napkin as another bout of nausea rose in her stomach.

Her eyes narrowed, she scanned the dimly lit parking lot for Adam, but she could only see shadowy figures of gray and black.

She considered beating her head against the stone exterior of the building beside her as penance for her sins and in question of her judgment. *It might do me well.* No time seemed appropriate to tell Adam about the baby. After all, it was an inappropriate thing to have to tell. But for him to find out here, from someone else, was perhaps the worst possible scenario.

She didn't know where the words came from or why they were pushed from her mouth with such urgency that they couldn't be silenced, but there they were—spewed like the vomit now spread on the dew-covered lawn below.

Absentmindedly, she ambled along the edge of the building, further into the darkness, her hands brushing against the cold stone exterior. At the back, light filtered through a partially opened door. It caught her attention, and she moved closer to peer inside. The entrance opened into a large kitchen with shiny, metal, industrial-sized refrigerators and ovens, and the temperature of the air escaping through the doorway must have been at least ninety degrees. The room was alive with workers bustling about in formal uniforms—white pressed shirts adorned with black bow ties and tuxedo pants. Because Ellie knew she couldn't possibly reenter the party through the front door, she hesitated, stepped over an old plastic milk crate, and walked in. To her dismay, a young girl, maybe twenty and dressed in the same restaurant-issued attire, spotted her instantly.

"Ma'am," the girl said, stopping in front of Ellie, "this isn't a public entrance."

Ellie caught a glimpse of herself in a stainless steel backsplash as she stepped further into the light. Her reflection explained the girl's horrified expression. Eyeliner was smeared down her tear-stained cheeks, her lipstick smudged from the cocktail napkin spattered with vomit.

"I'm sorry," Ellie said, wringing her shaky hands together. "I couldn't go through the front." She attempted a weak smile, hoping for an empathic response.

The girl hesitated, still and silent. Then she looked around cautiously. "Come with me." She led Ellie down the side of the kitchen and into a small area toward the back. "This is an employee bathroom." She opened the door and flipped the light switch. "When you're done you can get back to the ballroom through there." She pointed toward another door.

"Thank you *so* much," Ellie said, unable to find words strong enough to express her gratitude.

"Just try not to let anyone else see you." The girl's face, etched with pity, made Ellie want to disappear.

Ellie nodded, closed the bathroom door, and latched the lock. She inhaled and exhaled, deep and slow. Cleansing breaths. Trying to pull herself together. Trying to find even an ounce of strength. She would need it to get through what might come next.

Not knowing exactly *what* would come next scared her to death.

She pulled paper towels from a white metal dispenser on the wall, wetted them, and blotted her face. She fished makeup from her purse and dabbed at her cheeks with powder. In the chaos of her mind she said a silent prayer, thankful for her purse. She rinsed her mouth with water—careful not to splash her dress, surprised it wasn't already dotted with the contents of her stomach—and reapplied her lipstick.

She paused to examine her reflection in the mirror. Better. But even with an exterior semblance of normalcy, the distress inside remained.

She exited the bathroom and discreetly made her way around the back edge of the kitchen toward the alternate entrance she was shown. Shoulders back, she took another deep breath, stepped out of the swinging doors into the ballroom, and attempted to find her table. As she wove her way through a sea of seated guests, a few reached out to pat her on the arm or say a friendly hello. She attempted to smile and return each acknowledgment with the same calm cheerfulness, even though her insides were twisting into knots. Just as she took her seat, Sam approached the stage and began his opening remarks. The room fell silent.

"Welcome friends, to our annual Hospital Ball," Sam said. "I want to thank each and every one of you for coming, and I'd like to give special recognition to our gala committee members, led by Bonnie Singleton, for all of their hard work in making tonight possible."

Warm applause filled the room.

"Before we begin the festivities, I want to take a moment and acknowledge what I know is on the minds of many of us tonight." Sam paused, his eyes fell to the podium, and his face crumpled slightly. "Most of us have had the privilege of knowing Marc and Toni Walsh personally, and many of us have kids who attended school and played sports with their son, John, who was taken from us far too early after a car accident a little more than two weeks ago."

Heads nodded, and low murmurs rippled through the crowd.

"Can I ask that we have a moment of silence for Marc, Toni, John, and the rest of the Walsh family?" Sam asked.

The room was more silent than Ellie thought possible for a gathering of close to three hundred people. The significance of the quiet surrounding her towered in comparison to her own grief, filling her with even more guilt.

Sam cleared his throat before beginning again. "I want you to know I spoke with Marc this morning, and he asked me to express their family's gratitude to our community for all of your support during this difficult time. He assured me they're doing what they can to heal, and although they're absent tonight, he gave strict instructions to have fun and raise loads of money. So let's do him proud, folks—drink your drinks, and open your wallets."

Applause filled the room again, the somber mood lifting toward the sky with each echoing hand.

"Great job, honey," Suzanne said with a supportive peck on the cheek as Sam arrived at their table and took his seat. Everyone nodded their agreement, and Sam breathed an audible sigh of relief.

"This may be the toughest year ever," he said, reaching out for Suzanne's hand. After giving it a squeeze, he turned his attention to Ellie. "What happened to Adam?" Sam asked. "I was going to ask him if he wanted to say a few words, but I couldn't find him."

Ellie glanced at the empty chair beside her. In spite of the nerves filling her stomach, she smiled at the other guests around the table.

"He probably got stuck talking to someone at the bar," she said, hoping to sound nonchalant.

"Well, he'd better get back soon, or he'll miss our Emerald Glen rock stars being auctioned off," Kathy said, patting her husband, Tom, on the back with an affectionate smile.

"I don't think you can put chamber of commerce and hospital executives in the same class as rock stars, honey," Tom said, laughing.

Sam and Suzanne joined them in laughter, and Ellie tried to participate as well, but how could she enjoy light-hearted humor when her head was buzzing? And where *was* Adam? She didn't think he would leave the ball, but then again, *anything* was possible now. And she was fully to blame.

Waiters delivered food, and the room came alive with chatter and silver clinking against ivory china plates. Anthony lifted a decanter of chardonnay from the center of the table and topped off each wine glass. First himself, next his wife, then Kathy, and Tom, and . . . he was almost to Ellie.

Mental panic kicked in. Somehow she managed to avoid attention when the first round was served up. What to do?

Oh God, she was next.

Ellie placed her hand over the rim. "I've already had my fill, but thank you," she said.

"That's unlike you, Ellie," Kathy said.

"Oh, leave the woman be, Kathy! More for us," Suzanne said, cheerfully outstretching her glass for a refill.

Ellie and Suzanne exchanged a knowing look, and Ellie was filled with gratitude for their friendship. She excused herself and headed to the restroom, discreetly searching for Adam on the way, but even as she returned he was nowhere to be found.

At last, Adam appeared just as the waiter served each of them a piece of cheesecake topped with strawberry sauce.

Ellie had barely touched her dinner, and the sight of dessert made her stomach turn again. Or maybe it was the sight of Adam.

She couldn't decide if she was happy or disappointed that he had finally arrived. Or maybe she was worried.

It had something to do with the look in his eyes. They were the same familiar shade of blue she knew so well, but a dark anger had settled into them that made her squirm. And his posture had taken on a stiffness, so faint it was seemingly unrecognizable to everyone else, like a shield made exclusively for her.

"There you are, Adam," Sam said. "Everything okay?"

"Fine," Adam said. "Just some unexpected business I had to take care of." His relaxed smile surprised Ellie. Then again, he hadn't looked her direction yet.

"You've missed your meal," Sam said, scanning the area for a waiter.

"Oh, thanks, Sam. I'm not hungry."

Sam flashed a look of concern, and Adam quickly shifted his eyes to the crowded room. Ellie kept her attention on him, desperately seeking his acknowledgement, but he refused to look her way.

"It's about time for the auction to begin anyway," Kathy said. "You boys ready to hit the stage?"

Kathy's eager attitude grated Ellie's frazzled nerves. How could she be so casual about having her husband—all of their husbands—auctioned off? About another woman commissioning Tom's time? Then she wondered if she'd still feel threatened if she and Adam were still okay instead of only pretending to be. The fleeting thought transformed her annoyance toward Kathy into jealousy. Adam was right—she *was* jealous. It was an emotion she was always proud to say didn't exist in her marriage . . . once upon a time.

"Hello, ladies and gentlemen, and welcome to the twenty-second annual Greater Valley Medical Center Ball!" Bonnie announced enthusiastically from the microphone on stage.

Applause filled the room, and it was instantly clear Bonnie enjoyed the limelight. She waved to the crowd, a bright, lipstick-painted smile stretched wide across her face.

Ellie's anxiety increased as Bonnie rattled through the first few auction items. By the time she announced that Emerald Glen's successful men were next up, Ellie felt thoroughly ill. She glanced to her right and caught sight of Jackie sitting two tables away. Her blue eyes were fixed on Adam, her shimmering lips curved into a broad smile.

"Now remember ladies, you get these wonderful men for one night, all to yourself. Their wives have agreed to let them go for a good cause, but within reason, of course, ladies, within reason!"

Their wives have agreed? Ellie didn't remember anyone asking *her* permission.

The crowd laughed and whistled, the excitement more intense than Ellie had ever seen at an event that was habitually dull and proper.

Tom was up first, Sam second, and Anthony third. They all did the normal bit of pacing back and forth on the stage and flexing a muscle you couldn't see through their tuxedo jackets. Each of them kissed the backside of Bonnie's hand and flashed polite smiles. Tom sold for three hundred seventy five dollars, Sam for five hundred twenty five dollars, and Anthony for four hundred dollars.

"And now the best for last! With his Minnesota charm, please welcome Mr. Adam Thomas!" The joy in Bonnie's voice made Ellie's skin crawl.

Best for last. Ha! Ellie had an overwhelming urge to run onto the stage and slap the smirk from Bonnie's pudgy face. Instead, she placed a hand on her stomach and took a deep, shaky breath.

Hormones. That's all it is—just pregnant irrationality.

Ellie feigned approval and joined in applause as Adam walked toward the stage, still without even a glance toward her. He stopped at Jackie's table on the way, picked a single red rose from the centerpiece, and handed it to her before kissing her on the cheek. Jackie turned toward Ellie, her face beaming with pride. Ellie's head filled with anger, although she wasn't sure who to be most angry with: herself, Adam, or Jackie. Or maybe Bonnie.

Adam leapt up the steps and headed straight for the band, consulting with them in front of a flashy black and chrome drum set. Then he took center stage and faced the crowd, waving and blowing kisses to his audience. The band began to play, and George Thorogood's "Bad to the Bone" filled the air. Adam's body moved fluidly with the music. In all of their years together, Ellie had never seen him dance quite like this. He slithered out of his coat and threw it into audience. The women went crazy—whistling and pulling dollar bills from their purses.

Filled with horror, Ellie glanced between Adam and the crowd. High-to-do women had practically manifested into strip show groupies, spitting catcalls into the air.

It was . . . alarming. And humiliating. She was in shock.

Determined to protect her pride, she straightened her back. She would not show her discomfort. Across the table, Suzanne caught her eye and flashed a look of concern, but everyone else around her seemed to be enjoying the show.

Jackie was now on stage, pushing a dollar bill between the buttons of Adam's tuxedo shirt, and dancing beside him in her slinky gold gown. She tugged on his bowtie until it came unfastened, and then she waved it like a lasso above her head. Adam played the crowd and placed a hand over his mouth in mock shock, but the smile on his face and the look in his eyes as he finally glanced in Ellie's direction told her that this charade, and Jackie's response to it, was not at all unintended.

CHAPTER 18

ADAM

Adam sat behind his desk, staring at a computer screen that appeared to display nothing in particular—only words that blurred together like the recent empty days of his life.

It had been four days since he last saw Ellie. Since he found out she was carrying a baby he didn't help to make. His loneliness and a longing for the Ellie of old made the days drag on eternally, but the raw pain of her betrayal was still fresh, like a wound sliced open only moments before.

He had reviewed it again and again in his mind, trying to understand how she could be comfortable with another man and why she would keep such a monumental secret from him. And he couldn't decide which betrayal was worse.

The phone rang, interrupting his thoughts. He sighed at the persistent tone, goading him to participate in the present reality he despised. Finally, he answered flatly.

Jackie's voice sounded just as sugarcoated as it did at the ball, and he could almost see her seductive smile through the phone. "I just wanted to touch base. About our date."

Adam cringed at the word. He thought he was through with dating two decades ago.

"You have directions to my house, right?" she asked.

"I sure do," Adam said, dreading the night ahead. "I got all five of your emails." His eyes darted to the ceiling.

God help me.

"Okay, well, I'll just . . . see you tomorrow night." She finished the sentence but paused, an effort to stall and lengthen their conversation obvious. Before she could detain him any longer, Adam made an excuse about work and hung up while shaking his head.

He knew the auctioned off "date" was supposed to be a casual good time, if not a downright good laugh, but Jackie made it clear from the beginning she was interested in much more. Considering the recent downward spiral of his marriage, he found himself nervous and unsure of how to handle her ambition.

A tapping at the door took him away from his thoughts, and he looked up to see that it was Marc entering the room without waiting for an invitation.

"Hey there boss, I looked over those reports you gave me this morning. Not bad."

Adam studied Marc's face. His complexion was a little less gray, his eyes a little bit brighter than they were a couple of days ago when he returned to work. It was good to have him back.

"If you're comfortable with it, let's propose it at the next board meeting," Adam suggested.

"I'll get it ready," Marc said, heading for the door.

"Hey Marc?"

"Yeah?" Marc stopped.

"How are you holding up?"

Marc's shoulders dropped an inch. "We're getting through it, one day at a time." He glanced at the floor and looked up again. "That's what the counselor told us, and that's all I can do right now."

"You know if you need *anything* . . . "

Marc nodded, and Adam knew he didn't need to finish.

"And I appreciate that offer you put on the table a couple of months ago when you told me I should take more time off. Toni and I are thinking about planning a trip. Time to get out of Dodge, ya know?"

Adam nodded. "Just let me know when, and we'll work it out. Your family needs to come first."

As soon as the words left his mouth, a pain cinched Adam's chest. It was a truth he knew Charlie would've insisted on, words that could have saved him and his family a lot of pain if he would have lived by the action they demanded. Only, he didn't recognize it until now—a little too late.

"Thanks." Marc smiled and offered a salute before he walked out of the room.

Adam sat, staring at the door and brooding over his conflicted torture, filled with a broad range of emotions.

Anger. Jealousy. Ego. Love. Regret. Betrayal.

They were all fighting for center stage.

He wanted to explode. A piece of him was mad at Ellie, another angry with himself.

CHAPTER 19

ELLIE

E llie woke to a pounding head and a sight that turned her stomach sour. Empty wooden hangers spilled from Adam's closet, reminding her that if he wasn't gone before, he certainly was now.

She pulled the blanket over her face and squeezed her eyes closed, wanting to sleep through the nightmare her life had become. But her alarm clock buzzed loudly, commanding her to throw the covers back and start the day.

She splashed water on her face and winced at the moisture that burned her dry, red eyes. She dressed in athletic attire and sneakers, pulled her hair into a ponytail, and decided a run after school drop-off would be a good way to decompress.

As usual, getting the kids out the door was a chore. She nagged them to stay on task while they seemed consistently distracted and determined to be late to school.

Afterward, she returned to the house and surveyed the kitchen: a sink full of dirty dishes, a floor full of crumbs, spilled milk on the counter, and sticky napkins stained with syrup.

It can wait.

"Buster," she yelled through the empty house.

Immediately, his nails clicked against the wooden floor and tags hanging from his collar jingled as he ran toward her voice. He appeared at her side in seconds. She bent down and rewarded him with a scratch behind the ears.

"Hey buddy, you wanna go for a run?" she asked. He cocked his head and panted. She considered that this brown ball of fur may be her very best friend in the world at this moment, and her shoulders slumped.

They started down the street together. Soon, she was watching the trees and fences meld into the background, losing herself in the sound of her heartbeat echoing through her ears in rhythm to her feet pounding methodically on the pavement below.

"Ellie!" a voice called from the window of a white Mercedes as it slowly rolled by. Brake lights illuminated, and it pulled toward the side of the road.

Ellie slowed down and jogged toward the car with irritation, instructing Buster to follow her.

One run. One peaceful run is all I ask for.

Gravel crunched under the tires before it came to a stop, and another car sped by. Rays from a full sun above sent bright light bouncing off of the shiny metal roof.

"Hi Ellie!" Kathy yelled from the driver's side window of the car. "How about that Adam up there on stage," she said with a care-free laugh. "Who knew he could bring in fifteen hundred dollars for the hospital? I should've told Tom to work it a little more!" Her enthusiasm and delight were salt to Ellie's wounds.

"Yeah … who knew?" Ellie asked through a forced smile. She held two thumbs up while jogging in place with labored breath. If only she could feel so nonchalant.

"You're *so* good, Ellie. I wish I were better at exercising," Kathy said, as she pulled saucer-sized tortoiseshell sunglasses away from her eyes. She allowed them to rest on the bridge of her nose. "And what a beautiful dog!"

"Thanks." Ellie resisted the urge to roll her eyes and argue at Kathie's nonsensical comment about exercise. While, perhaps, Kathy would benefit from some toning, she was one of the thinnest people Ellie knew. Even at sixty years old, it seemed Kathy's body had the metabolism of a child, burning calories the very second they were consumed.

"Anyway, I won't keep you," Kathy said. "I'm just *so* excited we won your meal for ten at the auction! Do you think the beginning of May would work? I know it's not far off, but Tom's niece graduates from college the middle of the month, and his other sister will be visiting from Wisconsin, so we thought that'd be a nice time to have a small family get together."

"No problem," Ellie said, anxious to move on. Her mind was still on Adam rather than the dinner she agreed to make. "Okay Kathy, gotta go now before I cool off." She forced another smile, hoping it looked genuine.

"I'll call you, and we'll chat." Kathy slid her sunglasses back into place and waved a perfectly manicured hand at Ellie. Stones kicked up from the ground as she accelerated and sped away.

Ellie resumed her run, filled with more frustration than when she'd started. Mid-April used to be a time when she was too busy to be anything but tired. Days were filled with looming tax-filing deadlines and clients who had too many needs, far too late into an already short timeline.

Oh, how things have changed. Now your biggest concern is the messy kitchen you left at home.

Well, that and your marriage is in the toilet.

And soon you'll be raising a stranger's baby on your own.

She stared at the mountainous landscape ahead, but she didn't see the puffy white clouds and green rolling hills. Instead, she saw Jackie dancing with Adam in her slinky, gold gown. She saw him flirting with her, kissing her on the cheek, and she didn't know whether to be furious, jealous, or ashamed.

The trees and sky blurred behind tears that stung her eyes once again, and her legs turned weak. She slowed, folded forward, and rested her hands on her knees in an attempt to steady her weary body. Then the angry tears fell, filled with fear and disappointment for a love she could never imagine not feeling, for the man she imagined would never forgive her.

CHAPTER 20

ADAM

Jackie's house was a simple white ranch with black shutters. Neatly positioned three-foot-high square hedges flanked the front beside a small porch, built to shelter the entrance.

Adam forced himself to keep moving, one step at a time, on the gray stone walkway set into the top of a gently sloped grassy yard. He checked his watch and rang the doorbell—right on time—6 p.m. In his phone conversations with Jackie, she'd seemed harmless, but he was struggling to enter a state of mind kind enough to get him through tonight. It was one thing to dance on stage and flirt with her in an attempt to make Ellie jealous and take away his own pain by indulging in childish revenge, but spending an entire evening with any woman other than Ellie was a foreign, uncomfortable concept.

When the black-painted door opened, Adam was surprised at the image standing before him. Curls fell out of a playful ponytail and framed Jackie's face, her skin sheer in comparison to the heavy makeup she wore at the ball. Her cheekbones were highlighted with the slightest bit of pink, her eyes illuminated with subtle sparkle, pale lip-gloss painted across her lips.

Her attire was just as unexpected. A white cotton top layered under a jean jacket was snug but not low cut and provocative, as he would have anticipated. And a long black linen skirt playfully fell around her ankles above pretty pink toenails that peeked out from colorful beaded sandals.

"The weather's been so nice, I couldn't resist," Jackie said, following Adam's gaze to her feet.

Adam's eyes darted back up and latched onto hers. He stared, bemused by her transformation into the stereotypical girl-next-door.

"You did say casual, right?" Jackie asked. An anxious look flashed across her face.

He suddenly realized he hadn't said a word since she opened the door. "Yah sure . . . sorry . . . " He shook the surprise from his head. "You look fine," he said, smiling. He motioned toward his own attire: khakis, a white, pressed, button-down shirt, and loafers with no socks. "I'm casual!" Silently, he scolded the uneasy tone in his voice.

She sighed with relief.

Nerves welled up in his stomach, and Adam instantly felt like a sixteen-year-old again. He realized all at once that he knew nothing about this woman and wondered if he should have brought her something. Flowers, maybe?

She stood, waiting, her expression anxious. He shifted his weight and fumbled through his thoughts. Maybe he expected Jackie to take the lead? Or maybe he was just really, *really* out of practice?

"Should we go?" he finally asked, motioning toward the BMW.

She grabbed her purse, and they walked together in awkward silence. He opened her door first, before walking to the driver's side. Climbing in, he was greeted by the unexpected scent of her vanilla musk perfume. His heightened senses reminded him again that he was not surrounded by Ellie's familiarity.

The drive to the *Apollo Grill* in Bethlehem was short. And thank God. The quiet space between them was more uncomfortable by the minute, and Adam wondered if Jackie felt it, too. He had been absent from the dating world for such a long time that he was certain his instincts were untrustworthy.

When they entered the modern-decorated restaurant, Adam noticed people staring. His chest instinctively filled with guilt. Was it that obvious, even to strangers, that he was out with someone other than his wife?

But he quickly realized they weren't staring at him at all—they were staring at *her*. As they walked through the room to be seated, he watched several men hold their gaze on Jackie far longer than necessary. Faces of more than a few women hardened and filled with jealousy. But Jackie seemed oblivious as she sat and thanked the waiter. Her lip-gloss-coated smile was once again reflecting the light, but this time from a candle at the center of the table. Not only was she beautiful in a natural, innocent way in that moment, but she seemed sweet and genuine as well—not at all like the woman he met at the ball.

"What's good here?" Jackie asked, opening her menu.

Adam was aware he hadn't been very perceptive lately—*obviously*—but if he wasn't mistaken, it seemed there may be a hint of nervousness hidden behind her cool façade.

"Everything," he said, taking a drink of water.

Surrounded by full, long lashes, her round, blue eyes looked out above the top of her opened menu, as if in search of a hidden meaning. Wondering if she had misinterpreted his comment, he nearly spit out a mouthful of water. Shame at his attraction to her washed over him, and he tried to decide if he was being suggestive without even noticing.

"I've never had a bad meal here," he said, shrugging his shoulders, trying to backpedal.

She smiled and lowered her menu. "What *is* that accent?"

"Pardon?"

"Your accent? I just love to hear you talk. I forget, where are you from?"

"Oh," Adam said, chuckling, surprisingly at ease with her change of topic. Maybe his nerves were getting the best of him. "Minneapolis, Minnesota. You'd think with all the years I've been in Pennsylvania, it wouldn't still be so noticeable. Old habits die hard, I suppose."

"I think it's great that you still have it. It's charming."

Her compliment brought heat to his cheeks, although he wasn't sure why, and the unexpected rush of blood immediately sent his attention back to the menu. The internal tug of war between calm and anxiety was unsettling.

The waiter came to take their order, and a few minutes later Adam was feeling composed and confident again.

"So, you already know about my job, obviously, since you won me at the ball," Adam said, raising his eyebrows, "but I have no idea what you do?"

"I'm an interior designer."

"Oh." His eyes widened with surprise and unexpected respect. "Do you like it?"

"I do." Her eyes lit up. "I love it, actually. I work on a lot of projects, mostly homes, which is how I first met Bonnie about five years ago. She commissioned me to do some work when she was remodeling. Sometimes I do commercial jobs, and that's fun in a different way."

"What do you think about this place?" Adam asked, scanning the room. "Does the décor in here pass?"

She paused, but she didn't look anywhere except straight at him. Adam first noticed her eyes the night of the ball—their ability to communicate was stronger and more unique than any he'd ever seen—and as she looked at him now, he was drawn into their blue, playful shimmer, inviting his challenge.

"It's okay," she said.

"Okay?" He chortled.

Her eyes held fast to his.

"Their branding is one of the best I've seen, the lighting is attractive with an inviting glow, the art is interesting and in line with the theme and brand. The fabric and carpets could use some updating and perhaps a few minor changes to renovate the bar, but overall it's pretty good. But we didn't come here to eat any of that, now did we?"

Adam laughed out loud—a genuine laugh from deep in his stomach—and realized that he was having a good time. Jackie was smarter than he'd expected, her humor came easily, and he was relieved to find that the night was moving in a direction far from what he had imagined.

Their food was served with perhaps more flair and attention to detail than the room surrounding them. Swirls of puree and spice danced around their appetizers, salads, and dinners alike, each one as new and exciting as those that came before. They declined dessert, too caught up in conversation that moved easily from topic to topic, and Adam found the time passing quickly.

"Are you ready for me to take this yet, sir?" the waiter asked, approaching their table for the third time.

Reluctantly, Adam looked up to acknowledge him. How long ago did he first deliver the check? It had definitely been a while.

"You know, I didn't get it yet, but let me give it to you now," he said, reaching for his wallet and handing the waiter a credit card.

"I think they're politely asking us to get out," Jackie whispered, as she leaned forward and smiled.

"Yah, I think so," Adam said. The unexpected disappointment in his voice was obviously not lost on Jackie.

Her smile turned up higher at the corners. "Why don't we go for a walk down Main Street? I don't come often enough, but they have the best stores to wander through," she said.

Adam agreed. The realization that he didn't want this night to end yet brought both relief and apprehension, but he couldn't say no.

They wandered the street, walked through the Moravian Book Shop, and visited Donegal Square, all while fighting fits of laughter as they people-watched. They stopped for ice cream, and Adam observed Jackie as she studied a girl licking a cone, maybe three-years-old.

"Do you have kids?" he asked.

She shook her head and smiled.

"Want them?"

She paused, wearing an expression he was unable to read. Most women were an open-book when it came to their desires for children, and Adam was surprised at the unusual mysteriousness behind Jackie's eyes.

"I don't know," she finally said. "I used to. Sometimes I think about it, and I think maybe, but then other times, I'm not so sure as I grow older. I do love to be around them, though."

"Give motherhood a try, and you may not love being around them anymore." He chuckled.

"That's a horrible thing to say!" She gasped.

Adam held up a palm in surrender. "I'm not saying I don't love my kids. I do. To the moon and back. But it's tough. Not that I wouldn't do it all over again."

"Are you saying *I'm* not cut out for it then?" she asked, challenge and tease blinking behind her big blue eyes.

"No, of course not." Horrified, Adam tried to decide how to untangle himself from the unintended insinuation. Before he could speak in an effort to clarify, an older boy on a skateboard barreled down the sidewalk behind Jackie and knocked her off balance. Adam reached out to steady her while he watched both of their ice cream cones hurl toward the ground and smash onto the concrete.

"Are you okay?" he asked, glancing over his shoulder at the kid dressed in all black, speeding away from them.

"I think so," she said.

Her palm, warm and soft, was leaning against his chest. She looked up, and their eyes locked. An intense shiver rippled through Adam's middle section.

"Well, that was unfortunate," Adam said, clearing his throat.

"Was it?" Jackie asked. She straightened, once again firm on her feet, but her eyes were still on his.

Warmth spread across Adam's cheeks, down to his feet.

"Thanks for catching me," she said.

Adam was suddenly aware that he was holding his breath. Her eyes—the way they seemed to talk, their expressive nature—intrigued him. They had changed once more, now screaming sensuality, even appearing a darker shade of blue. His pulse was racing, and he knew it would be wise to call it a night. He cleared his throat.

"You know, it's getting late and the stores are closing for the night. You ready to head home?" he asked.

"Sure," she said.

The return car ride to Jackie's house was as quiet as the first, but this time the air was charged with a tension that made Adam sweat. Thoughts in his head had moved from a state of conflict to one of war. A tiny voice in his left ear reminded him of his love for Ellie and their children. The one on the right told him it was too late to save his marriage and justified his attraction to Jackie.

After all, Ellie had her romp.

Rocks crunched under the tires as they entered Jackie's driveway, a sound magnified in the silence between them. Adam slid the transmission into park, and breathed into the butterflies forming in his stomach. Jackie moved a hand to the keys that hung above his right knee and cut the engine with a swift flick of her wrist.

"Why don't you come in?" Her voice was laced with so much seduction that Adam thought he might burst.

Without a word, he exited the car and followed her.

Once inside, she closed the door, pushed him against it with surprising force, and leaned into him with a slow, probing kiss. All shyness had evidently disappeared.

Her lips were thinner than Ellie's, but soft and skillful. Again, he noticed her unfamiliar, sweet musky scent.

She tugged at his shirt and unbuttoned it with fervor as he pushed thoughts of Ellie from his mind, maddened by their persistence. Her lips moved down the hair of his chest, toward his navel. He gasped in anticipation. She unbuttoned his pants and ran her fingers over a small tattoo inked many years ago into his midriff, reminding him again of Ellie, the person he was thinking of when he branded his body, the person who owned the other half of his heart.

CHAPTER 21

ELLIE

E llie held a bright red tomato to her nose, inhaled its sweet-
earthy aroma, and gave it a gentle squeeze, a final test for ripe-
ness. She loved the farmers market at this time of year when food
was fresh and at its best flavor. A cozy warmth beat on her head
from the sun, making her hair sparkle. As a low breeze pushed
through the sky, she took a deep breath, realizing she hadn't felt
this content in longer than she could remember.

Her basket was full of red leaf lettuce, arugula, soft round balls
of fresh mozzarella, plump tomatoes, garlic cloves, and brick oven
baked bread. She found canned marmalades and homemade pes-
to from another stand to compliment the bread, and that distinc-
tive earthy-minty-anise scent from long stems of deep green basil
wafted into the air around her.

May always brought the promise that summer was near, but
warm weather arrived early this year and it felt more like the beginning of June. Flowers that bloomed a month premature gave
Ellie the opportunity to add freshly cut color to her agenda for the
dinner planned at Kathy and Tom's later that night.

Selecting food, planning a menu, and preparing a feast were
some of the things she did best. Although it was hard work, she

found herself getting lost in the joy behind the magic that made it all come together.

When she arrived home, she carefully washed and prepared each ingredient. She assembled as much as she could ahead of time before leaving for Tom and Kathy's to organize things there.

First on the list: Transform the Spleck home into an intimate, charming dining area for ten.

She pressed her finger to the doorbell, and Kathy answered almost immediately.

"I come with lots of baggage," Ellie said, balancing two cardboard boxes in her arms on the doorstep. The words were spoken without a thought, but they rang in her mind, leaving her no choice but to acknowledge the unintentional double meaning.

She pushed the thought aside and forced a smile.

"Let me help," Kathy said, removing the top box.

Already familiar with the layout of the house, Ellie breezed in and quickly moved from room to room, calculating what she needed to do as Kathy clucked behind her about how excited she was.

This chair will need to be moved, that table will have to go, and this one will need to be turned sideways.

"What do you need from me?" Kathy asked, her cheeks flushed, an eager smile spread across her face.

A few minutes later, Tom and his brother-in-law, Dave, were hauling boxes out of the car and Ellie was already moving furniture.

"Let us do that," Tom said, lowering the box in his hand to the floor. He rushed to the other end of the table Ellie was wrestling with in the living room. "Dave, lend a hand," he called to his brother-in-law.

At six feet tall, Tom was slender other than a small potbelly at his middle. As he approached, Ellie couldn't be sure, but his eyes seemed to linger longer than usual on her middle section, and she wondered if he noticed the difference. Her abdomen had finally started to thicken, not so much that she looked obviously pregnant, but definitely not the thin waistline she was used to. Hell, it wasn't even the slightly larger one of last month. She dressed this morning in a loose navy blue top that was gathered just below the bust, her best effort to deter any potential attention.

Dave sidled up next to Ellie and took her end of the table. "You didn't tell me she was such a pretty cook," Dave said. He was bald with a large red nose that sat boldly at the center of his face above a broad, but genuine smile.

"Never mind him, he's harmless," Tom said. Dave's plump body jiggled as he laughed at Tom. "Dave and my sister, Sue, came in last night from Wisconsin."

"Oh," Ellie said, offering a smile but only half paying attention. She was already eying the arbor outside the back door. Yes, the yard was the perfect place for dinner. She dug into her box of decorations—white lights would be just the thing—and pulled out a brand new string she had intended to use over the holidays, before she realized she didn't have it in her to decorate any more than absolutely necessary.

She found a stepladder in the garage and meticulously strung the lights through the wooden framework of the arbor. As an accountant, she learned that attention to detail was of upmost importance, applicable to most things in life. The atmosphere tonight would be almost as important as the food.

Lost in thought, Ellie nearly lost her balance when Kathy appeared with a gasp. "I had no idea you were going to . . . Ellie, this is above and beyond."

"It's a special occasion," Ellie said.

"Still, it's too much."

"It's already done, don't give it another thought." Ellie slipped the last wire through and descended from the ladder.

Ellie took Kathy's reaction in stride, but secretly she was filled with pride. It *was* going to look amazing. Once she was done setting the table with scattered candles, the fresh flowers from the market, and some ivy she'd clipped from the side of Kathy and Tom's garage, she had just enough time to race home for a shower before returning for the arrival of guests at five o'clock.

Tom and Kathy's niece, Kelly (the guest of honor), arrived right on time with her parents, Jake and Jennifer.

"Thanks *so* much for planning this dinner. Everything's so beautiful, and we haven't even had dinner yet," Kelly said when she was introduced to Ellie. She looked and talked more like a woman in her mid-thirties than a girl just getting ready to enter the world on her own. Dressed in a classy indigo blue three-quarter sleeve wrap dress, her brown shoulder-length bob cut matched her mother's and screamed 'soccer mom.'

Silently, Ellie scolded herself. She would probably be a soccer mom soon.

An old soccer mom. Alone. Forever.

"It's my pleasure. I hope you enjoy it." Ellie's smile came sincerely. Little else filled her heart with more pride than to nurture people with food, to bask in their appreciation. "And congratulations on your graduation."

Kelly's face beamed with pride as she thanked Ellie again, before she moved toward the makeshift bar in the dining room. Ellie watched her choose a wine glass from the side bar and fill it with Greco di Tufo, a white wine from the Campania region of Italy. It was perfect for the tapas and salads. Ellie's chest expanded with pride. She spent hours researching wine before making selections, careful to include choices that would complement each phase of the menu.

She considered Kelly's youth—probably just old enough to legally drink—and wondered if Kelly would make wise decisions in life. To make wiser decisions than Ellie would perhaps be easy, but it never seemed so simple when you were in the thick of things.

The doorbell chimed again, and Ellie was introduced to Kathy's sister, Colleen, and her husband, John. When John shook her hand, it completely disappeared inside of his. He was a creature of contradiction; his hands thick and calloused with a grip that was soft, the look of a giant with green eyes that were gentle and warm.

Colleen had kind eyes and a broad smile, her glossy auburn hair similar to Kathy's, but a shade lighter in color. Like Kathy, she was thin without looking frail, her skin soft and creamy.

Colleen and Kathy moved to the dining room, and Colleen fussed over the table that was set with tiered shiny metal plates and platters made of natural, earthy woods holding cheeses, crackers, and fruits. They stood side-by-side laughing and chatting, bearing a strong sisterly resemblance. Watching them, Ellie was reminded for the millionth time that she was an only child. For as long as she could remember, she felt like she had missed out on an important piece of life by not having a sibling.

Dismissing the thought, Ellie moved back to the kitchen, checked the food in the oven, and put finishing touches on the salads and side dishes. Once everything looked perfect, she returned to collect everyone for dinner, motioning to the door that opened into the back yard.

Jennifer and Kelly walked through first, under the arbors that extended from the back of the house. They paused to look up and coo at how beautifully the white Christmas lights twinkled against the dusk sky above, confirmation that Ellie's tedious work was worth the effort.

Kathy was seated first at the long, linen covered table situated on the lawn and surrounded by various dining chairs from the house.

Tom was next. He stopped and plucked a brilliant pink Gerber daisy from one of the bouquets of freshly cut flowers that lined the center of the table, handed it to Kathy, and kissed her on the cheek. A pain of nostalgia toward Adam shot through Ellie's body like a jolt of electricity.

Once the rest of the guests were seated, chatting, and content, Ellie took a deep breath, walked to Kathy, and bent down to whisper in her ear. "If you're okay, I think I'll start cleaning up the kitchen while you eat," Ellie said.

"Nonsense," Kathy objected before the words were completely out. "Sit and eat with us, Ellie."

"Oh, no, I couldn't. Really, I'm fine," she argued, "I made this for you. Enjoy it."

"We won't hear of it," Tom said. "There are ten chairs, and since Kelly's here alone, we're only using nine. Sit and have a meal with us. After all, we have a lot of wonderful food."

His argument for her to stay had now captured an audience. Everyone agreed, urging Ellie to take a seat in the empty chair beside Colleen. Colleen pulled the chair away from the table as if to finalize the decision. "Please," she said.

Ellie surrendered, happy to rest her tired feet, especially since they were beginning to swell, no doubt from the one thing she tried most not to think about. But she initially felt awkward in a do-not-fornicate-with-the-hired-help sort of way. Colleen was quick to put her at ease though, and almost immediately she could imagine them becoming friends. She found herself relaxing, dinner a huge success, all of the guests gracious and complimentary, fussing over the food and the ambiance alike from beginning to end.

Jennifer shared stories about their recent visit to Italy and proclaimed she was in love with the Italian Barbera wine Ellie chose to serve with the pasta. Dave seemed to like it too, maybe too much, and Ellie wondered for a moment if someone should cut him off. It was obvious he wasn't one to become loud or obnoxious, but rather more endearing with each additional glass of alcohol. Nevertheless, Ellie found herself worrying about him and then she wondered why, thinking it odd that people she barely knew had quickly become such comfortable companions.

Jennifer attempted to top off Ellie's glass of wine, and Ellie felt awkward for the first time since she sat down. *Dèjá vu all over again.* Ellie placed her hand on the rim and pasted a smile on her face. "Thank you, but I'm working."

Jennifer began to argue, but Ellie shook her head. "Really, you enjoy it," Ellie said, her smile set in place. She had already excused herself once, when she carried her first glass of wine to the kitchen and discreetly emptied it into the sink.

"As long as you're pouring." Dave tipped his glass toward Jennifer.

Relieved, Ellie turned her attention to Jake, who had picked up where Jennifer left off with the details of their trip to Italy.

"Even I thought it was romantic," he said.

"Don't listen to him," Jennifer said. "What he liked most was that all the girls greeted everyone with a kiss on each cheek."

Everyone chuckled, and Ellie was overcome by a sensation she couldn't quite place—it seemed so strange, so awkward among people she had only just met hours ago. If she weren't pregnant and she *had* swallowed a glass of Barbera, she'd believe it was the wine warming her from within.

She watched the glow from candles scattered about the tabletop dance on faces filled with animation at each new bite, and it hit her as her own words echoed in her mind.

"Thank you, but I'm working."

It was the satisfactory feeling of accomplishment that she had almost forgotten existed.

A bout of laughter interrupted her thoughts, and Ellie realized everyone's attention had turned to Tom's sister, Sue.

"The bush went up in flames instantly, and Tom just stood there staring at it, as if he didn't really believe the matches would actually start a fire," Sue said.

Laughter swept across the table again, and Jennifer's face took on a look of remembrance, her cheeks rosy from the alcohol. "And then in an attempt to snuff it out, he ripped off his t-shirt and threw it on top." Everyone laughed so hard that some of them had a hard time swallowing their most recent gulp of wine.

"I was six!" Tom said, mock irritation lacing the words.

"He spent the rest of his childhood trying to convince our mom he wasn't a pyromaniac," Sue said.

The banter continued for another twenty minutes. When Ellie finally rose from the table, there were tears welling in her eyes and her mouth hurt from smiling too hard. Her ears were ringing against the loud laughter surrounding her.

"Okay everyone," Kathy said, tapping a spoon against her glass to gather everyone's attention. "Let's follow Ellie, like she said, and go see if we can satisfy our sweet tooth, shall we?"

"I don't know if I can stuff in another thing." Jake stood and stretched as if he was attempting to make more room in his stomach.

Once inside, Dave helped himself to a large dose of caffeine from the coffee urn resting on a sturdy table in the center of the living room, and Ellie thought it a good idea considering the amount of alcohol he had consumed.

"It's so hard to decide," Jennifer said, standing next to Kelly, examining the delicately displayed desserts.

Aware of the fatigue that had crept into every muscle, Ellie fought the urge to indulge in some much needed sugar and headed to the kitchen to start her cleanup. A half hour passed, then the kitchen filled with guests eager to help, carrying trays and dishes.

"You all really don't have to do that!" One at a time, Ellie took the trays from them in protest, insisting that everyone continue to enjoy the night.

"Stop arguing. It's the least we can do after the wonderful night you've provided," Tom said, exiting the room in search of more things to tidy.

People continued to move around her, helping with the mess. Jennifer walked by and raised a brow that suggested Ellie accept defeat. Ellie sighed and placed a tray on the butcher-block counter-top. Although she wanted to deny it, she was somewhat relieved—too weary to argue with the offer of help, too tired not to accept it.

Once the dishes were washed, the platters were cleaned, and everything was packed away, the men carried boxes to Ellie's car.

"Ellie, thank you so much again for everything!" Kathy exclaimed, hugging her tight. "It really was just so wonderful, really!"

"It was nice sharing a meal with you and your family. They're all lovely." Ellie smiled with pride, filled with satisfaction in the knowledge that it really *was* wonderful.

She was light on her feet. She had a second wind. She felt young. And happy. And for a moment, all of her troubles were far away. She hopped off the doorstep with the enthusiasm of a child just as the headlamps of a car entering the driveway temporarily blinded her path. Squinting, she held her arm up, attempting to block the light.

The vehicle stopped, and a voice called out from the dark. "Well hello Ellie dear!"

Bonnie Singleton.

And the happy moment was gone.

Bonnie stepped out, closed the driver side door, and waved with an eagerness that made Ellie uncomfortable, although she wasn't sure why.

"Bonnie," she deadpanned. "What are you doing here?" Ellie forced a smile that felt awkward after the genuine one that had lived on her face most of the night.

"Well . . . " Bonnie stopped in front of Ellie, holding a hand to her chest, dramatically pausing to catch her breath. She held up a pink shiny bag from her boutique. "Kathy ordered this pretty little top from my store, and I wanted to get it right over to her soon as I could. I know she's been lookin' forward to it."

"At nine-thirty?" Ellie asked, looking at her watch.

"You know how it is—the life of a small business woman. I actually just left the store. Had some paperwork to do."

Ellie scrunched her forehead at Bonnie, unable to find her late night visit anything but odd. She said good night and started toward her car again, but Bonnie stopped her.

"I *am* sorry that I missed your little dinner, Ellie. I presume everyone was just over the moon with your meal?" Bonnie asked.

Ah, and here's the real reason for her visit.

Ellie spun around on the ball of her foot, wishing Bonnie were under the sole of her shoe.

"I think it went well, but why don't you ask the guests? I mean, since you're here." Ellie smiled and shrugged her shoulders.

Moving toward her car once more, a smile crept up in her mind as she visualized her dinner companions who would no doubt sing her praises once Bonnie was on the other side of that door.

"Yes, well, I'm sure they'll all have good things to say," Bonnie clucked, as she started on the sidewalk toward the house. "And by the way, your husband has done it again. He is just full of surprises isn't he?"

Ellie froze and turned her head slowly toward Bonnie.

"What's that?" she asked.

"Adam. I never would've taken him for the tattoo type." Bonnie said, laughing, amused at herself, at Ellie's expense.

Goose bumps raced over Ellie's skin. She stood speechless and watched Bonnie enter the house. She realized she was holding her breath when she began to feel dizzy. Releasing the air held tightly in her chest, she felt like a balloon, moving through the sky, plunged to the ground as fast as the metal point of a pin could prick its rubber exterior.

"Yes, he's full of fucking surprises," Ellie mumbled under her breath in the dark of night, as she yanked on the car door handle. She drove home without hearing what song was playing on the radio or taking notice of the scenery around her, everything blurring together in her mind.

"How'd it go?" Suzanne asked, greeting her at the door when she arrived at home.

Tommy and Lizzie ran from the hall and grabbed onto Ellie's leg, screaming with joy.

"Mommy, I missed you," Lizzie said.

Ellie suddenly regretted telling Suzanne the kids could stay up until she got home, and then she felt guilty all at the same time.

"Didn't you have fun with Aunt Suzie?" Ellie asked, fluffing her daughter's curly hair.

"We had fun," Tommy said. "She gave us ice cream sundaes!"

Suzanne shrugged her shoulders and flashed a look of guilt. "Sorry, isn't that what I'm supposed to do? Spoil them and then give them back to you?" she asked. "So, *how'd* it go? I'm dying to hear."

"Good, but I'm tired. Can we talk about it in the morning?" Ellie asked.

Suzanne looked disappointed, but Ellie gave her a pleading look, and they agreed to talk no later than nine the next morning. Suzanne picked up her keys, slid on a sweater, and paused to study Ellie's face. "You look exhausted."

"I am. We'll talk tomorrow; don't worry. And thanks again for watching the kids." Ellie leaned forward and gave Suzanne a quick, reassuring hug.

"Anytime," Suzanne said as they separated, but her concerned expression remained. She shifted her attention to the children. "C'mere kids, Aunt Suzie needs a hug." Suzanne scooped Tommy and Lizzie up for a hug, and gave Ellie a cautionary glance. "You sure you're okay?"

No! She wanted to scream. But she couldn't.

Ellie gave a pointed nod. "Just tired," she said. "Tomorrow, okay?" She pulled her lips into a tight smile.

Ellie watched Suzanne walk into the darkness before she closed the door and leaned on it for support, Bonnie's words echoing again in her mind, too upsetting to repeat, even to Suzanne.

As she walked down the hall toward the half bath, Lizzie screamed for her. "Mommy, I'm hungry."

"I'll be right there."

On the other side of the door, she lifted her shirt and stared at her reflection in the mirror. Her skin was stretching slightly across her developing belly, but it was still right where it belonged, below her navel. She studied it, half of a tiny red heart with a zigzag center. The matching half of her puzzle piece was missing; displayed in the very same spot on the person she had always thought completed the other half of her.

"Mommy, I want some cereal," Lizzie cried from the hallway.

Ellie lowered her shirt, opened the door, and found her daughter in a heap on the floor at her feet.

"Come on, I'll get you some," she said, heading for the kitchen with a sigh of exhaustion.

"I'm hungry, too," Tommy said, jumping up onto a stool at the counter.

"Of course you are," Ellie mumbled under her breath. She opened the refrigerator and peered inside.

Great.

"There's no milk, guys. You'll have to eat it dry."

Both kids started whining.

She opened the door to the pantry and realized the cereal was gone, too. She returned to the refrigerator, but it was just as empty.

Great. Great. Great.

She had been so distracted with the dinner party that she forgot to do her own shopping. She rested her forehead against the cold metal of the stainless steel refrigerator and squeezed her eyes together as tightly as possible before turning back toward the children.

"Okay guys, no bread, no cereal, no milk, and no leftovers. Are you two *really* that hungry?" She looked at her watch—10:14 p.m. "You should've been asleep a long time ago. How about if we all go to bed, and I'll take you out for pancakes in the morning?" She clapped her hands together in excitement and spoke in her most enthusiastic voice, desperate to convince the kids to end this exhausting night. Now.

"But I'm *hungry!*" Lizzie cried from her chair, crocodile tears threatening to spill over.

Ellie's head hurt, her heart ached, and all she wanted to do was fall into her bed and sleep forever. Dealing with whining children was almost too much to bear.

"Okay, everybody get your shoes on," she said, relenting, picking up her purse.

The kids squealed with delight and raced to the back foyer, where they slipped on their shoes and thin jackets.

The sky opened up, and rain began to fall just as they left the driveway, making it impossible for Ellie to open the car windows even though it felt as if she was suffocating. Her mind was buzzing: Anger. Regret. Jealousy.

Had Ryan seen her tattoo?

Obviously, he must have.

It was something she hadn't thought of until now. Even in the face of her own guilt, even after the charade at the hospital ball, she could not believe Adam would share another woman's bed.

Particularly a woman like Jackie.

The thought made her physically sick. She considered it might have been a good idea to take a painkiller for her throbbing head before leaving the house, even though her stomach was twisting into a knot. It felt as if someone was sitting on her chest. She found it so hard to breathe that she wondered if she was having a panic attack.

The rattling in her mind was loud enough that she didn't hear the siren screaming toward the back of her vehicle until Lizzie screamed herself.

"Mommy I have to *pee!*" Lizzie screeched.

The unmistakable glow of flashing red and blue lights brought her attention to the rearview mirror.

"Lizzie, you're just going to have to hold it. How many times have I told you to use the bathroom before you leave the house?" Her words were impatient, her mind exhausted. Her attention shifted between the road and the lights in the rearview mirror.

"But I *can't* hold it. I really have to *go!*" Lizzie cried again.

The police car continued to follow her, and Ellie wondered why he hadn't passed by yet.

"Mom, I think he wants you to pull over," Tommy said. "Like cops and robbers. This is cool!"

"Tommy, he isn't pulling me over!" Ellie said.

Is he?

The rain pounded against her windshield, harder, making it difficult to see, even with the wipers at max speed. As she approached an intersection, she glanced in the rearview mirror again, wondering if Tommy was right. She made a mental review of their trip, trying to decipher if she had done something wrong.

"Mommy, I have to *peeeeeeee!*" This time Lizzie screamed at the top of her lungs.

"Lizzie, stop!" Ellie yelled, turning her head toward the backseat.

Headlights flashed. From the side. In her peripheral vision. Just for a moment. A split-second. The sky filled with the sound of rubber screeching against wet blacktop. Ellie slammed on the breaks, but her efforts were canceled as another vehicle collided with hers. A loud bang rang through the darkness. A jolt hard enough to deploy the airbags. Her car pushed sideways through the intersection. The windshield crushed into a thousand pieces. Somehow, it momentarily maintained its flat shape. Then it imploded, as if a bomb had exploded above it.

Tommy's screams and Lizzie's sobs from the back seat, jumbled together with high-pitched tones of metal crushing metal.

And then everything was silent, and everything was black.

PART V

In Sickness and In Health

CHAPTER 22

ADAM

Adam tossed in bed, restless, agitated, exhausted from days and nights that blended together and offered no promise of sleep. Residual anger brewed in his veins, but the feelings were directed at so many different things all at the same time that his head was throbbing.

He didn't want to think about Ellie or Jackie anymore. He didn't want to think about the mess his life had become, but he couldn't escape the turmoil. And there was little Bobby Fleich. That might be worse.

It had been months since Adam stood outside of Bobby's window in the ICU unit of the Greater Valley Medical Center, hands shoved into his pockets, shoulders slumped. Bobby's tiny, lifeless body was hooked up to more wires and tubes than he could count, his face hidden under an oxygen mask.

Life can be so unfair. The thought settled into Adam's mind, self-pity blanketing him so it was literally hard to breathe.

He wondered what would happen to the boy. As far as Adam knew, they still hadn't heard from next of kin. He imagined Bobby spending the next eleven years in a foster home, and his body shuddered at the thought.

He'd talk to him. See how he was doing. He could be there for Bobby—in a way no one was there for him. He'd do all of that when Bobby woke up.

But then the machines came to life. Alarms began to sound, and nurses ran into his room, scurrying around. At first, Adam mistook their frenzy for panic, and he was gripped with fear. But then he saw it—the excitement, the sparkle in their eyes, the smiles on their faces. Bobby was recovering.

Adam smiled, then frowned. His emotions swung between relief and fear. Fear and relief. And he fled. He nearly ran out of the hospital—as far away from Bobby as he could go.

Because he couldn't talk to Bobby. How could he when he didn't even have an explanation for himself? And how the hell was it that after years on the hospital board he'd not come across another young child who lost both of his parents in an accident? How was it nothing had ever affected him quite this way? Was it as odd as he thought? Was he as alone as he'd felt? Was Bobby?

The answers haunted him.

They were still haunting him.

He punched the pillow under his head, threw it across the room, and watched it hit the wall with a thump before it fell to the floor. His cell phone buzzed on the sheets beside him, demanding attention despite his self-indulgent sorrows. He glanced at the bedside clock—11:31 p.m. and checked the phone's screen—*Sam.*

"Isn't it past your bedtime?" Adam said, secretly thankful for the distraction.

"Everything's fine, but I need you to come down to the hospital," Sam said, his tone familiar, collected.

A million unconnected scenarios ran through Adam's mind. Only one thing stood out with clarity. Sam wouldn't be calling at that hour if everything was fine.

"What happened?"

"Ellie and the kids were in a car accident."

"Wha—"

"Everyone's going to be okay, but you need to come." Sam's voice remained calm. Still, Adam's heart began to pump hard enough for the sound to echo through his ears.

"I'll be there as soon as I can," Adam said. He clicked the off button, unable to ask anything further, his voice already drowning, his throat threatening to shut off his air supply.

Car accident.

Frantic, he gathered clothes and pulled on jeans and a shirt. His feet carried him in a sprint toward the car where he fought to cope with his keys in a hand that had suddenly taken to wild tremors.

. . . but you need to come.

Accelerator pushed to the floor, he drove with purpose, Sam's voice playing through his mind, repeating itself endlessly, like a scratched record spinning on a turntable. He wondered how much of *"everything's fine"* to believe. Sam was a veteran at handling "unfortunate circumstances" as they called them in the boardroom. Adults and children alike were rushed to his emergency room on a daily basis, many times gambling with life or death. He knew Sam's voice would be calm no matter *what* the situation. He knew Sam would tell him everything was fine even if it weren't, and the latter thought was terrifying.

His feet pounded through the hospital parking lot almost as fast as his racing heart. A layer of perspiration fell across his skin. Bright light from the hospital's interior escaped through windows, glass walls illuminating the otherwise dark surroundings of night as he closed in on the building. When he reached the entrance, he spotted Suzanne waiting in the emergency room lobby. She stood against a stark white wall, sipping from a paper cup. The automatic glass doors opened on command with a swoosh, and she looked up from her post.

"This way." She grabbed his arm and led him through large doors that required a pass for admittance.

Adam followed, unable to ask what he was dying to know. The telltale scent of antiseptic hit his nostrils, and he fought to suppress the nausea building in his stomach. He still couldn't find his voice, so he just kept moving.

They weaved their way down a hallway of curtain-drawn cubicles. When they turned the corner, Sam came into view. He was standing outside of a room at the end of the hall, fingers pressed into his temples, talking to a police officer.

"Adam," Sam said, turning toward them as they made their way closer. The officer nodded at Sam, at Adam, then turned to walk away, toward the nurse's station.

"Where are they?" Adam managed to ask, even though he was breathless. The officer's keys and handcuffs clinked against his belt as he walked away. Adam watched him go, turned back to Sam. "Police, Sam? You said everything was fine."

Sam shifted his weight and cradled one arm on the other. Raising his hand to his face, he took on a thoughtful pose. "Try to calm dow—"

"I don't want to calm down, Sam." Adam felt his teeth grind together. "I want you to just *tell* me what's really going on here, and I want to see them. What happened? Where's Ellie? And where are the kids?" The questions came one after another, succinct and rapid, like his still-racing mind, the wild rhythm of his heart battering his chest with every agonizing beat.

Ellie. In an instant, he could sense her presence. The overwhelming feeling hit him with a swift force, strong enough that he struggled to steady himself.

He looked past Sam and walked toward the room's entrance, but Sam placed a hand on Adam's shoulder to stop him.

"Don't be alarmed. It looks worse than it is," Sam said.

Adam's throat constricted tighter than ever before, making it impossible to speak. He braced himself and entered the room. Ellie was lying on a hospital bed with an IV inserted into her arm. A plastic mask covered her face, and round disks attached to dangling wires were strapped to the top of her slightly bulging stomach.

He walked to the bed, gently touched her hand. The icy feel of her skin sent a shiver through his body.

"She's cold," he said, barely managing the words, his throat tangled. "She needs a blanket."

Suzanne nodded. "I'll ask a nurse," she said, disappearing into the hallway.

Adam turned to Sam, puddles building in his eyes. "Tell me the truth, Sam. What are we talking about here?"

"She hasn't responded completely yet, but she's improved. They have her on fluids, oxygen, and some pain medication."

"Will she?"—Adam's eyes fell to the floor. He forced himself to choke out the words—"respond completely, I mean. What if . . . what if she doesn't?" His voice cracked. He could barely finish the sentence much less withstand the pain that filled him at the thought.

"Don't," Sam said gently. He remained silent for a moment, as if waiting for Adam's full attention before he continued.

Finally, Adam looked up to meet Sam's eyes again.

"We have no reason to believe she won't recover."

Adam turned back to Ellie and swallowed hard. He wanted Sam to be right. He wanted to believe everything would be fine. *But all the machines. All the tubes.* She looked so fragile, not like the Ellie he was used to. The Ellie he knew always had everything together and running smoothly. She was the glue. He *needed* Sam to be right. If something happened to her, then what? What about the kids?

The kids . . .

Oh God.

Adam's mind raced again.

"Where are the kids?" Adam asked, wondering why no one had mentioned them yet. Scenarios flooded his thoughts from bad, to worse, to unthinkable, each of them rushing by in a fraction of a second.

"They're down the hall. They were banged up and scared, but they're preoccupied right now with coloring books and toys. We didn't think it'd be a good idea for them to see Ellie like this."

A nurse appeared with a blanket, draped it over Ellie, and began to tuck it under the edges of her bed.

"I can do that," Adam said to the nurse.

"It's okay, it's my job." Her voice was cheerful. She looked at Adam with a smile and went about her duties.

"Please." He took a firm hold of the white cotton.

The nurse's movement came to a halt, and her eyes moved from Adam's face to his hand. She gave him an understanding nod and left the room. Adam glanced at Sam and shifted his attention back to the blanket.

"And the baby?" Adam's throat constricted again, every word a struggle. He wasn't sure why he cared, but somehow he found himself concerned and hopeful that the life inside of Ellie was safe and healthy. He continued tucking the blanket around the edges of the bed, anxious to busy himself with anything other than standing around, feeling helpless.

"We're monitoring things." Sam's mouth bunched together, and he became introspective. Adam could see perplexity and disappointment etched into every line of Sam's facial expression. "We want to make sure Ellie doesn't start with any contractions, and they did an ultrasound to check on the baby. So far everything looks okay, but only time will tell." Sam paused. "Why didn't you tell me she was pregnant?"

"We didn't tell anyone." Adam, unsure of how to explain and with no energy to figure it out, decided not to elaborate. Instead, he stared down at Ellie, trying to suppress his tears.

"Are you reconciling?" Sam asked.

"I don't know." It was an honest answer. Adam didn't feel like he knew anything anymore.

With the exception of a black and white clock that ticked on the wall, the room was silent before Sam continued.

"I think you need to move back into the house," Sam said.

A tear finally escaped, rolled down Adam's face. He swiped it away and looked up at Sam. How could he explain the magnitude of their problems to Sam when he was unable to face them himself?

"When she gets out of here, she's going to need help," Sam said.

"When. Not if?"

Sam didn't acknowledge the question. "In the meantime, your kids are going to need you."

"Where are they?"

"There's one more thing," Sam said.

Adam was weary, unsure of whether he could handle *one more thing*.

"That police officer—the one in the hall earlier—was behind Ellie when she had the accident. He was attempting to pull her over, but he claimed she wasn't stopping."

Adam sunk into the chair by Ellie's bedside, placed his elbows on his knees, and raked a hand through his hair.

"He said he was following her, sirens on, but she just kept going. Then she ran a red light, and a car coming through the intersection plowed into her."

Adam flinched at the word *plowed*.

"Sorry," Sam said, his expression empathetic. "Anyway, it was probably a good thing he was behind her, because he called EMTs to the scene. Without their quick response, we may be having a very different conversation right now."

"Why was he pulling her over?"

"Her taillight was out."

Adam stared in disbelief, and Sam shrugged his shoulders.

"What about the people in the other car?" Adam asked, suddenly realizing they could be facing a legal situation in addition to a medical one.

"Young driver. Sixteen years old. He was speeding, not to mention they found a can of beer in the car, so they've decided not to press charges. Besides, his injuries were minimal, and well, you know how it goes. Even though Ellie ran the light, I don't think the parents want more trouble to deal with than they already have."

Adam sighed with relief.

"The officer does want to talk to Ellie when she wakes, though. He said he couldn't understand why she didn't pull over."

"Is *he* going to bring her up on charges?" Adam asked.

"He didn't say. I gave him my personal assurance that I know Ellie as a friend, and this was highly unusual. He did ask us to take a blood sample from her to test for drugs and alcohol."

Adam looked at Sam, waiting for confirmation that she was clean, then his eyes darted to the floor with immediate guilt. Ellie would never operate a vehicle carrying their children while under the influence of anything.

On the other hand, she's full of surprises lately.

"Of course it was negative," Sam said, looking bewildered.

"The kids?" Adam asked again.

"I think Suzanne was headed that way. She should be with them by now. I can take you."

Adam followed Sam, filled with a mixture of nervousness and sorrow. A mental picture of Ellie lying in the hospital bed haunted him as they walked. Her body, pale and almost lifeless, was a far cry from the wife he had shared a life with for seventeen years.

He considered, perhaps for the first time, what life would be like if Ellie weren't there to care for, if there were no decisions on whether or not to reconcile.

They reached the end of a long, white tiled hallway, and Adam heard the sound of Lizzie's laugh—it was enough to stir excitement inside of him. At an all time low, he realized that Lizzie and Tommy were the only ones who could make his heart smile.

"Daddy!" Lizzie screeched in her high-pitched voice. She jumped off a bench, and books spilled from her lap to the floor as she ran toward his open arms. He picked her up and hugged her tight, wanting to hold on forever.

"Daddy's here, sweetie. I miss you so much munchkin," he said, stroking her hair, holding her close.

Tommy quickly appeared at his pant leg, squeezing Adam's thigh for dear life.

"Oh, hey there Buddy." Adam tousled the top of Tommy's hair. No response.

Adam gave Lizzie a kiss on the check. "Daddy has to put you down for a minute, okay?" he said, lowering her to her feet.

Gently, he pried Tommy from his leg and put a hand under his chin, forcing his son to look up. Tears fell from Tommy's cheeks and spilled onto the floor, transporting Adam again to his past. His own eyes became blurry, but he fought to maintain control for the sake of his son.

"Mommy's going to be okay, Tommy. It's going to be okay," he said.

Tommy jumped into Adam's arms and cried with an unbridled fear that made Adam's heart melt.

"Are they going to take Mommy to jail?" Tommy asked, his words disjointed, coming slowly between sobs.

With a gentle hold, Adam pushed Tommy far enough away so they could speak face to face. "Why would you think that?"

"Because the police officer was chasing us," he blubbered.

"No, Tommy, no one's going to take Mommy to jail."

"Where is she? I want to see her," he said.

"Mommy isn't feeling well after the car accident, so she's resting. But as soon as she wakes up and feels better you can see her. I promise, okay?"

Adam gathered both children into his arms and hugged them tight.

"Everything's going to be okay, I promise. Daddy's going to come home, and everything's going to be fine." As the words left his mouth, he silently hoped that he could follow through on his word.

Adam felt a hand resting on his shoulder and looked up to see Sam standing above him.

"Kids, how about if Aunt Suzie takes you to the cafeteria for some ice pops?" Sam asked.

"Yay!" Lizzie said, her eyes wide.

Tommy looked first at Sam and then at Adam for reassurance. Tommy's increased awareness compared to Lizzie's innocence reminded Adam that his son's boyishness was slipping away, a thought that scared and saddened him at the same time.

"It's okay. Go get an ice pop, and I'll see you when you come back."

Tommy slowly turned toward Suzanne, but Adam could sense his lingering hesitation.

"Tommy?" Adam called.

Tommy stopped and turned to look back.

"You know I love you?"

"Love you too, Dad," he said. Adam watched him leave the room with Suzanne and Lizzie, wondering how his seven-year-old son grew up so fast.

"She's awake," Sam said to Adam, turning to walk out the door.

Adam's followed, his pulse accelerating as they stepped closer to Ellie's room. But when they arrived, his heart sank. They could hear her halfway down the hall.

"Where are my babies?" Ellie yelled at a nurse standing beside her bed.

"Your baby's fine," the nurse replied. "We've been monitoring both of you, and everything looks okay. Try to calm down now."

"I want my babies! Where are Tommy and Lizzie?" Her piercing screams bounced off the sterile walls surrounding them. With wide eyes and a wild expression, her attention zeroed in on Sam as he and Adam entered the room.

"Sam," she said, "they won't let me see my babies. I want to see my babies!"

The nurse shook her head and exited the room, visibly thankful for the relief.

"Tommy and Lizzie are fine. They just went with Suzanne to get some popsicles," he said, placing a hand on her arm. "You have to stay calm or you're going to be in this bed longer than I know you want to be."

Her head fell back onto a pillow, her hysteria replaced by heavy sobs that shook through to her core. "Thank God," she said, covering her face with her hands. "Thank God." She repeated it over and over, the words barely audible.

Adam stepped toward her bedside, understanding the depth of her relief.

"I'll let you two have some time," Sam said, glancing at Adam and walking into the hallway.

Adam reached down and took hold of Ellie's hand. She looked up at him, her face hardening. She yanked her hand away and turned her head toward the wall.

"Ellie?" He was overwhelmed by the variety of raw emotions swimming through his body.

"You didn't have to come," she said.

"Of course I came. You're my wife."

She turned toward him, an icy expression chiseled onto her face. "What *exactly* does that mean? You left us, Adam. You don't live with us anymore, so who are you trying to impress here?"

Adam's body tensed, and he struggled to keep up with the far swinging pendulum of her disposition. Before he could respond, she continued.

"Oh that's right, you wouldn't want to look bad to the outside world, would you? Maybe you should've thought about that before you got up on stage, dancing around with that tramp you're sharing a bed with."

Stunned by the hatred in her words, even more dumbfounded by her insinuation of Jackie, Adam's forehead wrinkled as he tried to decipher her accusation. He was unable to piece together how she would possess any details of his date with Jackie or the fact that it even happened to begin with.

"Don't be so—"

He was interrupted by a knock at the door. It was another nurse, this one wearing a shirt filled with pink hearts of various shapes and sizes.

How ironic.

"Hello Mrs. Thompson, my name is Abigail, and I'll be your nurse for the next seven hours. I just need to get some vitals." She strapped a blood pressure sleeve to Ellie's arm.

"That's okay," Ellie said. She looked at Adam with contempt, her face hard as stone. "We're finished here anyway."

CHAPTER 23
ELLIE

E llie winced as Suzanne helped her settle into a wheelchair. A nurse handed her a clipboard asking her to sign the discharge form on top, and Ellie scribbled a frantic signature. Three days in the hospital was more than enough. Suzanne gathered Ellie's bag and placed it on her lap before wheeling her down the hall toward an elevator.

"I spoke to Adam this morning," Suzanne said as she walked.

Ellie sighed. "Please tell me you've reconsidered, and he's not at my house."

"It's his house too, El. And no, I haven't changed my mind. I'm not leaving my family to come take care of you and the kids when you have a husband who's more than willing to do it." Suzanne stopped in front of the elevator, pushed the down button, and gave Ellie a look that matched her reprimanding tone. "Besides, you need to talk to him."

The elevator doors opened, and Suzanne wheeled Ellie in. Ellie stared at the illuminated L as the doors closed, thankful that at least they were alone for her lecture.

"Not to mention the fact that your kids need him," Suzanne continued. "And if I remember correctly, last time we talked about this, you said you still loved him."

They reached the main entrance, the exit, and Ellie squinted in the bright sunlight. It was the first time she'd been outside in days, and she greedily gulped in the fresh spring air.

A burst of wind lifted and whipped her hair around, against her face. Suzanne placed Ellie's things in the trunk while Ellie slid into the front passenger seat. Her breath caught at the pain. On second thought, maybe she didn't want to leave—a motionless position in bed was much more comfortable.

And besides, she didn't want to face Adam. No matter what Suzanne said.

Suzanne got into the car, started the engine, and looked at Ellie with a sigh.

"So, do you want to tell me what the real problem is?"

Ellie shifted her attention to the landscape outside of her window. The grass was greener, flowers blooming in newly mulched beds that surround the hospital. It seemed everything else was beginning to thrive just as her world was crumbling around her.

"It's over," Ellie said.

"No it isn't."

"Can't be fixed."

"Ellie, stop talking in code and just spit it out." Suzanne put the car in drive and checked her side view mirror, waiting for an opportunity to merge into traffic while other cars passed.

"He slept with Jackie."

Suzanne's eyes darted back to Ellie, and she returned the gearshift to park. "I don't believe it." Her eyes widened then narrowed. "Besides, how do you know?"

Ellie looked at her lap and blinked back tears. "Bonnie Singleton."

Suzanne wrinkled her forehead and laughed. "I think that car accident did some damage to your brain. When did you ever start believing a word Bonnie had to say?"

Ellie sighed. "Adam has a tattoo—same one as me—a broken half of a heart. We got them one night, right after we were engaged. We were drunk, and young, and ..."

"And?" Suzanne stared at Ellie as if she'd lost her mind. "What does this have to do with anything?"

"It's *below* his waistline." Ellie said, raising her eyebrows. "Jackie told Bonnie about the tattoo. Of course, Bonnie was only too eager to bring the news back to me." Ellie turned back to her window, a lump in her throat. "There's only one reason Jackie would've known."

Suzanne sat silent for a moment, staring out the windshield, straight ahead, at nothing in particular. Finally, she started to drive.

"You're quiet," Ellie said.

"When you wanted Adam back—after Ryan—did you think your relationship could be fixed then?" Suzanne asked.

"That was different, we were—"

Suzanne held up a hand to stop Ellie, keeping her eyes on the road. "It's not different. I love you, Ellie. You're my best friend. But you're wrong. Adam having a thing or whatever this is with Jackie may not be ideal, but what happened at the hospital ball, well . . . " Suzanne shook her head, said no more.

"Are you saying this is *my* fault?"

"Ellie," Susanne said, glancing at her now, "you're pregnant."

The lump in Ellie's throat grew larger still, making it difficult to swallow. Tears blurred her vision, and the anger filling her head made her dizzy. She wondered if her pregnancy hormones were really completely out of control, or if things were genuinely as bad as they felt.

CHAPTER 24

ADAM

Adam rushed into his office, and his secretary, Nancy, did a double-take as he passed by her desk. He managed a smile bred purely from embarrassment but didn't slow down.

Once inside, he closed the door and leaned against the sturdy maple wood, allowing his head to rest against the cold, hard surface. He was forty-five minutes late, his tie—the third one this morning—wasn't yet tied around his neck, and somehow Lizzie managed to spill—or rather dump—lemonade on his second pair of suit pants when he dropped her off at preschool, leaving the entire front of his right thigh soaking wet.

He was exhausted, he was a mess, and he was madder than hell.

He walked to his desk. After shrugging off his suit coat, he tossed his keys and tie onto a credenza behind him. He sat and sorted through papers, balling some of them up and tossing them into the trash as if he were in the midst of an aggressive game of dodge ball. He wanted to hit something.

He stood and considered a walk down the hall for a cup of coffee like he would normally do, but the last thing he needed coursing through his veins was caffeine, the adrenaline already more than he could handle.

He fell back into his chair and leaned forward, elbows resting on his knees, head cradled in his hands, feeling utterly defeated.

CHAPTER 25

ELLIE

E llie stared at the walls of her bedroom—her new prison. For the first time in her life, she had nothing to do but rest. *Mandatory* rest. She tried to move her leg, and pain coursed through her body.

A shiny metal walker stood beside the bed in case she needed to use the bathroom. "Just something to lean on in case you need the extra support," Dr. Van Linden had said. She rolled her eyes. Pregnant at forty-one and suddenly she had joined the ranks of the elderly. They may as well have shoved her into a nursing home.

She glanced at her cell phone on the bedside table. Suzanne would be back in less than two hours with Lizzie. She had rearranged her schedule to pick up Lizzie from preschool every day at noon and spend afternoons at Ellie's house until Adam got home to take over. Until things got back to normal.

Whatever *normal* was.

Ellie hated that Suzanne had to take time away from her career for them. It reminded her of sacrificing her own career, but Suzanne dismissed the thought of any inconvenience. "Remember last year?" Suzanne asked. "When I had the stomach flu and you bailed me out by completing a week's worth of tax returns up against a deadline?"

Of course Ellie remembered. That was what friends did. Even still, why didn't Adam step up for once? As far as Ellie was concerned, he was to blame. On both counts.

And then there was Jackie.

She closed her eyes.

"All you need to do is call if you need anything," Adam said earlier that morning as he slid the cell phone across the bedside table, placing it an inch closer to her.

He also brought hot coffee, made just the way she liked—sweet with a little bit of milk. It smelled heavenly, but she'd never admit it.

Besides . . . coffee? Was he teasing her on purpose? Or was he just too self-involved to remember?

"I'm pretty sure you were standing there when the doctor said no caffeine," she snipped, refusing to take the cup he'd extended to her.

"It's decaf. I called the nurse, and she said decaf was fine."

His thoughtfulness took her off-guard. She didn't know what to say, but she remained rigid, still refusing to accept.

"You love coffee. I thought it might make you feel better," he added.

The hope in his eyes began to chip away at her anger, but only for a moment before she used it against him.

"Actually, it's making me nauseous." She stared at him, her eyes cold as stone. "Can you just take it away?"

Adam left the room, and she had to force her own silence. She wanted to call him back. She wanted to taste the warm liquid she loved so much. She wanted the comfort of it filling her stomach, even if it was only temporary.

But she wanted to lash out at Adam more.

She wanted to punish him for Jackie, and she wanted to punish herself for Ryan.

And so, she led this march for the last three days.

Most of the time, when Adam entered the bedroom, she pretended to sleep. Other times, she mercilessly hung him out to dry. He was clueless. He had a lot of questions about the kids. And she knew it.

The first day, Adam laid out the kids' school clothes the night before as she had instructed, but she purposely sent him to a drawer in Lizzie's room full of socks that were too small. Lizzie had a sock fetish to begin with, and the mishap sent her on a thirty-minute rant the next morning.

Later that same night, Tommy came to visit her before Adam tucked him in, and Ellie gave him permission to play his video games in bed. "Under the covers though ... our secret," she said with a wink.

Tommy's eyes grew wide as saucers. "Thanks Mom!" he said, racing out of the room. The next morning, Adam had a heck of a time waking their seven-year-old up for school.

And then earlier that morning Adam asked what kind of juice to pack in Lizzie's thermos. Apple juice, she thought. It was always the same—it was the only thing Lizzie would drink. How could he not know that already?

"Lemonade," she said without rolling over. She could only imagine the fit Lizzie must have thrown when she realized her thermos was filled with the thing she hated most.

CHAPTER 26

ADAM

Adam checked his watch—5:06 p.m. He should have left the office by now, but he dreaded going home. Suzanne was waiting at the house with Ellie and the kids, and he knew it was unfair, but thirty minutes ago, he had sent Suzanne an apologetic text explaining he was swamped. She sent a reassuring reply, telling him not to worry, offering to make dinner. Truth be told, he was overwhelmed at the office, but it didn't even begin to compare to how flabbergasted he was on the home front.

And he had no idea what to do about it. He was trying, he really was. After the accident, he was convinced they would make it work. But the last three days had left him with nothing but a dark sense of hopelessness toward his marriage. Ellie was clearly no longer in love with him, regardless of his intentions.

He clicked on his email and composed a reply to Marc regarding the quarterly earnings report. He was totally engrossed in his thoughts and halfway through typing his response when the scent of vanilla musk hit his nose. Small hands gently landed on his shoulders, and she leaned into him from behind.

"Hey there stranger," Jackie whispered, her breath tickling his earlobe.

He hadn't even heard her come in. His breath caught in his throat, his body ridged. Still, excitement bubbled in his stomach.

"How'd you get in?" Adam asked, recalling the time. It was after hours. The building would have been locked up by now.

Jackie spun his chair around so they were facing each other. She was wearing black cotton tights and shiny gray ballet flats. Her curves were hard to miss, tucked into a white tank top layered under a flowy long sleeved, sheer blue shirt.

"I ran into your secretary. Nancy, I think? Nice lady," Jackie said.

Adam looked toward the door, wondering who was left in the office.

"Don't worry, she was leaving for the day. Everyone else is gone, so it's just us," she said, answering his unasked question.

Jackie walked around his desk, running a finger dressed in pink nail polish along the smooth wooden top as she went. Her blue eyes, accentuated by her blue top, were trained on him seductively the whole time. His midsection tightened, and he forced himself to breathe. She came full circle and pushed his laptop forward on the desk without taking her eyes from Adam. Then she took a seat in its place.

"You're a hard man to get ahold of," she said finally.

Adam cleared his throat, trying to find his voice. Somehow she had managed to work him into a ball of sexual tension again—in the space of less than five minutes—and he was fairly certain she knew it.

"I heard about the accident. I hope Ellie's okay."

"I suppose she will be," Adam said, a pang of resentment stabbing him in a hundred places at once. If nothing else, Ellie was a survivor.

Rumors of their split had spread through at least some of the town; this Adam knew. In one of her recent messages, Jackie was sure to let him know she'd been informed.

"I had to move back in to help with the kids," he offered.

What?

The words were out before he could consider the insinuation they held. He wondered why he was leading Jackie on. He moved back in because he loved Ellie.

Right?

"I mean . . . " He wiped his sweaty palms against his suit pants. The fabric under his right hand was stiff from the lemonade Lizzie soaked him with that morning. His thoughts returned to the anger—no the hatred—Ellie had displayed toward him, and he wondered what it was he'd been fighting for.

"Adam?"

He looked up and met Jackie's big blue eyes. They were beautiful, passionate, staring at him with open acceptance and kindness . . .

"I thought we may have had something," she said, continuing.

. . . and lust . . .

"I was hoping maybe you felt it, too."

Adam rose from his chair. Without hesitating, he sunk his fingers into the back of her blonde hair and pulled her lips to his. He kissed her, hard, passionate. Her response was unrestrained, her tongue eagerly exploring his. His lips skimmed over the soft skin on her neck, his hands moving up her shirt, a finger brushing over her nipple, through the thin fabric of her tank top. She moaned and tugged greedily at his belt buckle, then yanked on his zipper and slid a hand into his pants. He gasped, sweeping papers onto the floor, pushing her further onto the desk, leaning into her. Frantically, she unbuttoned his dress shirt halfway down. He pulled the blue top over her head.

She felt so good, so open and willing. Unlike Ellie, who loathed him and reminded him of his inadequacy every chance she got. With Jackie he was interesting and sexy. He was tired of feeling less-than and beat-down. Loving someone who couldn't love him back was exhausting.

The thoughts clouded his head, but he pushed them away. He wanted only to focus on the feeling of Jackie's hands roaming his chest, her lips moving against his. A faint chime in the background fought for his attention, but it was vague, and he was too preoccupied to care. He reached down and removed Jackie's flats, then slid his feet free from his dress shoes, allowing his pants to fall to the floor. A loud thump in the hallway made them both jump. Somewhere in the building a door slammed, and Adam froze, realizing the chime was the elevator. Jackie bolted upright on the desk. Adam's heart raced. Physically, he was about to explode. More noise echoed from the other side of his office door. He fought to think clearly and checked the time—5:34 p.m.

"Shit," he said. "The cleaning people." They came three evenings a week. It was their night.

Jackie's eyes darted to the ceiling. She took a deep breath and exhaled slowly, looking as disappointed as he felt.

Silently, they both collected their clothing and dressed in a hurry. Just as they finished, Gasper walked into Adam's office and stopped abruptly.

"I sorry," Gasper said in his usual broken English. He looked from Adam to Jackie and back to Adam again, a sheepish expression blanketing his round face. "I come back later."

Gasper had worked for the cleaning company Exactitude used for the last three years. Because Adam was often in the office late they ran into each other regularly, but never before had there been a woman there when he'd arrived.

"It's okay, Gasper. Come in," Adam said, silently scolding himself. He should've expected this visit for God's sake.

Gasper offered an awkward nod and wheeled his cleaning cart into the room. He grabbed a duster and went to work on a set of bookshelves on the other side of Adam's large office. Mercifully, he kept his back to them.

Adam gave Jackie an apologetic look and silently mouthed, *I'm sorry.* She lifted a pen from his desk and scribbled something on a small white piece of paper. She folded it twice before pressing it into the palm of his hand. Then she left without a word.

He unfolded the note and swallowed hard, trying to suppress the lust that threatened to consume him.

My place. Tomorrow. 2pm.

CHAPTER 27

ELLIE

It was nearly six, and Adam wasn't home yet. Suzanne brought Ellie a bowl of beef stew ten minutes ago, but she had barely touched it. She'd been plagued with guilt all day, and it seemed to have taken her appetite hostage as well. Sabotaging Adam seemed like a good idea, a way to show him how much she really did as the main caretaker, but seeing him suffer wasn't giving her the pleasure she had expected.

The door to her bedroom swung open and Lizzie appeared, her curly blonde pigtails bouncing up and down with each enthusiastic hop toward her bedside.

"I wanna come up," she said.

Ellie patted the bed. "Just be careful not to bump Mommy," she said.

Lizzie's pudgy hands grasped fistfuls of the quilt as she climbed onto the mattress. She rested her small head on the pillow next to Ellie.

"When's Daddy gonna be home?" Lizzie asked.

"Soon," Ellie said, stroking her daughter's silky blonde hair. "Why?"

Lizzie shrugged. "Daddy gave me lemonade today," she said, scrunching her face.

A fresh wave of guilt washed over Ellie. "Oh?"

"I hate lemonade."

"I know."

"Do you think Daddy's still mad at me?"

"For what?"

"I spilled lemonade on his pants," Lizzie said.

Oh boy. The waves of guilt were churning now, forming white-caps, as she realized she'd brought the kids down right along with Adam.

"I love Daddy, though," Lizzie said, her eyelashes fluttering as Ellie continued to stroke her hair. Then her eyelids sprung open, and she looked up at Ellie. "Do you love Daddy, Mommy?"

Ellie's throat tightened. "Of course I do," she said softly.

Of course I do.

CHAPTER 28

ADAM

Adam stood at the kitchen counter, spreading grape jelly on a piece of toast for Lizzie. Behind him, Buster barked frantically at a squirrel on the other side of the window. He slid the plate in front of Lizzie and opened the back door for the dog. He was pouring orange juice for Tommy when his cell phone chimed with a text message from Ellie.

If you made decaf, I'd love some.

A fresh surge of anger flashed before his eyes. It was the first morning he hadn't stopped to check on her right after his shower. He was done trying to please her.

He set the cup of orange juice in front of Tommy and walked upstairs toward the master bedroom. He paused outside the door, about to knock as he normally would, but instead he pushed the door open without announcing himself. This was, after all, *his* house and his bedroom just as much as it was hers.

The scent of Ellie's familiar jasmine lotion filled the room. She managed to pull herself into a sitting position on the bed where Adam found her tugging a brush through her brown hair. She stopped, and her lips moved into a sheepish half-smile.

"Hey," she said softly.

"I didn't make coffee today," Adam said abruptly.

And I don't plan on making some just because you've decided you want it.

He stood rigid in the doorway.

"Oh." Ellie looked like she'd just had the wind knocked out of her.

"I'm off in a few minutes then." He placed his hand on the doorknob and turned to leave without asking if there was anything she needed.

"Adam?" Ellie called.

He stopped and took a deep breath, hoping the fresh oxygen would subside some of the anger filling his lungs.

"I'm really sorry."

He turned to face her. "For what?"

Her eyes cast downward toward the cream and tan paisley bedspread. "For being such a bitch."

His forehead crinkled, and his eyes searched her face for some kind of explanation. Ellie didn't admit guilt easily, and her apology blindsided him.

"Maybe we could . . . you know . . . try?" It was obvious the words didn't come easy for her by the way the broken sentence fell from her lips.

He stood quiet for a beat. There was only one thing he could imagine she was referring to—them as a couple, married, and in love—but at the same time he couldn't imagine she would be referring to that at all, with the way she'd been acting.

"Try what?" he asked, finally, refusing to get caught up in assumptions. Besides, he wanted to hear her spell it out.

"Us?" Her brown eyes were undeniably hopeful.

Why? The question nagged him. Why the sudden change of heart?

He nodded, as if he was following, even though he was not. "For the kids?" he suggested agreeably.

Ellie sighed and smiled. "Yeah, for the kids," she said, pushing a piece of hair behind her ear.

Adam walked toward her and picked up her cell phone. He glanced at the screen. "Full charge," he said, setting it on the table beside her with a thump. He leaned down, stopping a few inches from her face. "How about you just work on getting better? I suppose then we'll all be able to move on, and everyone'll be happy."

Ellie's face was stricken. He stood and turned to leave again.

"Not because of the kids," she blurted out when he was halfway across the room. Because I . . . I—"

"You what, Ellie?" he shouted, turning on the ball of his foot, staring her down with steely eyes.

The muscles in her throat were visibly tense, her eyes welling up with tears, her expression full of conflicted emotion.

"Love you," she finally managed to say, the words sounding strangled.

He didn't think she'd say the words. He doubted she was even thinking them, not really. Mostly, though, he still wondered *why* she said them.

Worst of all, he wished she meant it. But how could she, when she acted like she hated him?

"Yah well, you have a funny way of showing it." He exited the room and pulled the door closed with a thud.

He paused in the hallway and jammed his fists into his pockets. His right hand collided with the folded piece of paper he'd slipped into his suit earlier this morning. He fingered it and fished it out. He had already reread Jackie's note half a dozen times this morning, but he examined it again anyway.

My place. Tomorrow. 2pm.

He pursed his lips, recalled the feeling of her mouth on his. Excitement bubbled in his stomach again. Glancing at the bedroom door once more, he refolded the note and returned it to his pocket.

On his way down the steps, he dialed Nancy and left her a message, instructing her to clear his schedule today after two.

It was time to get the kids to school.

CHAPTER 29

ELLIE

When Ellie heard Suzanne and Lizzie enter the house a little after noon, she was staring at nothing in particular, running the smooth bed sheet between her fingers. She'd been stuck in bed for hours, tortured by a self-imposed state of mental and emotional chaos.

"Hey sweetie," Suzanne said from the doorway, a cup of hot decaffeinated tea in her hand.

Ellie slid her legs closer to the edge of the bed and used her arms to hoist her body weight up.

"Whoa!" Suzanne said, now at her side. "Slow down," she scolded.

This was what it was like most every time she headed for the bathroom, but she refused to wear a catheter. Ellie's injuries were already sending angry surges through her body. The pain was less intense with every passing day, but the difference was minuscule; and coupled with her ongoing inability to function normally, it offered little consolation. She fell back gently against the pillows behind her.

"I'm so tired of being stuck here." She looked at Suzanne, her face twisted into a pout. "And I need your help with something."

Ellie decided not delve into the details of her transgressions. Not now. Instead, she explained to Suzanne that Adam had been struggling with the kids, and asked for another favor. Suzanne was more than happy to help, agreeing to pack the kids' lunches, fill their thermoses, and lay out their school clothes the night before. For the first time, Ellie desperately wished she could do it herself. She was even more surprised to find her motives weren't predominately born from guilt, but from genuine desire to help make Adam's life easier.

Adam arrived home at least an hour early, and Ellie hoped it was a sign that he understood her this morning. She never was good at apologies. Her pride had a habit of sabotage, despite her best intentions.

The bedroom door stood ajar, allowing her to observe sound bites of commotion coming from the kitchen. Dishes clattered in the sink, and the kids' voices rose with excitement as they greeted Adam. She smiled at the depth of their love for him. Together, they made a good family—it was a truth she could feel in the deepest part of her soul. She just needed to figure out how to get past the mess they'd made of things.

She promised herself she would work on changing the pride and sabotage bit. Later, she'd make the same promise to Adam.

Maybe.

If her brain could get her mouth to speak the words aloud.

CHAPTER 30

ADAM

A dam was flat on his back in bed, staring at the ceiling, mentally reviewing a checklist of what needed to be done in the morning. It was a habit he'd gotten accustomed to since he came home and took charge of the house and the kids—or *tried* to take charge as best he could.

Earlier tonight, when Suzanne explained that lunches were packed, thermoses were filled, and clothes were laid out, he was first inclined to hug her.

His face lit up. "You're a lifesaver." As soon as the words were out, he reconsidered. "Yah, but you're already doing so much, Suzanne. I don't want to—"

She rested a hand on his arm. "It's fine. Ellie asked me to."

And with just four words, his incompetence was verified in spades. His face fell, and it was clear Suzanne took notice. She shook her head and stood squarely in front of him, her hands grasping both of his shoulders as if to ensure she had his full attention.

"She loves you, Adam. She's my best friend, and I can honestly say that even if she's a total whack right now, she loves you. It's tearing her up that you're on your own, and I'm happy to help."

Her words stung. He said nothing and stood perfectly still while he watched her say goodbye to the kids. She slung a shiny red leather purse over her arm and kissed him on the cheek before she left him there, still frozen in the middle of the kitchen, the scent of vanilla musk clinging to his white dress shirt.

CHAPTER 31

ELLIE

E llie's eyes popped open to a clinking sound in the kitchen. She'd been home now for more than a week, but each morning she still woke with the same initial thought—she needs to rush out of bed and take care of kids, a house, and a dog. And then she would realize she couldn't.

Mornings were when she was sorest and stiffest—always a harsh reminder that she was in bed for a reason. She moved a bare leg over the sheets beneath her, relishing the softness of the fabric against her black-and-blue skin. The surface bruising looked worse a week out, but the residual pain was more of an ache that settled in her muscles, bones, and joints. The doctors said those injuries would take longer to heal.

The faint smell of coffee wafted into her bedroom, and if she wasn't mistaken . . . she sniffed the air . . . burnt bacon? Panic gripped her thoughts for a moment as a picture flashed through her mind—the house was on fire, about to turn to ash, while she lingered in bed. She wondered again if she should attempt to get up.

The hallway outside her closed bedroom door filled with noise, and a giggling Lizzie sped through the entrance then leapt onto the bed.

"Lizzie, be careful not to jump near Mommy—gentle!" Adam yelled.

Close behind, seven-year-old Tommy struggled to carry a tray of food into the room. On it, a glass was filled with orange juice. It sloshed back and forth, threatening to spill over the edge with every small step he took. Adam did his best to guide Tommy toward her while still allowing him to complete the task independently.

"Happy Mother's Day, Mommy!" Lizzie said, sporting a smile that melted Ellie's heart.

"We made this for you," Tommy said, finally approaching the bedside. "Breakfast in bed!" His eyes sparkled, his boyish face beaming with pride.

Adam took the tray from Tommy and waited while Ellie struggled to sit up against some pillows. Gently, he lowered it onto her lap.

"This is a surprise," Ellie said, smiling at the kids. "And a first," she mumbled, looking up at Adam with an accusatory glare. His eyes fell to the floor.

She reminded herself to play nice. Despite her efforts, she was still fighting a swinging pendulum of feelings—love, then anger, then love—tick then tock, like a bomb waiting to detonate.

"So whose idea was this? Yours?" she asked, playfully poking Lizzie in the belly, making her squeal.

"Or yours?" She poked Tommy on the forehead.

"It was Dad's idea." Tommy flashed a brilliant smile and glanced back and forth between Adam and Ellie.

Adam looked up sheepishly and shrugged his shoulders.

"Oh," Ellie said. In the last couple of days, she had tried to be as helpful and kind as she could, considering she was still stuck in bed. She hoped Adam had noticed. She thought he had because he'd taken to a newfound thoughtfulness. The thing was, it still caught her by surprise every time. And she was still trying to quiet the ticking inside.

She looked at the food displayed before her: decaf coffee made just the way she liked, eggs that looked too done, a slice of toast that, no doubt, one of the kids spread gobs of jelly on, and . . .

"We ate the rest of the bacon," Lizzie said, pointing to a half strip of bacon, the remaining item on Ellie's plate. "It was really good!"

"Quiet Gizzard!" Tommy yelled, giving Lizzie a push that knocked her off the bed. She tumbled to the floor and started to cry.

Adam collected Lizzie and carried her out of the room, promising an ice pack.

"That wasn't very nice." Ellie looked at Tommy, her brow furrowed.

His eyes cast downward, and guilt filled his face.

At least she still had that. She'd long ago learned that sometimes making her kids feel guilty was the best way to give them an understanding of right and wrong.

Tommy slid across the bed, carefully inching his body closer before resting his head on the pillow next to Ellie.

"Thanks for the breakfast, honey," Ellie said, tousling Tommy's hair.

"Welcome." Tommy opened his mouth then closed it again. He opened it a second time, but still didn't speak.

"What's wrong?" she asked.

Tommy's face wrinkled up in a ball. "Are you and Dad getting divorced?"

Ellie's chest tightened, and she had to remind herself to breathe. With everything that had happened over the last few months, neither child had broached this topic. Honestly, it amazed her that it took this long, but it didn't make it any easier.

"Oh honey—"

"Cause I really don't want you to get a divorce."

Her throat constricted. Tommy suddenly looked years younger than he did moments ago. Her own childhood memories and a fresh sense of missing her mom the way she did during those initial days after she left washed over her like a tidal wave. She set the orange juice and coffee on the nightstand, struggled to sit straighter, and moved the tray to an empty space on the bed. "C'mere, sweetie." She held her arms out for him.

"But your bruises," he said.

She hated the way he looked at her—as if she wasn't *herself* anymore.

"Just be gentle."

Tommy slowly moved closer and carefully settled against her body. She held him as tight as her pain would allow and kissed the top of his head, rubbing his small back.

"It's going to be okay. Mommy and Daddy have messed some things up, but we're trying to figure it out."

I think.

She was busy wondering if she even knew what she's talking about, when Tommy started wriggling around.

"You'd better eat your breakfast, Mom," he said, announcing he was going to play a video game.

She struggled to clear the clutter from her mind at his quick change of topic. The kids often seemed to move from one thing to the next with a speed that left her perplexed and scrambling to collect her thoughts. She was reluctant to release him, but holding him that long had been painful enough—her body began screaming at his weight against hers as soon as he came into her arms.

She dropped one more kiss on top of his head before he jumped up and off of the bed.

"Make sure you apologize to your sister," she called out as he ran out the door.

For the second time she surveyed the tray that now sat beside her on the bed. Two handmade Mother's Day cards were partially tucked under the plate. She pulled them out to study them. She ran her fingers over a paper doily cut into a heart and pasted to red construction paper. It reminded her of her tattoo. It reminded her of the baby. A reminder that her heart felt like it was breaking nearly every day for the last few months, holes pierced through it like the doily under her hand.

She was tired.

And she had to pee.

She rolled onto her side and swung her legs over the edge of the bed, bracing against the pain.

Oh, the joys of being pregnant. Even getting out of bed was a task. Even on a normal day without scrapes and bruises. Even without a walker.

Her walker. She glanced to her right and realized she'd left it behind on her last trip to the bathroom. It was getting easier to move around—thank God—but in return she hadn't been as cautious.

Finally, she decided she could make it without the additional support of a metal contraption, but when she tried to stand, a shooting pain coursed through her stomach and air caught in her lungs. She was bent over, holding her breath at the side of the bed, when Adam entered the room. He immediately rushed to her side and grabbed her arm, encouraging her to lean on him for support.

His grasp was reassuring, yet she still felt betrayed. Her feelings began to shift again without warning. It was all so confusing. She wanted to push him away, and she wanted to pull him close at the same time. Regardless, she knew she needed him, and that thought angered her even more. She didn't want to need anyone. She learned, at the age of just eight years old, that it was safer to be independent.

Adam helped her to the bathroom and, although she refused to let him accompany her to the toilet, he was waiting outside the door when she returned.

"You okay?" he asked, following her even though she now had her walker.

She stopped and took a moment to study his face. The familiarity of every line and angle made it even harder to live with the distance between them. She wanted to reach out and hold onto him, and at the same time, she wanted to slap him.

She hated herself. She hated Adam. Round and round she went, unable to jump off of the carousel.

"Ellie?" Adam looked at her expectantly. She realized she was still staring, both of them standing, frozen in the middle of the bedroom.

"I'm fine." She shook her head as if to clear the cobwebs from her brain and started toward the bed again.

Once she reached the edge of the mattress she shooed Adam away. He took a step back, hesitated, and his expression turned pensive.

"Ellie . . . about Jackie—"

"Don't!" Ellie's head whipped up, and blood rushed to her cheeks. Pain lashed through her neck at the movement. "Don't even speak her name to me." Her hand trembled, and she dropped the bed sheet.

"But—"

"Get out," she said, holding her stomach and cringing as the baby gave her a hard kick in the ribs.

"Are you kidding me?" Adam looked like someone had slapped him in the face, and Ellie figured he was mad. Her whole body tightened in response, anger welling up inside. She was ready to fight, but he didn't continue. Instead, the color drained from Adam's face, and his shoulders sank. He left and closed the door quietly behind him.

Ellie sat on the edge of the bed and dropped her head into her hands before she let out a long sigh that quickly turned into sobs.

Why do you keep doing that?

PART VI

To Love and To Cherish

CHAPTER 32

ADAM

"Daddy, I neeeed a napkin!" Lizzie's high-pitched squeal sent pain shooting through Adam's already aching head.

He spun from the sink where he was filling Buster's metal water bowl in a jagged movement that sent water into the air before it sloshed onto his tie.

"Great," he said, dropping the bowl into the sink with a clatter.

He wet a paper towel and rushed to Lizzie's side but, by the time he reached her, blobs of grape jelly had run down her chin and toppled off, her pink cotton shirt now dotted with splotches of purple. Adam looked at his watch and sighed.

"Okay, we're late. And now we both need to change."

He hadn't even had coffee yet, and he desperately needed a cup.

Carefully, he removed Lizzie's sticky shirt. Once her face was wiped clean, he hoisted her tiny frame from the kitchen stool and started down the hall, his daughter dangling over his shoulder. Lizzie was busy squealing and playing drums on his back when he spotted Tommy on the couch in the living room and stopped.

"What are you doing?" he asked, exasperated.

Tommy's fingers continued to move over the controls of his hand-held video game at warp speed. "Hey Dad," Tommy said without looking up.

"Hey *Dad?*" Adam asked. "*Hey Dad?*" His tone reflected his impatience and frustration, but Tommy didn't seem to notice.

Adam walked to the back of the couch where Tommy was lounging in his pajamas and realized he hadn't seen his son in the kitchen for breakfast. He took the game from Tommy's hand and flicked it off.

Tommy bolted upright on the couch, crossed his arms, and scowled at Adam. "You just made me *die*, Dad! Now, I probably lost the game!"

He inhaled, slow and deep, trying to remain calm, and lowered Lizzie to her feet. With a stern expression, he shook his index finger at both kids, trying to convey his seriousness. "Okay, I've had it with you two. Every day, we're late. You know what you're supposed to do, and I expect you to do it. Tommy, get to your room and get dressed. You'll have to eat something in the car. Lizzie, get upstairs. We need to change your shirt."

Large tears sprung to Lizzie's eyes. She sobbed aloud and ran to her room. Tommy stomped to the staircase, his feet heavy enough to crack the wooden floorboards, and paused. "When's Mom gonna be better?" he asked, before continuing. "This stinks," he yelled as he climbed the steps. A moment later, his bedroom door slammed shut.

Adam tossed the game onto the couch and raked his fingers through his hair. Even with Suzanne's' help and Ellie's newfound cooperation, he was in way over his head. Shoulders slumped forward, he carried his heavy body upstairs to change his tie—where he lived—in the spare room of his own house.

―⟨+ +⟩―

Two hours later, Adam sat at his desk, staring at his inbox—forty-three new emails were waiting for him. In addition, he had already listened to thirteen voicemail messages.

Three were from Jackie. Pushing the thought from his mind, he turned his attention back to that morning.

Trying to keep up with the kids and work was wearing him out. *Who are you kidding?*

Okay, keeping up with the kids would wear him out even if he weren't working.

And the ever-shifting emotions between him and Ellie weren't helping.

His mind jumped back to Mother's Day, a couple of weeks ago. Until Jackie's name came up he thought he and Ellie were doing okay. And then she went berserk.

He wanted to yell back. What right did she have to admonish and then dismiss him from her bedroom? From *their* bedroom? After all, she was the one pregnant with someone else's child.

But then the guilt of Jackie crept in again. He looked at the red scratches on Ellie's pale face, the dark bruises on her skin from the car accident, and the fight just . . . vanished. He didn't know if he had anything left inside, and he often found himself wondering if it was because of his problems with Ellie or his exhaustion from trying to take care of everything from the house to work to the kids.

He lifted the phone and dialed the number for home. Ellie answered on the third ring.

"I think we should get a nanny," he said.

"Adam?"

Adam released a frustrated sigh. "Were you expecting someone else?" The words escaped his mouth before he could think them through, and he immediately grimaced.

Ellie remained silent.

"Sorry, I—"

"It's fine," she said. "I just never imagined my husband calling me in the middle of the day to announce we need a nanny. Besides, you know how I feel about someone else raising the kids. As hard as it is, *I* need to do that."

Husband.

The word lingered in Adam's mind. He was still her husband, and she was acknowledging him as such. At least that was some kind of consolation.

Wasn't it?

"Okay, a housekeeper then. Someone—anyone—to help you." He sat back in his chair. "El, I'm sorry."

"For what?"

"That it took me this long to get it. I mean, the kids—they're a mess and a handful. And the house—it's just—it's a lot. I never thought you sat around all day and did nothing. I really didn't. But I suppose . . . " He paused, trying to choose his words carefully so as not to upset her again.

He shook his head, raked his fingers through his hair, and studied his hand. How many times had he unconsciously pushed those fingers through his hair? Especially lately? Absentmindedly, he wondered if he might end up bald as a result.

"So let me get this straight—you want to get a nanny, or a house-keeper, or whatever—because you can't handle being Mr. Mom for a couple of weeks?"

Although her tone was sarcastic, he thought she might be quietly laughing on the other end of the phone, but he couldn't be sure, and even if she was, he knew it would serve him right.

"No. I want to get a nanny because I think you deserve some help. This isn't about me, El, okay? Even after you're better, I think you should, you know, be able to relax a little. Or at least not be so stressed out and run ragged."

Silence.

"El?"

Ellie cleared her throat, and Adam gave her a minute, but she still didn't say anything. He wondered again if he chose the wrong words.

"Ellie?" He straightened in his chair, and his lower back caught. He ran a hand up and down the muscle for relief. The spare room bed was killing him—mentally, emotionally, *and* physically.

"I'm here," she said. He had listened to the sound of his wife's voice for many years and, by her throaty reply, he knew she was crying.

"Oh, El, I'm so sorry. I'm sorry for everything."

When they hung up a few minutes later, Adam took a deep breath.

She said thank you.

She didn't yell, and she wasn't cross. She was . . .

He scrunched his forehead, analyzing Ellie's response. She'd been emotional for months, and this was no exception, but she genuinely seemed touched by the suggestion. Or maybe it was the admission that she had a hard job. No matter, he felt like an idiot, the little-too-late kind.

He scowled.

She'd been warmer lately, not so quick to snap, but he was careful not to give her a reason. Even though she was moving around better on her own now, he still waited on her as much as he could. At the same time, he was mindful to give her plenty of space. He took care of the kids and tried to keep them quiet (though it was an impossible task). He ran the house (even if it was kind of a mess), and got the kids out to school (granted, they were always late), and fed the dog (although he did pour dog food into Tommy's cereal bowl one morning when he was particularly tired. Lucky for him, Tommy and Buster were paying attention).

He closed his eyes. In his mind, he could see Ellie as if she were standing in front of him. There was no disguising or hiding the pregnancy now. Her stomach had expanded, a size larger than what he remembered with either of their other two children at thirty-weeks. (She thought he didn't keep track, but of course he did.)

The thing was, he didn't care anymore. He didn't feel like a bystander. He felt like a husband. He felt like a father. And although the thought of losing her in spite of it all scared him to death, he knew he had to lay his emotions on the table. They got along okay, but they tiptoed around each other, and they still hadn't discussed Jackie or Ryan. That halfway scenario wasn't enough for him. Not anymore. They both needed to be willingly vulnerable or it would never work.

But there was one thing he needed to do first.

His cell phone vibrated against the desk in front of him. He picked it up and glanced at the screen.

Jackie.

Again.

He pressed IGNORE and tossed it back onto the desk.

Make that two more things.

CHAPTER 33

ELLIE

E llie checked her watch—10:41 a.m. "I gotta go, Suz. I'm already going to ruin Ryan's day. I should at least try to be on time."

"How are you holding up?" Suzanne asked from the other end of the phone.

"The best I can." Ellie rubbed a hand over her bulging stomach and the baby kicked as if it could sense her nervousness. "At least I'm not on bed rest anymore."

"You should've done this a long time ago."

"Better late than never. Isn't that what they say?" Ellie scrunched her forehead and frowned. Hearing the words out loud didn't make her believe them.

"How's everything going at home? Adam still practicing the 'in sickness and in health' part of his vows?"

"He's really trying," Ellie leaned against the wall of her kitchen and looked at the ceiling dreamily. "He told me he thinks we should hire a nanny, can you believe that?"

It had been weeks, and Ellie kept waiting to wake up from the dream she was convinced she must have been having. But Adam was still at home. He'd been a trouper with the kids, although he struggled every day. He was kind and sensitive, and most of all he was present.

"Hmm, the kids must really be getting to him." Suzanne laughed.

"I think it may be more than that. It's almost . . . "

An image of Adam wearing a pressed white button-down jelly-stained shirt from this morning popped into Ellie's mind, and she smiled. He didn't even seem to know it was there until she pointed it out.

"You still there?" Suzanne asked.

"Yeah," she said, bringing herself back to Suzanne. "Listen, I gotta run."

⊷⊶

Ellie chose a table in the back corner of the small coffee shop in town. Her body had healed a great deal in the weeks since the accident, but she had some deep bruising that could still be felt occasionally—like now, when she slid against the unforgiving frame of a hard, wooden seat. At least the light was dim, the funky-deco tabletop tall enough to hide her telltale stomach.

The morning rush was over, but the staff behind the counter still hustled to fill orders. Two new mothers sat at a corner table opposite her, behind baby strollers they absentmindedly rocked back and forth while they talked. She recognized the dark half moons under their eyes, their puffy faces, and barely brushed hair, and she sank into her seat at the thought of going through it all over again.

A few minutes later, Ryan walked through the door, and her breath caught in her throat. He was still all muscle beneath a tight black t-shirt, but he looked like a baby—probably half her age.

What was I thinking?

She watched him scan the room in search of her and wondered if this was a bad idea. Spotting her, he waved and smiled.

Too late.

As he made his way toward Ellie, three different girls flashed him broad smiles and sweeping glances. Without stopping, he nodded and smiled at each of them. When he reached the table, he bent down and kissed Ellie on the cheek. His gesture took her off-guard, and she wasn't the only one. The facial expression of girl number two, perched on a stool near a window in the middle of the room, quickly progressed from a smile to a frown to a glare. Ryan didn't seem to notice. As he moved away, Ellie inhaled a whiff of his cologne, a scent that had no familiarity.

Of course it doesn't!

But you did sleep with the guy.

When you were drunk.

Her nerves flared up again at the thought of how much worse her unfamiliarity with Ryan made their situation, and she squirmed in her seat.

He smiled and pulled out a chair. She flinched at the sound of its metal legs scraping against the concrete floor. Graceful, he was not. And now that he was closer, Ellie could see what looked like part of this morning's breakfast smeared on his wrinkled jeans.

At least Adam has a three-year-old to blame.

"I got you some water," she said motioning toward two bottles on the table between them. "I'm not much of a caffeine drinker lately."

"Cool." Ryan took one of the waters from the table and thanked her.

She twisted off the top of the other and took a few gulps, wishing it were a bottle of wine. Even if she could have caffeine, she wouldn't. Her hands were already trembling so badly that she found she had to sit on them to force them still.

"So, what's up?" Ryan asked, in the deep voice that she *did* remember from their one night together. He flashed her another million-dollar smile. "I was kinda surprised to get your phone call. It's been what?" His face became thoughtful, perplexed. He focused on the ceiling, deep in thought. She half expected him to start counting on his fingers.

"About six months," she said.

"Yeeeaaahhh," Ryan said, a slow smile sliding across his face. "That's right." He held the water bottle out, lifted one finger from his grasp on it to point at her. His eyes lit up at the recollection. "A few weeks before Christmas." He winked at her as if he and Ellie shared some sort of top-secret information. "Wow." He nodded and took a long swig of water. "I wondered what happened to you. I woke up and you were just, like, gone, dude. And like, dude, you were really messed up that night."

Ellie grimaced at the way Ryan used the words "*dude*" and "*like*." His body may have been dense with muscle, but the space in his head seemed to be filled with air where a brain should have been.

How could he possibly have made me laugh as hard as he did that night at the bar?

Then again, maybe it was the liquor.

"About that night . . . " she couldn't find the words to continue.

Ryan looked at her expectantly, a huge white smile still plastered on his face. His eyes lingered on her chest for a beat, and Ellie cringed. She tried to begin again, but she wasn't sure how.

She stood up, and his eyes followed her face. Slowly, his smile began to fade, confusion settling in its place. She pointed to her stomach and rested her hands on it.

"Whoooaaa, congratulations, dude. That's heavy. You got kids already?"

Ellie sunk back into her seat, exasperated.

"What I'm trying to say is—"

"Ryan!" A slim, twenty-something girl with a swinging blonde ponytail appeared at Ryan's side, unapologetically interrupting their conversation. She placed her hand on his shoulder, a starstruck expression settled on her face. Ryan looked up and smiled at her. He jumped from his chair and hugged her, lifting her off her feet in the process. Ellie looked on in silent confusion and disbelief.

"Hey, Rachel," he said, returning her to the ground. He was still smiling, their eyes locked. "The other night was—"

Ellie cleared her throat. Ryan and Rachel both stared at each other a moment longer before they turned their attention to her. As if suddenly remembering he was here with someone else, Ryan released his hold on Rachel and took a step back.

"This is . . . um . . . " He looked from Rachel to Ellie, briefly perplexed, and Ellie wondered if he'd forgotten her name. "This is my, ah, friend, Ellie."

Friend? Ellie felt like someone had dropped her into *The Twilight Zone.*

"Hi." Ellie forced a smile and wondered how Ryan could keep his.

Rachel studied Ellie, confusion spreading across her young face—undoubtedly from the wrinkles staring back at her. It was immediately clear that she'd concluded Ellie was age-inappropriate for her the-other-night-was-so-wonderful-stud-muffin-Ryan.

"Dude, this is such a coincidence," Ryan said, breaking the silence between them.

Please don't let the baby get his brains—or lack thereof!

Ellie wondered again if telling him about the baby was wise. Actually, it seemed like the worst possible idea.

"Isn't it, though?" Ellie asked.

Ryan gave her a blank look, clearly not keeping up.

"A coincidence?" Ellie said, trying to clarify.

Geez.

He smiled and nodded in return.

Ellie pretended to check her watch and placed another smile on her face. "I have to run and get some errands done. Why don't you go buy your . . . Rachel . . . a coffee, and we'll catch up later."

Rachel's glare softened, and she beamed at Ryan.

"Good idea," he said. "You're like, the coolest, Ellie. Catch ya later." He draped his arm around Rachel's shoulder, and they walked away, exchanging a disgustingly graphic open-mouthed kiss.

Ellie hung her head in her hands. She finished her water and started for the door, wondering what to do now that this conversation hadn't gone exactly the way she'd planned. Not that she had every word mapped out, but never had she envisioned this.

She grabbed her purse and made her way toward the exit, but just as she almost reached the daylight streaming in through the glass door, she bumped into someone.

Literally.

Her protruding stomach knocked a cup of coffee from a woman's hand, sent it flying to the floor.

"Oh God!" Ellie turned toward the woman, exasperated. "I'm so sorry." Their eyes met, and she recognized a familiarity that she couldn't immediately place.

"Ellie!" The woman called, her tone warm, welcoming.

Ellie blinked her eyes and it clicked—her glossy auburn hair, creamy skin, thin frame. Kathy's sister.

"Colleen, how nice to see you." Ellie surveyed the damage around their feet. Coffee was splattered all over their shoes, their pants, the floor …

And how unfortunate for you to see me.

"I'm really so sorry," Ellie said in horror. An employee had already appeared with a mop, and she and Colleen were trying to step out of the way. "I'm sort of a physical hazard these days," Ellie said, motioning to her large stomach.

"I see," Colleen said. "I had no idea, but congratulations."

Colleen's warm smile offered a marginal sense of relief after the bizarre start to her day, but her words rattled in Ellie's mind. *Congratulations* would normally be the appropriate response, but under the circumstances Ellie wasn't feeling celebratory.

"Thanks," Ellie said, trying to mask her unease. "I just . . . I feel terrible." She looked at the mess, both of them covered with coffee from the ankles down. She grabbed a bunch of napkins, and they began to blot themselves dry.

"Stop apologizing." Colleen offered a dismissive wave. "That's what dry cleaners are for. Besides, I've been thinking a lot about you lately, so this is perfect."

Perfect?

Ellie stared at Colleen, amazed. It was easy to recall how welcoming and friendly Colleen was at the dinner party, but how could anyone be *this* friendly *for real?*

"I've been playing phone tag with Kathy for days. I wanted to get your number from her because John and I have a proposition for you. Do you have time for a cup of coffee?" Colleen asked.

"Oh, no, you don't have to—"

"I want to. Actually, I just left Kathy another message." Colleen rolled her eyes. "It's been impossible for us to connect."

"I've already had my decaf for the day," Ellie, said, placing a hand on her stomach, another apologetic smile.

"Of course." Colleen was agreeable, but determined. "Well, I wanted to ask you . . . "

Something caught Ellie's attention at the back of the coffee shop, and Colleen's words began to fade away. From the corner of her eye, Ellie could see Ryan and Rachel. Their smiles were gone, replaced by angry, accusatory expressions. Rachel was pointing her finger at him, a redhead now standing between them. Ryan scoffed, dismissively waved his hand, and looked in Ellie's direction. He began to walk toward her.

Ellie's pulse raced. She felt the need to run.

How many girls are following this guy around, anyway?

"I have to go," she said, looking at Colleen, who was still talking, although Ellie hadn't heard a word she'd said.

"What?" Colleen looked quizzically at Ellie before scanning the coffee shop for nothing in particular. She clearly had no idea what was happening, and Ellie planned to keep it that way.

"Sorry." Ellie's eyes were apologetic. She felt bad, but . . .

She glanced toward the back of the coffee shop again. Ryan was still walking toward them, the redhead now on his heels.

"I'll call you," Ellie said to Colleen, not waiting for a response before she ran out the door and toward her car.

Toward something normal.

Normal.

Whatever that was.

CHAPTER 34

ADAM

A dam's cell phone rang, and he said a silent prayer, hoping it wasn't Jackie again. He glanced expectantly at the screen, as he had every time it had chimed in the last few days.

Sam. Finally.

He spun around in the leather seat behind his large wooden desk and answered.

"Did you get it?" Adam asked.

"Hello to you, too," Sam said. "Just so we're clear, I could get in serious trouble for this. Are you sure you know what you're doing, Adam?"

"I've never been surer."

"Bobby went to live with his aunt in Minneapolis."

"As in Minnesota?"

"Is there another?" Sam let out an exasperated sigh.

After swearing Sam to secrecy yet again, Adam had an address for Bobby scribbled on a piece of paper, tucked safely in his pocket. Searching the Internet, he went about mapping out his plan.

Half an hour later, Marc and Adam's secretary, Nancy, stared at him as if he'd gone mad when he announced he had to leave and may not be back for a couple of days.

"And don't say anything to Ellie," he said to Nancy. "If you hear from her, just ask her to call my cell." Bewildered, Nancy began to protest, but he shut her down with a firm hand, signaling her to stop.

Nancy shook her head, surrendering. Adam continued to his office, Marc on his heels.

"Do you want to tell me what's going on?" Marc asked, following him in, standing in front of Adam's desk.

"Later," Adam said, preoccupied. He pulled his suit coat from the back of his chair and slid it on.

"Are you in some kind of trouble?" Marc persisted, concern and confusion spread across his face as he watched Adam approach the door.

Adam turned back to face Marc and paused. He gave Marc's shoulder a reassuring squeeze. "You're a good friend, Marc. I just need you to trust me on this."

With that, he was on his way. Racing down Route 476 South toward the Philadelphia Airport, Adam's sweaty hands clung tightly to the steering wheel.

Minnesota. With his Aunt.

How can all of this be a coincidence? Surely, it isn't.

The overnight bag in the backseat had been packed for days, waiting. When he called Ellie, he found he was relieved when she didn't answer. His kept his message brief.

So what if a last-minute flight cost almost fourteen hundred dollars?

So what!

He glanced at the time—12:35 p.m.—and silently pled with the universe, hoping he wouldn't get stuck in the all-too-common Philly traffic. His flight was scheduled to depart in two hours.

He was cutting it close.

Cindy.

That was her name—Bobby's aunt.

Not Bev. It's not the same.

But what if it was?

He had to be sure.

He took a deep breath and tried to focus on the road.

He had done his homework. He'd talked to attorneys. He knew what to do and who to call. He had a basic understanding of the agencies and how they could help. He would make sure what happened to him wouldn't happen to Bobby. He ran a company, for God's sake. He could do this.

His chest tightened with guilt, knowing he should have gone to visit Bobby while he was in the hospital. He should've figured all of this out before the boy was gone.

He merged left, changing lanes, speeding past a green truck to his right. Determination filled every drop of blood running through his veins, his grip on the steering wheel tighter with the "what if" questions that ran through his mind.

What if Cindy's not interested in raising a kid?

What if Bobby's not happy?

Then he would fix it.

Surely, if he could love a baby that wasn't his own, if he and Ellie could make it through everything that had happened in the past year, then they could love a child who needed a home, a family. He was positive Ellie would be as willing as he was to adopt.

Right?

If they could make it.

He could only hope.

—+– –+—

At the Minneapolis airport, Adam sped through the terminal, impatient. Adrenaline continued to course through his system, even after three hours on the plane. It was now almost seven o'clock, and he was hungry.

Good, no line at the car rental. He followed the roped-off aisle to the counter and a young kid, probably not even twenty, greeted him with a lopsided smile. Adam guessed he was probably fresh out of high school. A work-issued polo shirt hung from his thin frame, acne dotted his forehead. The boy went through the motions of assigning him a car, but Adam barely heard a word he was saying, agreeing to whatever seemed like the quickest way to finish and get on with his plan.

Gas? Sure, that rate is fine.

Insurance? Yah sure, whatever …

Ten minutes later, rental papers in hand, he exited the airport and sucked the Minnesota air into his lungs, almost as if it were his first breath.

Home. It had been years since he'd been there, and he wondered why he stayed away so long. During his second year at Exactitude, he was assigned to attend a business conference in Minneapolis. In the weeks before his impending trip, he searched for, and finally found, a satellite image of his childhood home on the Internet. He studied it carefully, noting how much larger the trees were, examining cars parked in the driveway, trying to imagine the people who resided there.

But when he arrived in the city, he couldn't bring himself to visit the neighborhood of his youth. He tried every day, but less than halfway there, he'd always turn the car around and start back toward the hotel.

He did, however, continue to study the image after he returned home. He watched the seasons change as satellite images were updated, and he still studied the vehicles, wondered about the people. New roads became visible in areas nearby, the landscape changing with a growing community. Then, a few years later, the neighborhood was demolished. The county was making room for a chain of outlet shopping stores and nationally franchised restaurants.

And that was that.

After settling into a silver sedan, he made three quick stops before continuing: fast food, a bar, and a small corner store, then onto the interstate.

As he exited the freeway, his body became heavy. The rest of his drive was slow, as he tried to remember the way. Eventually, he turned off of the paved road, the tires crunching against a gravel path as he wound through the manicured grounds, toward the far side of the cemetery. He stopped the car and silenced the engine. As he opened the door, his chest tightened. He forced oxygen into his lungs.

It didn't take long to find their tombstones, one beside the other—Clark and Mary Thomas—just as he remembered. The sun was getting lower in the sky, but the air was still warm, the slight breeze that passed over him calming his nerves. He knelt and placed the flowers he purchased on the grass in front of him. The brown paper bag he'd been carrying was now wilted with moisture. He peeled it away from a cold bottle of beer and popped off the top.

"Here's to you mom and dad," he said, tipping the bottle toward the gray marble stones. He took a long swig, forcing the liquid past a lump in his throat. Settling onto the soft earth, he allowed his back to rest against the engraved tombstone that bore his mother's name, and thoughts of his parents flooded his mind.

A smile tugged at the corner of his mouth. He was a small boy, his mother chasing him. Round and round the partition separating the kitchen and the living room they went. She finally caught him, tickled him until he couldn't breathe. It was almost a nightly ritual for the two of them, and though he squirmed and squealed and protested, his favorite part was when she caught him, when he could feel her soft skin against his, hear her heartbeat racing, when he could smell the powder-scented lotion she always wore. He could almost smell it now, even after all of these years.

His father's attempt at humor was often found in conversation rather than roughhousing. In the morning, he'd enter the kitchen and, in a playful tone, ask Adam if he ate his '*brestick*' yet. In turn, Adam would respond with a quick eye roll, an exasperated, *Dad*, followed by an enunciated correction. *It's breakfast, Dad, break-fast!*

In turn, his dad would challenge him to spell the word and then offer his standard line, *You're getting even smarter than your old man, you know?* Adam often wondered if his dad was only trying to be funny, or if it was really a ploy meant to assure him that Adam was actually learning something at school. *High five,* his dad would say, after each lighthearted vocabulary lesson. His father's skin was more like soft rawhide, his scent spicy and salty at the same time.

Lazy Sunday mornings—those were his favorite. At the start of each new week they would lounge in his parents' bed. Adam would recline against his father, his head propped up on his chest so he could see the book his dad was reading aloud. His mother was always on the other side—behind him, leaning in to participate while she softly stroked her fingernails in circles against Adam's small back. Powder and spice and salt, the softness of his mother, his father's leathery skin . . . together it was the smell and feel of love, pure and true.

And just like that, it was gone. Forever.

Memories began to fragment into shards of sorrow, forcing silent tears down the sides of Adam's cheeks for what never was and what could have been.

As an adolescent, he was angry, and he sometimes wondered if he would've been better off had he been even younger when they died. That way, maybe he wouldn't have remembered them at all. But now . . .

Even though he didn't have them for long, he had two of the best parents a child could ever hope for. He realized, perhaps for the first time, that they gave him a gift by setting an example, by showing him what a parent should be. The thought sunk deep into his soul. They showed him how to love. It had been the basis for almost every decision he'd made in life, whether he was aware of it or not.

The sun inched lower, and brilliant rays fell beneath the clouds, illuminating them with color. The vibrant pinks remind him of how beautiful his mother was. She never wore much makeup, but she always carried a tube of pink lipstick, something Adam watched her apply countless times.

He continued to sit and consider them, deliberately remaining present in recollections of the parents he lost so long ago.

He *wanted* to remember.

He *needed* to remember.

And he found himself embracing his past in a way he was never brave enough to do before that day.

Finally, when darkness blanketed the sky, he drove to a motel where he fell into bed, thinking about Ellie. Solemnly, he considered their text exchange earlier, but he just couldn't deal with an explanation. He couldn't put what he was doing into words. Not yet.

CHAPTER 35
ELLIE

Morning sunlight cut through the window as Ellie stepped out of the shower and found the notification waiting on her cell phone.

Adam
Missed Call & Voicemail

She played the message and listened to Adam rattle on about a business meeting. He said he was flying out that afternoon and should probably be back tomorrow night.

She hung up. He didn't say where he was going.

She tried him back, but the call was immediately sent to voicemail.

She blotted at her wet hair with a soft white towel and scowled in the mirror. She slathered lotion on her legs, spread powder over her face, and dotted her cheeks with blush, but her mind wouldn't stop buzzing.

She knew Adam owed her no explanation. Sure, things were marginally better. But they'd made no promises. They had yet to have any kind of a *let's talk about the future* conversation.

Regardless, her nerves unraveled, and she wasn't sure why. She sent Adam a text.

Where are you?

She stared at the phone for a beat, but no response. She dressed, dried her hair, and spent some time clanking around the kitchen, but forty-five minutes later, there was still nothing.

It wasn't until after dinner that her phone finally chimed.

Don't worry. See you tomorrow.

She stared at the cryptic message, unsure of the proper response. Should she be angry or scared? Or maybe both?

She dialed his number and waited.

Voicemail. Again.

Her patience was running thin. Her fingers raced across the keys.

Adam?

His reply was immediate.

Can't talk.

What? What kind of crap was that?

What's this about?

She was tapping her fingernail on the phone when it chimed another reply.

Ellie … don't.

J. Renee Olson

And then again.

I'll see you tomorrow. Nite.

Had he just shut her down? She stared in disbelief, wondering if the union she thought they had started to repair was a figment of her imagination.

The cartoon Lizzie and Tommy were watching on television ended, and they appeared at her feet, pleading for ice pops. For the next two hours, she did her best to shove the anxiety from her mind and focus on tedious tasks around the house. Then she tucked the kids into bed.

She didn't look at her phone again until she slid in between the sheets of her bed. She was examining their exchange, the terse, clipped sentences from Adam, when it hit her: *Jackie.*

She was no longer on bed rest, which meant she no longer needed Adam's help in the same way she did before. Maybe he'd decided his new role as doting husband and father wasn't so great after all. And who could blame him? She was an emotional basket case with a bulging stomach, an aching back. The kids, much as she loves them, were a handful and more than a mess, to say the least.

Jackie, in contrast, was a slinky blonde goddess with a flat stomach and no circles under her eyes. And she was waiting for him somewhere away from the turmoil that Ellie had created.

Where was the choice in that?

CHAPTER 36

ADAM

A dam checked the address again on the tiny paper he'd fold-ed and unfolded countless times and slowly turned onto Oak Street. Inching along, he scanned the houses one at a time, searching for #73. It was just before nine on Saturday morning, and even though he didn't get much sleep, he was wide-awake, his body restless with nervous energy.

Finally, he spied the house number posted on a mossy-green ranch-style home. Near the street, irises and daisies surrounded the base of a mailbox; ivy climbed its post. The modest house was well kept and guarded by neatly squared hedges. Carefully spaced peonies filled a raised, large flowerbed.

Adam slowed the car and hesitated before parking along the curb across the street. The middle-class neighborhood was nice, full of one-story and Cape Cod-style homes. Sidewalks ran along a street flanked by oak trees. In the distance, at the end of the block, tall wil-low trees towered over a pond, blowing gracefully in the soft breeze.

He pulled on the door handle, about to get out, but the front door to house #73 swung open. A boy ran out, wearing a baseball uniform, *Johnny's Pizza* written across his red t-shirt. A dark mop of hair covered his head and bounced with each step.

Bobby?

Adam closed the car door and sat back against the seat. His heart hammered in his chest, and he wondered if he had the courage to go through with what he had planned.

He watched the boy toss a baseball in the air, catch it several times, then jump into a white mini-van parked in the driveway, a dealership sticker still stuck to its window. Close behind, a petite woman with brunette hair and bright blue eyes followed, a bat and helmet in her hand. She tossed the gear into the back of the van and slid into the driver's seat.

The van came to life, backed out of the driveway, and started down the street. Adam followed, and five minutes later they arrived at an elementary school baseball field. He parked four cars away and watched as the boy ran onto the field toward several other kids wearing the same red *Johnny's Pizza* t-shirt.

After a few minutes of self-debate, Adam exited the car and discreetly headed toward parents and fans of the opposing team. Lucky for him, the jeans and t-shirt he'd hastily tossed into his overnight bag made it easy to blend in. Dark sunglasses helped fight the bright morning glare, but most of all, they helped him avoid eye contact.

The air smelled of freshly cut grass, and a warm June breeze occasionally swirled through, lifting dust from bases on the field. He stood near small metal bleachers, watching kids and coaches warm up with practice pitches and swings. Bobby wound up and threw, but for a moment he was no longer watching Bobby—instead, Adam was six years old again, playing catch in the backyard with his father.

He blinked several times and kicked his toe into the grass, contemplating again what to say and how to say it.

Soon, the game was underway. Bobby slid into second base and leapt up, a proud smile stretched across his face, his white pants covered in dirt. The woman he assumed was Cindy clapped and cheered as if Bobby was her own child. Her dark hair was thick and glossy against the sun, bouncing up and down as she jumped enthusiastically, her skin colored with the honeyed kiss of summer.

Halfway through the game, a tall man with sandy-blonde hair and brown eyes walked to Cindy's side and casually slid an arm around her waist. Adam watched him bend down and kiss the top of her head. He was thin but muscular, his skin tanned and weathered, as if regularly exposed to the sun, wind, and rain.

On Bobby's next bat, he fouled on the first pitch but made contact on the second. A crushing sound echoed through the air, and he sprinted to first base. A lanky boy scrambled for the ball and threw it to first base, the play close enough to be questionable.

"*Safe!*"

The brunette jumped up and down with excitement, and the man beside her thrust his hands in the air and released a loud whistle.

When the game was over, Adam quickly returned to his car and waited. He followed the white van and a blue SUV back to house #73, then watched the three of them go inside, a screen door at the side of the house slamming closed behind them.

Through partially opened windows, Adam could hear laughter, the clanking of kitchen dishes. He looked at the wedding ring on his left hand and closed his eyes, visualizing his parents, searching for courage. He sucked in a deep breath. The car door felt heavy, as did his feet. He followed a concrete walkway, to a single step at the base of the entrance. A wrought iron doorknocker hung at the center of the front door, painted the same glossy cream color as the trim that bordered each double-hung window. He stopped abruptly and paused.

Everything seems fine. Maybe it's best to just go home.

He took a hesitant step backward.

No. He wouldn't be a coward again.

He leapt forward and pulled on the doorknocker before he could change his mind. The woman appeared almost immediately, a dishtowel in her hand. Up close, her dark brown hair and bright blue eyes were stunning. She was young, maybe late twenties. A broad smile on her face slowly relaxed, her expression melting into confusion as she studied Adam.

"Can I help you?" she asked.

Adam shook his head, realizing he hadn't said a word. "Oh, I'm sorry, I'm . . . "

The man with the sandy-blonde hair appeared at her side, his protective hand resting on her shoulder. He peered at Adam suspiciously.

Adam shoved his hands in his jeans pockets. His pulse skipped, quickened. "I was hoping to talk to Bobby."

"And you are? Who?" the man asked with a scowl. He was slightly older; Adam guessed early thirties.

"I know this is unusual, but I'm from the *Greater Valley Medical Center.*"

The woman looked puzzled for a moment, as if trying to connect the dots in her mind.

"Yah sure, from Pennsylvania?" she asked.

"That's right," Adam said, smiling.

"What do you want with Bobby?" the man asked.

Adam looked at the ground, shifted his weight. "I suppose I really should've gone to see him when he was awake in the hospital, I just"—he cleared his throat—"couldn't. But I'd like to talk to him now, if that's okay? Just for a few minutes?"

The man was still scowling, suspicious.

What did you think was going to happen?

Adam found himself stumbling over his own words.

"We, um, you see, I'm on the board at the hospital, so I . . . that's how I know about the . . . situation. And, well, I had a similar experience as a child." He raked a hand through his hair and looked into the woman's blue eyes. "Are you Cindy?" he asked.

She nodded.

"I thought maybe it would help him to talk to someone who understands."

Her blue eyes softened, and Adam was relived to see the kindness in them, not for himself, but for Bobby.

"And I think it'll help me, too." Adam shrugged his shoulders. Not knowing what else to say, he finished with, "I was born in Minneapolis. It's good to be home."

What does that have to do with anything?

The man opened his mouth to speak, but Cindy placed a hand on his chest, stopping him. On her fourth finger, a diamond engagement ring and gold wedding band caught in the sunlight.

"Okay then, Mr. . . . ?" she searched Adam's face for information.

"Adam." Adam smiled. "Adam Thomas."

She extended her arm. "Okay, Adam, it's nice to meet you."

Adam shook her hand. "Same here." He followed her down a narrow hallway to a bedroom where they found Bobby sprawled across a bed. He was drawing a picture of what looked to be rocket ships and asteroids. Cindy introduced Adam as a friend from the hospital that took care of him before she could make it to Pennsylvania. She told them she'd be back in a few minutes, and then she disappeared into the hallway, leaving the door halfway open.

Adam motioned to a space at the edge of the bed. "Do you mind if I sit?"

Bobby shrugged his shoulders and sat up. "You came all the way from Pennsylvania?"

"Sure did." Adam smiled as he took a seat.

"Your voice sounds kinda funny, like my Aunt Cindy and Uncle Dan's."

Adam laughed. "Oh, that's probably because I grew up around here a long time ago. Didn't your mom have the same accent? Or your dad?"

"No," Bobby said.

"Hmm," Adam said, scanning the room. The walls were painted blue, the bed covered in a blue and tan checkered quilt. Books and baseball memorabilia filled shelves and walls. "You like baseball?"

Bobby nodded.

"How are you settling into your new home here? Looks pretty comfortable?"

"It's okay."

"Not quite the same as being with Mom and Dad, though, right?"

Bobby looked at Adam, his eyes wide, innocent. The expression pulled hard on Adam's heart. "Yah, I understand."

Bobby's face soured. He stood, picked up a baseball glove, and slammed his small fist into it. "Nobody understands."

"My mom and dad died in a car crash when I was seven—same as you."

Bobby froze, and Adam watched the boy's throat visibly constrict. He could *feel* what Bobby was feeling.

"That's why I came, you see. I never had anyone to talk to when I was your age. I thought it might be nice for you to know that you can talk to me—if you need to."

Bobby remained silent for a long moment while he studied the hand still shoved into his baseball glove. He rubbed his knuckles against the leather.

"Do you still remember them?" Bobby finally asked.

Adam nodded. "You'll always remember them as long as you *want* to remember. They'll always be a part of you right here." Adam placed a fist over his heart, watched tears spring to Bobby's eyes. "It's important to make sure you hold onto the memories. They'll help you find your way to all the good things in life."

Adam studied Bobby's face. His cheeks were rosy. His long, thick eyelashes, now wet with tears, blinked above blue eyes that match Cindy's.

He was so . . . *young.*

"How about your Aunt? Is she good to you?"

Bobby nodded. "She's pretty cool. So's Uncle Dan."

Adam nodded in agreement. "C'mere," he said, patting an empty space on the bed. "I want to show you something."

Obediently, Bobby sat alongside Adam.

"Do you know what a pinky-swear is?"

"Yeah," Bobby said.

"My dad always said pinky-swears were for girls." Adam laughed at the memory. "So, we did a thumb-swear instead. Like this," he said, taking Bobby's small thumb and hooking around his. They shook and then pulled apart, and Bobby smiled. "You should teach that to your Aunt Cindy. Any time you need to talk to someone, I bet you could talk to her, and she could keep any secret with a thumb-swear. Any secret at all."

They talked a few minutes longer, and a sense of peace fell over Adam. It was clear that Bobby was safe and loved with Cindy. When he realized that fifteen minutes had passed and Cindy hadn't returned, he bid farewell to Bobby and stepped into the hallway. He found Cindy standing a few feet away from the door, propped up against the wall, tears streaming down her face. She led him to the end of the hallway, several feet from Bobby's room.

"I suppose you didn't come just to talk, did you?" she asked, looking up at Adam.

Adam shook his head. "I wanted to make sure he was okay."

She nodded and inhaled, a long steadying breath.

"You're doing an amazing thing for that little boy you know," Adam said. He pulled a business card from his wallet and offered it her. "If you ever want to visit Pennsylvania, just give a call."

"To visit my sister's grave, you mean?"

Adam glanced at the floor. "It's important for him to remember where he came from. Besides, my wife and I have kids—our son is Bobby's age. I'm sure they'd have a blast together."

"Jill was ten years older than me—Bobby's mom. She wasn't only my sister; she was my best friend, you know? We were on our

honeymoon, for Christ's sake, and I get back to get the news that . . .
" She covered her face with her hands before taking a deep breath,
struggling to stand straighter. "I called Jill for everything. And now
I'm supposed to figure it all out? What if I don't know what I'm doing?
What if I do it all wrong?" Her glossy eyes searched Adam's face for
an answer.

"I suppose as long as you always love him, you'll do it right." He
shrugged his shoulders. "If there's one thing I'm sure of, it's that."
Adam hesitated, but he had to ask. "There's something I can't figure out though. Bobby mentioned my accent. Same as yours. But
not your sister?"

Cindy managed a laugh. "Yah, Bobby thinks we sound funny.
My parents moved us here when Jill was sixteen and I was six. I was
still sopping things up like a sponge, but Jill hated them for tearing her away from her friends. A year and a half later she was off to
college and back in the Northeast."

Dishes clattered in the kitchen, and Adam wondered if sandy-
blonde-hair was trying to remind him he was still out there. *What
was his name?*

"How'd your husband take the news that you were going to
have an instant family?"

Cindy smiled, and her eyes lit up. "Dan? Surprisingly well, actually. I suppose I did *that* right the first time."

Adam smiled in return and nervously raked a hand through
his hair, wondering if he would be able to salvage his own relationship. He used to feel that way about Ellie—sure of himself, sure of
her. Sure that he did it right the first time. But that was once upon
a time.

CHAPTER 37
ELLIE

E llie placed Lizzie's favorite stuffed puppy in the overnight bag and turned to Suzanne. "Are you sure you want to keep them all night? You really don't have to."

"Don't be ridiculous, of course I want to keep them," Suzanne said. "Besides, you look like crap. You need a break."

"Gee thanks."

"Have you heard from Adam?"

"If that's what you want to call it," she mumbled. She pulled the zipper of the overnight bag closed, hard enough for it to rip it off, and Suzanne raised her eyebrows. Ellie dropped the bag on the floor. "I still don't even know where he is."

"He said he'd be back tonight, right?" Suzanne asked.

"Yeah, but . . . " She pulled at the cotton of her sweater, ran the hem back and forth in between her fingers.

Suzanne grabbed onto Ellie's shoulders and jostled her playfully. "Relax! Do something fun. You don't have anyone else to worry about till tomorrow. Adam's a big boy."

"That's what I'm afraid of. What if he's on the other side of the country with"— she swallowed against a lump in her throat that formed at the mere thought—"with *Jackie?*" She could barely manage the word. Saying it aloud made her legs suddenly weak and forced her onto the bench in the foyer.

The kids came barreling around the corner, Tommy shooting a play gun at the Barbie in Lizzie's hand while Lizzie screamed.

Suzanne clapped her hands, an effort to get their attention and stop the mayhem. "Aunt Suzie's ready to go. Who wants ice cream?"

They both screeched in delight, dropped their toys on the spot, and sprinted toward the front door.

Suzanne rushed them out the door and turned toward Ellie, sympathy etched into her face. "Just try to enjoy some free time."

Ninety minutes later, Ellie had eaten dinner, picked up the toys, and cleaned most of the house. She bent down and scratched at the gray hair around Buster's muzzle. He moaned and stretched lazily across the braided area rug he'd fallen asleep on an hour before. She straightened, and her hand instinctively moved to her aching lower back.

Just me and the dog—getting old together.

With a heavy sigh, she lowered herself onto the couch. After plucking the remote from in between the cushions, she flipped through every channel three times. Every picture was a blur, every sound muffled against the rattle in her mind. Finally, she turned it off and paged through a magazine, but she found herself reading the same line three times, not comprehending a single word.

The phone rang, and she nearly ran to get it, anxious to talk to anyone, desperately hoping it was Adam. But when she picked up, the line went dead. She had just made her way back to the couch and returned her attention to the magazine when it rang again. The person at the other end hung up a second time. She looked at the phone quizzically and dialed it back using *69. The female voice that answered wasn't one she immediately recognized, although it sounded vaguely familiar.

"Hello?" the woman asked again.

She still couldn't quite place it.

Until . . . she did.

Jackie.

She listened for a moment, straining to hear Adam's voice in the background, wondering if they were together. Blood rushed from her head to her toes and left her dizzy. She clicked the phone off and angrily yanked the cord from the jack. Her back slid against the wall until she was seated on the floor. Her heart was racing, her hands shaky. She released her hold on the phone, and it fell against the wooden floorboards beside her with a clatter.

When her legs finally felt stable enough to support her weight, she struggled to get to her feet, struck by the realization that it probably wasn't a good idea to sit on the floor in the first place this far into her pregnancy. She found her cell phone and dialed Adam's mobile. The call was sent straight to voice mail.

As soon as she hung up, Suzanne's number appeared on her screen.

"Hi, Mommy! Me and Tommy are getting ready for bed. Whatcha doin'?"

The sound of Lizzie's voice forced her to take a deep breath and reframe her thoughts. She talked to Lizzie and Tommy (who chattered away and sounded high on sugar) for a few minutes before Suzanne took the phone. She thanked her again for taking the kids (God knows she couldn't deal with them right now), but was careful not to disclose Jackie's call for fear that talking about it aloud might leave her in pieces. Besides, her phone was flashing a low battery warning.

With nothing else left to do, she tried to start a novel, but she couldn't seem to focus on the story, so she returned it to the shelf. One minute her hand was paused on the narrow spine, the next she was alphabetizing the entire bookcase. When she slid the last book into its proper place, she realized that her head was pounding, her lower back aching. She also had to pee for what seemed like the hundredth time that day.

That was when she decided to run a bath—not too hot, of course, even though she was tired of that pregnancy rule, too—but she was entirely edgy and jumpy. She needed to relax. Oddly, the baby had been kinder today, with fewer kicks to her ribcage.

She watched the silky bubble bath slide into the water and then slipped out of her clothes. Standing at the mirror, she released her hair from a ponytail—the pregnancy and prenatal vitamins had added gloss and volume to every strand. Her face had gone from oval to round, and her chest had nearly doubled in size. But her neck and shoulders were still slender, feminine. She looked like the Goddess of Curves, someone she barely recognized.

A moment later, she caught her mind wandering, playing a game in which it tallied her good and bad qualities before comparing them against Jackie's for review.

Oh God.

She massaged her temples, her forehead, trying to rid her mind of the thought. She'd been settled in the warm water less than a minute before her eye caught a flicker outside of the window, a set of headlights entering the driveway.

What'd the kids forget now?

Weary, she stepped out of the tub. She slipped into a silk robe, reviewing a mental checklist of what was packed in the kids' bag.

Lizzie can't sleep without her puppy, but she thought she stuffed that in. Or worse, what if something was wrong?

She neglected to plug the house phone back into the jack, her cell phone left charging on the counter downstairs.

By the time she reached the bathroom door, Adam was standing in front of her. Startled, she jumped backward. Adam's eyes swept from her head to her toes and back up again. Light from the candle she'd lit a few minutes before flashed against their blue centers. He took a step forward; she took a step back, confused by his silence, his serious expression. Slowly, his hand reached out for her. She flinched, not in fear but surprise. Gently, he wiped a patch of bubbles from her collarbone. His touch sent a chill racing down her spine.

"You look . . . beautiful, amazing."

Ellie managed a weak laugh and made a sweeping motion in front of her stomach with her arms. "I'm enormously pregnant. If you think this is the definition of beautiful or amazing, you might need glasses." Her body buzzed, nervous and edgy. She wanted to ask him where he'd been. She wanted to ask about Jackie, but she was frozen in place, in silence.

He moved a hand to her face and rubbed his thumb in circles on her cheek. Her heart skipped then raced as if it couldn't decide how to beat. She found herself staring into his eyes, wondering what made him tick—and then questioning why she didn't already know the answer.

She searched his face, trying to interpret his solemn expression, wondering where he'd come from.

"I tried to call. You didn't answer." His voice was quiet, almost a whisper.

"I didn't hear . . . I unplugged—"

His grasp on her cheek tightened, and she felt like she was losing her footing. He pulled her face toward his and bent down to meet her lips for a long, smooth kiss that took her breath away. His fingers moved to the belt around her robe, and he slipped the knot apart with ease. It fell open, and she stood exposed, but safe in a way she was sure she could only ever feel with Adam. Goosebumps raced over the surface of her skin, quickly cancelled out by a surge of heat that rushed through her veins. Gravity pulled on her stomach, and her back still ached, but her entire body was tingling, alive. Adam caressed her left breast, and despite the baby, and her bulging stomach, and the problems they'd had, and Ryan, and Jackie, and everything else, sensuality stirred within her—racing and spiraling deep in her core. Adam's fingers brushed the inside of her thigh, and a soft moan escaped her lips.

Then, his hand wrapped around hers and he guided her toward the bedroom. There were so many questions she wanted to ask, but she was afraid to break the spell between them. Besides, she didn't know if she could speak, even if she tried. So, she followed in silence and allowed her physical and emotional need for her husband to consume her.

Afterward, they fell onto the sheets, breathless. Absentmindedly, she ran her fingers through the hair on Adam's chest, a smile stretched across her face.

She was glowing. She could feel it from within, and she was sure Adam could see it in the way he returned her sated gaze. More than sex, more than satisfaction, something was buzzing, humming, lighting her up inside.

Just as her pulse began to slow, she found out what it was. A warm gush of moisture hit her legs, and she bolted upright.

Visibly startled, Adam did the same. "What's wrong?" he asked.

"I think my water just broke." She lifted the sheet that covered her stomach. Her head and her heart both began to pound, and she looked at Adam in horror. "It's too early, Adam. It's too soon!"

CHAPTER 38

ADAM

Hand pressed hard against his horn, four-way flashers on, Adam weaved around cars on the way to the hospital. It was the weekend, and everyone in the Valley seemed to be out. As soon as they pulled into the emergency lot he realized he was going the wrong way—entering near the area reserved for ambulances—but he kept going anyway.

When they reached the edge of the building, he slammed to a halt, shoved the gearshift into park, and jumped out of the BMW. An EMT was propped up against the brick exterior of the hospital, a paper cup cradled in his hand. Startled, he straightened and tossed the cup. Steaming coffee splashed onto the grass. The EMT sprinted toward the car while calling out for additional help, and seconds later two stocky men in white uniforms were placing Ellie on a stretcher. She moaned in pain while she held her stomach, her body curled into a fetal position.

Adam could only look on helplessly as a new surge of turbulence rushed through him—he had just begun to think he'd figured everything out.

"Go ahead and park your car, sir. We'll meet you inside," the coffee drinker said, motioning toward Adam as they wheeled Ellie away.

Adam drove to the crowded lot with a foggy head, his hands now shaky with adrenaline. He finally found a spot near the back, but he was the only person in sight as he exited the car. A crescent moon cast an eerie glow on large oak trees, and dark shadows hovered near their ancient wide trunks. The summer air was hot and thick with humidity, the lot dimly lit. Adam struggled to take a cleansing breath, feeling like a character dropped into a scene from a horror film, waiting, just waiting for something bad to materialize. He could feel it looming—the doom—with every step he took toward the entrance, and there was nothing he could do about it. He'd spent hours online, reading about the risks of pregnancy in women over forty. Of course, he hadn't shared this with Ellie. In his flustered state, there were too many to remember.

Not to mention the car accident. It instilled paranoia. When Ellie first came home, he watched her struggle, and he bargained with God, actually dropping to his knees, praying every night for the first time in his life. He had made sure she took all of the vitamins and medicines and supplements the doctors gave her, and he double-checked with them to make sure everything she did was normal, acceptable, in line with a full recovery.

As she grew stronger, and the bickering between them subsided, the possibility of hope felt stronger too. Relief inched in little by little, but he stayed vigilant, he still told her to rest, he still prayed she'd be okay, that the baby would healthy, that *all* of them would be happy.

And now he found himself at risk of losing them both. Again. And it felt as if all of the oxygen had been sucked from the air.

When he finally reached the building, a security guard dressed in a navy blue uniform was waiting for him just inside the door. Adam glanced absentmindedly over the shiny metal badge and hospital ID pinned to his shirt. Though he could see the man's mouth move, he couldn't hear any of the words, everything muffled in the fog clouding his brain. The guard turned and motioned for Adam to follow—instructions Adam silently obeyed. They walked down a sterile white hallway, Adam's view of anything ahead blocked by the tall broad frame of the guard. Fear gripped him, threatening to tear him apart and leave him lying in a heap right there on the hospital floor. Eventually, they stopped at a curtained room near the end of the hall where Ellie was arguing with a nurse.

Again.

Adam's heart jumped into his throat, and pressure built behind his eyes. She was talking—no, better than that, she was *yelling* at a nurse. He'd never been more relieved to hear her so angry, and the emotion that swept through him threatened to buckle his knees beneath his weight.

"Did you call him?" Ellie asked the nurse. She clenched her teeth, struggling to breathe through another contraction. "I *need* Dr. Van Linden."

"We're working on that." The nurse was busy placing round disks connected to wires on Ellie's stomach—the same disks Adam saw after the car accident. She explained to Ellie and Adam that they would help monitor the baby's heart rate.

Another contraction.

Adam wished he could be calm like the nurse.

A second nurse entered and inserted an IV into Ellie's arm. Monitors jumped to life, and a saline bag dripped fluid through a tube. A young, twenty-something girl with a blonde ponytail came in next, wheeling a portable cart that held a computer. She asked for Ellie's personal and insurance information. Since Ellie was still arched in pain, clutching her stomach and complaining about Dr. Van Linden, Adam answered her questions.

Outwardly, he was a picture-perfect, level-headed husband, the tone of his voice calm, even. He was shocked at his ability to pull this off, because physically and mentally, he was standing at the edge of a very high cliff. The conflict was overwhelming.

He finished providing admissions information to the girl, and they were whisked upstairs to the third floor maternity ward, placed in what Adam thought was a birthing room. Finally, they were alone, and the chaos calmed for a moment. Adam walked to Ellie's side and took ahold of her hand, relieved when she didn't pull away. It was icy cold, just as it was after the accident. This time, though, her face was beet red and she was very much alive. For her sake, he tried to keep tears from flooding his eyes, and he did his best not to cringe when she tightened in pain. He didn't remember it being this bad with Tommy and Lizzie.

"It's going to be okay," he said, wondering if he was trying to convince Ellie or himself.

She looked up, and the fear in her eyes increased his anxiety tenfold. Yes, for some reason, this felt different than the delivery of their other two children.

And not just because this child wasn't his.

It was a self-justifying thought that entered his mind without consciousness, and with it, came a wave of guilt. He tried again to shake his angst, but before he could collect his words, a tall, thin, redheaded man dressed in blue scrubs entered the room and introduced himself as Dr. Gibbs.

"Where's Dr. Van Linden?" Ellie asked, her tone terse.

"He's not on call tonight, but we understand you want to see him. We've attempted to reach him—"

"Please . . . " The desperation in Ellie's voice was audible, and it looked like she was about to cry.

Without responding, Dr. Gibbs glanced at the monitor screen. He held a stethoscope to Ellie's protruding stomach and moved it higher above her abdomen. Gently, he pressed on her tightly stretched skin, probing at the baby on the other side. His hand moved to rest on her arm, and his eyes met hers.

"Your baby appears to be breech, Ellie—feet down. And your amniotic sac has torn. That's not an ideal situation, but we're going to work on it, okay? We need to see if we can get the baby to turn around so you can deliver without further complications."

"Breech?" Ellie's face paled before she scrunched her body again, breathing through another contraction.

Guilt continued to badger Adam from every angle. Things with Ellie and him should never have gotten this bad. He should have seen to it. He should have known better, paid more attention. If he had, they wouldn't have been separated, she wouldn't even be pregnant. And then there was earlier tonight. For a moment he wondered if this happened as a result of his pulling her into their bedroom. That would be his fault, too. After all, her water broke just afterward.

"Could this have happened because . . . ?" His voice was barely audible, and he couldn't finish the question.

"No." Ellie shook her head before giving into another contraction. She gave Adam a knowing look. "That's not why," she said, straining to finish her sentence.

When Ellie was pregnant with Tommy and Lizzie, Dr. Van Linden said sex during pregnancy—even late term—was perfectly acceptable. Adam remembered being too scared to test the theory as her pregnancies had progressed. And that was when she was younger—under forty. To think he may have endangered this child . . . and Ellie . . . this could all be his fault.

Dizzy and nauseous, Adam steadied himself by gripping the bed rail.

Dr. Gibbs pulled a clipboard from a hook at the bottom of the bed and fingered through some papers. "Looks like you're a little early—"

"Thirty-three weeks," Adam said, struggling to stay focused.

Ellie shot Adam a look of surprise. Of course he'd kept track, even if she didn't think so.

"Okay, let's get this done." Dr. Gibbs smiled and replaced the clipboard.

At the command of Dr. Gibbs, an ultrasound technician and a nurse joined them in the room. Ellie received a shot they explained would help her uterus relax, and Dr. Gibbs attempted to guide the baby into a head-down position.

A gray and white shadowy image moved on the screen, and Adam's heart expanded in his chest. In that moment, he knew for certain DNA was no longer a factor. He would love this baby just as he loved Tommy and Lizzie; he would never again forget to cherish his wife.

Suddenly, the monitor beeped and shrilled with loud alarms. Adam's body jumped in response. He watched the screen light up with jagged lines and flashing lights.

"What's happening?" Adam asked.

"I think I'm going to be sick," Ellie said. Her body heaved, and a nurse appeared at her side with a plastic basin.

Nurses scurried around the room in haste. Dr. Gibbs stopped trying to move the baby, and everyone began to talk quickly. Adam found it hard to breathe in the midst of the frantic buzz.

"The baby's losing oxygen," Dr. Gibbs said, his voice calm but clipped. "We're going to have to do an emergency cesarean."

"What?" Ellie asked, her face stricken with panic. "No, I didn't want to have a C-section this time. I really want to see Dr. Van Linden." Her strength had all but vanished, replaced by exhaustion and vulnerability. Fear coursed through Adam, and he could only focus on the one thing that mattered—he would do anything not to lose her.

"Do what you need to do," Adam said with a pointed look at Dr. Gibbs.

Ellie's eyes darted to his, accusatory, clouded with betrayal. Fleetingly, he wondered if that would be the last look he ever saw on his wife's face. Panic threatened to cut off his air supply.

Adam shook his head. "El, I can't lose you. Either of you. You have to—"

"Excuse me, please." A nurse pushed in between Ellie and Adam and checked the drip flow through the IV that ran into her arm. She explained that the anesthesiologist would meet them in the OR and administer a local anesthetic—it would knock Ellie out completely.

Another nurse placed a hand on Adam's shoulder and asked him to back away. "We need to take her to the OR now."

"Adam," Ellie called, her voice weak, as they rolled her bed from the room.

He moved against the wall and leaned on it for support, breathing methodically. His head was spinning, his stomach nauseous. He blinked, and then he was standing in a big, white, sterile room full of medical equipment—alone.

⊱━⊰

Adam sat in a small waiting room, his elbows resting on his knees, his head in his hands. It had been an hour. He started to dial Sam's number three times, but was afraid he wouldn't be able to find his voice long enough to have a conversation. Thank God the kids were with Suzanne.

Finally, someone called his name. He looked up and saw Dr. Van Linden standing in the doorway, wearing a tuxedo. A tiny bundle was wrapped in a pink blanket, cradled in his arms, a broad smile stretched across his face, his eyes full of sparkle.

Adam jumped to his feet and found he still needed to balance himself on wobbly knees.

"It's a girl," Dr. Van Linden announced, his Dutch accent friendly and familiar.

Adam sighed, his shoulders relaxed. His breathing became heavy, and his eyes began to fill with tears. The anxiety of the last few months had taken its toll, and he was exhausted.

Dr. Van Linden stepped forward and gently placed the baby in his arms. Adam stared at her small round face, still blotchy from childbirth. He pulled back the edge of a pink hat on her head and discovered a thick patch of brown hair. When he reached out to touch her hand, she wrapped five small fingers around one of his, and his heart melted.

Everything about her was so small, so sweet, so . . . *perfect.*

He felt as if he'd taken a euphoric drug, his body light as a feather, everything in the room bright and crystal-clear but dream-like at exactly the same time, but the spell broke as the sequence of events from earlier that day rushed in, filling the forefront of his mind.

Adam turned his attention back to Dr. Van Linden, still standing in front of him, squeezed into a tuxedo and a smile, and he wondered if he really had lost his mind. Maybe he was dreaming, all of this an exhaustion and stress-induced illusion.

The baby stirred and murmured softly—a familiar sound that took him back to the births of Tommy and Lizzie. He glanced at her for a moment then focused hard, narrowing his eyes on Dr. Van Linden. A ruby-red bowtie hung loosely around his neck, and engraved platinum cufflinks sparkled at his wrists. The doctor's shiny, black dress shoes faced Adam's beat-up running sneakers.

Adam's forehead wrinkled in confusion. "Where did you . . . how did you . . . ? Dr. Gibbs was with Ellie." Adam exhaled, blinked hard.

"Oh," Dr. Van Linden said, his belly bouncing as he chuckled. He motioned to his formal attire. "My wife and I were at a charity event in New York City. I left as soon as I heard about Ellie, but I got here just as Dr. Gibbs was finishing up. I wish I could've come sooner."

A door opened behind the doctor, and a gust of air swept past them as a family of three walked by.

Not nuts. Thank God.

"Don't worry, my wife didn't really want to be there anyway," Dr. Van Linden said with a wink.

Adam remembered Ellie's insistence that Dr. Van Linden be contacted, her demanding behavior, and his cheeks flushed with embarrassment. Details of the night came rushing back to his conscious mind, one small wave after another, prompting Adam to stand straighter, hold the baby a little tighter.

"And Ellie?" Adam asked, his body stiff with concern. He braced himself, still expecting the worst, although he wasn't sure why.

Dr. Van Linden rested a hand on Adam's shoulder. "Gibbs is a good man. Ellie's going to be fine. She's in recovery now. They'll move her to a room, and then it'll take another hour or two for the anesthesia to fully wear off."

Relief sunk into his bones, his jaw, every muscle, every drop of blood. He didn't know whether to laugh or cry. And he was suddenly exhausted.

"She's so tiny," Adam said, looking back down at the bundle in his arms. "Shouldn't she be in one of those incubators or something?"

"No," Dr. Van Linden said, waving his hand dismissively. "You have yourself a fighter there. She weighed in at six pounds."

Adam tried to remember how big Tommy and Lizzie were when they were born, but it seemed like so long ago. "But Ellie was only thirty-three weeks." Adam was still convinced there had to be something to worry about.

Dr. Van Linden shoved his hands in his pockets, rocked back and forth on his feet. "These things happen," he said. He brought a hand to his chin and ran his thumb over the curve of his jawbone. "I think . . . "

Dr. Van Linden's words faded into the background. Adam couldn't seem to focus on anything but the small miracle cradled in his arms.

A minute later, he looked up at Dr. Van Linden's smile and wondered what he had just missed, if he should ask. But before he could, a nurse appeared, and Adam was led to Ellie's room. He found her sleeping peacefully, relieved to see there were no more tubes or wires stuck into or onto her body.

He settled into a chair by the window and marveled at the soft skin and red lips that peeked out from the blanket in his arms. Her tiny chest moved up and down with each inhale and exhale, and every breath felt like an extension of his own.

Twenty minutes later, fatigue settled into his muscles. He glanced at Ellie again, still wondering how to make things right. *If* they could make things right.

He considered the baby's father and wondered if he would have to compete for the love of this tiny being who'd already stolen his heart. He tried to decide how they would explain to the kids that he wasn't the father of their sister. And he worried that it could all be for naught; would Ellie really still love him all the same?

Then he rested his head back, too exhausted to think anymore.

CHAPTER 39

ELLIE

E llie's eyelids opened, and her surroundings slowly came into focus. The creamy yellow walls reminded her of soft, baby chicks. She tried to move her head and winced—it was heavy and foggy. Sluggish, her eyes scanned the length of her horizontal body. The bump she was used to seeing at her waistline was gone. Her hand moved over the blanket to her stomach, and she tightened at dull pain coming from a bandage at the inside bend of her arm, the staples pierced through the skin below her abdomen. Her mouth was dry, and she wasn't sure she could talk even if she tried.

A gurgling sound came from somewhere to her left, and she gradually managed enough strength to turn her head. Adam was asleep in a chair, holding what looked like a wadded up pink blanket. The sound got louder, and Adam stirred. His eyes opened and met hers.

"Hey," he said, holding the blanket in his arms, sitting up straight. He rose and walked to Ellie's bedside. "We have . . . um . . . it's another girl." His voice and facial expression were both filled with the unmistakable mark of pride.

Her mind cleared, sharpened, and she remembered being wheeled into surgery. She tried to reach out her arms, wanting to hold the baby, but they were heavy and weak. She could barely lift them off the blanket.

The baby made a sucking sound with her mouth and fussed in Adam's arms. "I think she's hungry," he said. "Do you want to try?"

Ellie did her best to force a small nod, and Adam pushed a button to raise the slope of the bed into a sitting position. Gently, he propped Ellie's arm up on a pillow and placed the baby in its bend. As Ellie helped the baby latch onto her breast, tears built in her eyes. As if he knew her thoughts, Adam lifted a yellow plastic pitcher from the bedside table. Condensation dripped from its base as he poured her a cup of water. He helped her drink through a straw, and the cool liquid allowed her to finally find her voice.

Her heart swelled with more love than she could ever imagine for this perfect tiny being, just as it did when she had Tommy and Lizzie, but the love was accompanied by pain this time around—full of complication and shame.

Adam reached up and touched her cheek. "Ellie, we should talk."

Her chest tightened. No good conversation ever started that way. She was still uncertain about the time they'd spent together earlier that night.

"Do you still love me?" he asked.

Her throat swelled so she could barely speak. "I think the question is do you still love me?"

"Why . . . " He shook his head in confusion, his forehead wrinkling the way it did when he was trying to figure out the crossword puzzle in the Sunday morning paper—something he was terrible at. "This whole thing is my fault," he said.

"Clearly I own some of the blame," she said, looking down at the baby, releasing a breath as a tear fell from her cheek.

"I've never loved you more." His voice was a low whisper, and she could hear the words catch in his throat. When she raised her head to look at him, she was surprised to find he was shedding his own set of tears.

"I've been trying to tell you for months, Ellie. I just haven't been able to. Every time I try, I seem to mess it up. If I hadn't let you down, if I hadn't let our family down, we wouldn't be having this conversation. I pushed you . . . to him." His eyes, sadder than she'd ever seen them, spurred a brand new wave of guilt.

She raised her hand to grab onto his, but the IV pulled at her skin. She grimaced and shook her head. "Still, I never should've . . . "

"We both have our own guilt to deal with. I know how overwhelmed you were now. I just wasn't paying attention before."

"And now it's going to start all over again," Ellie said, looking back down at the baby.

"I promise I'll be there this time, if you want me to be."

"What about work?"

He shrugged. "I'll figure it out. Marc can manage okay without me for a while. I'm not going to make the same mistake again."

"I never really wanted you to leave, you know?"

Adam pushed his hands into his pockets. "Why'd you tell me to go then?"

She scratched nervously at the white cotton blanket and scrunched her face. "I was really, *really* mad at you. And you weren't listening. I didn't know how to get through to you."

His eyes fell to the floor. "I'm so sorry."

Three words, a simple acknowledgment she'd been waiting to hear for what felt like an eternity. The sincerity behind them overwhelmed her with emotion. She nodded and bit her lip. "Me too."

"Do you think we can make it work?" Adam asked.

"I hope so."

"She's perfect you know," he said, looking at the baby.

Another tear ran down Ellie's face, as she looked at her new daughter, fast asleep in her arms.

"I'm not surprised, though. She's a part of you, so how could she be anything but perfect?" Adam stroked Ellie's tear-stained cheek with the outside of his hand. She leaned into the comforting feel of it.

"There is one thing," he said, clearing his throat.

"Anything," she said, looking up at him with a half-crooked smile.

It was obvious he was struggling to get the words out before he could change his mind, and once they were spoken, she wished he'd reconsidered. "The baby's father . . . "

Anything but that.

CHAPTER 40

ADAM

Adam woke to the sound of a crying baby, momentarily convinced he must be dreaming. Moving slightly, he winced at the pain in his back and realized he wasn't.

Didn't they all just fall asleep?

And he'd thought the spare room bed was bad.

He wasn't sure what time it was, but dim light peeked in from behind the window shades. Ellie stirred in the hospital bed, and Adam stood. Approaching the bassinet, he looked down on Mary. Her face, scrunched up, wrinkled, and bright red as she expressed her desire to eat.

Mary.

He stared at her with amazement, as he did each time she captured his attention, every time he touched her. They named her after his mother. He told Ellie about his trip to Minnesota, and she'd insisted. While she may not be his, he was proud to give her the name.

He lifted her tiny body and took her to Ellie, who had already begun to inch her way into a sitting position on the hospital bed.

"Thanks," Ellie said, her voice groggy. She took the baby, greedy for milk.

This had become their ritual. Adam made a conscious effort to be more present this time around. Instead of going home and taking the easy way out, he'd spent two nights on a hospital cot in Ellie's room. He would retrieve the baby for Ellie, quick to get her anything she needed. He even changed most of the diapers.

He realized that his business wouldn't fail without him for a few days, or even a couple of weeks. Marc was only a phone call away.

His priority now was his wife, his family.

Just as Mary finished feeding, a nurse entered the room to take Ellie's vital signs again, and a pediatrician arrived to take one last look at Mary before they went home.

Sam and Suzanne had already visited three times and brought the children twice. Tommy and Lizzie knew they had a sister, and for now Adam and Ellie agreed that was all they needed to know. Mary's father and the pending conversation he knew they would eventually need to have with the kids still crowded the back of his mind, but their new motto was 'one step at a time.'

At ten o'clock, Ellie had her first proper shower in two days. She emerged refreshed with shiny hair, pink cheeks, and smooth, radiant skin. Adam smiled at her. Before he had the chance to pay her a compliment, there was a knock on the partially opened door. It swung open.

Tom, Kathy, and another woman he didn't recognize entered the room carrying an enormous bunch of fresh flowers.

"Ellie! I'm so glad we caught you," Kathy said.

"Yes!" the other woman agreed, looking more than excited to be there. "You said you'd call, Ellie, but I never heard from you. I got worried, and when I called Kathy and found out about the baby . . . well, I just had to come see. Congratulations!"

She reminded Adam of Kathy in a way, and it was evident the pair had been friends for a very long time. But he'd never met her before.

"Colleen, what a surprise," Ellie said with a smile.

Adam wondered how they could've allowed this much space to build between them—enough that Ellie would have new friends he knew nothing about. How much had Ellie's life moved forward since they'd been apart? A million different possibilities surfaced in seconds. Maybe she'd hired a divorce lawyer and he didn't know it. Maybe she went to Kathy for help and she and Tom knew about everything.

The women crowded around Mary's bassinet while Tom shook Adam's hand, congratulating him. Next, he was introduced to Kathy's sister, Colleen.

Of course . . . the resemblance . . .

Adam shook her hand and his body relaxed, although he still struggled to place her connection with Ellie.

"So, Ellie," Colleen said, "I know the timing may be bad, but I've just been dying to know—did you give any thought to my offer?"

Tom was going on about local Chamber of Commerce initiatives, but Adam couldn't focus on what he's saying. He was too busy eavesdropping on Ellie and Colleen. Kathy walked Mary around the room, fussing over her with soft cooing sounds, laughing at nothing in particular.

Ellie looked confused. "Offer?" she asked.

"At the coffee shop."

"I . . . " Ellie's face flushed. "You know, things were crazy that day. I'm embarrassed to say it, but I was having a hard time focusing on our conversation," she said, motioning to the Mary, "you know, with the baby getting ready to come and all, and early, to our surprise." She let out a nervous laugh, and Adam could tell she was trying to compensate. He knew her too well.

"Of course," Colleen said with a smile. She let out a dramatic sigh and flicked her thin wrist theatrically, signaling her dismissal of any worry on Ellie's part. "Well, at least I know you didn't decide against it."

Ellie raised her eyebrows in question.

"Maybe I should start at the beginning?" Colleen asked.

"That'd be great." Ellie flashed an apologetic smile.

"Have you ever heard of Block Farms?"

Ellie shook her head.

"It's in Nazareth—a small farm, but great soil. John and I bought it ten years ago, and it's been good to us. It's one hundred percent organic, and three years ago, we started a small market on the property. Lately, we've considered doing some catering using what we harvest in the menu." Colleen paused and smiled. "That's where you come in. We'd like you to be our caterer."

Ellie wrinkled her forehead. "Me?"

"Oh come on, Ellie, I'm surprised you aren't already cooking professionally. The dinner you prepared at Kathy and Tom's was one of best meals I've ever had." Colleen held up her hand and proceeded to tick items off on her long, slender fingers as she spoke. "You're talented, you're bright, you're personable, and you have an impeccable eye for detail. All together, that's pretty valuable."

Tom was still chatting away . . . something about potential tourist activities on the Lehigh River, or the Lehigh Canal, or something. Adam nodded politely, but he was focused on the smile that had just spread across Ellie's face.

In response to Ellie's silence, Colleen continued pleading her case. "We have very loyal customers, and many of them have asked about catering."

Ellie shook her head. "Wouldn't you want someone with more experience? Or *any* experience for that matter?"

Colleen laughed as if Ellie had just made the most ridiculous comment. "We saw everything we needed to see. And taste."

Ellie glanced at Adam, and he looked away, hoping she didn't notice him listening. He knew what she was thinking—she was wondering if he'd approve.

"I think I may have my hands full for a while," Ellie said, looking toward Kathy and Mary who were still entertaining each other.

Colleen's face fell. "I hope you'll at least think about it. You're our first choice, but we'd like to start taking on small jobs by fall."

Just before noon, their guests had finally left, the discharge papers had been signed, and Adam and Ellie placed the last of their belongings into their overnight bags.

"I'll go tell the nurse we're all set," Adam said on his way across the room.

His cell phone rang from a table by the window where Ellie stood, softly bouncing Mary up and down in her arms.

"It's probably Marc," he called out to her. "Just tell him I'll call him right back."

He returned a minute later and found Ellie motionless at the window. She was still cradling Mary, but the color had drained from her face. For a moment, Adam worried she was ill—she almost looked unsteady on her feet.

She held up his cell phone.

"It was Jackie," she said.

CHAPTER 41

ELLIE

Ellie stood frozen in place, her legs heavy, almost as if they were concreted to the floor. Just a couple of days ago, Adam said he loved her. He said he wanted to try again. They talked about Ryan, but they hadn't talked about Jackie.

Okay, so they only talked briefly about Ryan, but at least they'd started the conversation. But Jackie had completely fallen from her radar. And now she felt like a fool.

Jackie.

Just the thought of the woman's name made her feel nauseous, made her question whether or not things could really be fixed between them.

And why is she still calling him anyway?

Adam's face fell, and the butterflies filling her stomach multiplied.

"I'm sorry about that," he said, walking toward her, taking his cell phone.

"What's going on, Adam? With the two of you?"

She didn't really want to know, but she had to ask.

Before he could answer, a nurse entered into room with a wheelchair, explaining she'd come to escort them out.

"I can walk just fine," Ellie said.

"Hospital procedure." The nurse, clearly not going anywhere, adjusted the footrests of the wheelchair.

Ellie gave Adam a sideways glance, and he shifted his attention to the floor. Then he gathered their things and left to retrieve the car, avoiding eye contact the entire time.

CHAPTER 42

ADAM

Adam walked through the parking lot, barely aware of the warm summer breeze gracing his face or the brilliant purple wildflowers landscaped through the hospital grounds. At the moment, his mind was set on one thing and one thing alone.

Jackie—and what to do about her.

It had been more than two months since their mid-afternoon rendezvous—an event he wished he could erase from time or at least from his memory.

⚔ ⚔

That morning, Adam had left the house consumed by an overwhelming sense of chaos. His mind raced with rage as he thought of Ellie's harsh temperament, their constant bitter exchanges, and his stomach churned with excitement and as he recalled his encounter with the Jackie in his office the night before.

I . . . love you. Ellie's words echoed in his mind, and he harrumphed out loud. Who was she kidding? And why did he care? That was what pissed him off most—that he still cared. That he still wanted to believe her. But he couldn't. Not anymore.

He arrived at work and confirmed that Nancy had cleared his afternoon schedule as he'd requested. He took a seat at his desk and tried to busy himself, but he couldn't focus on anything other than Jackie's note and the minutes that ticked by at an agonizingly slow pace.

Anxious, he fingered the white piece of paper, folding it and unfolding it before reading it again.

My place. Tomorrow. 2pm.

His heart sped, desire surging through every inch of him.

He left ten minutes earlier than he had to, unwilling and unable to stay at the office a second longer than necessary.

The thud of his heart galloped against his chest as he hopped up the final step in front of Jackie's white ranch house and rang the bell.

She opened the door, and Adam's breath caught, stuck in his throat. Black lace fell all the way to her ankles. The material, sheer and tight, hugged her curves and left little to the imagination. Her bare feet were tucked into black stiletto heels.

Without a word, she reached out for his hand and pulled him inside. Her kiss was intense. She pressed her chest against his, her hands roaming freely.

He inhaled her vanilla musk, and his senses skipped to the scent of Ellie's jasmine lotion. The unconscious betrayal was maddening. His mind clouded.

Jackie's fingers loosened the buttons of his dress shirt, his hands threaded through her hair. He continued to kiss her, pushing the thought away.

But his confrontation with Ellie resurfaced. *Maybe we could . . . you know . . . try?*

Jackie tugged at his shirt and pulled his arms free. It fell, a white heap on the floor.

"Adam," she whispered. Somehow, the sound of her voice was alarming, intimate, and out of context. He felt her breath against his ear, and goose bumps raced across his skin.

"I want you," Jackie murmured. She kissed his earlobe.

I . . . love you, Ellie said.

His mind whirled. He felt dizzy. Ellie was in his head. Jackie was pulling at his belt buckle. He was brimming with frustration, enough to shout, but he could barely find his voice.

He grabbed onto Jackie's shoulders, held her at a distance, while he attempted to compose himself. His pulse throbbed against his neck.

Jackie looked up, the desire in her eyes slowly softening, replaced by confusion.

Adam shook his head.

"Not again," she pleaded, her forehead creased with disappointment.

This was exactly what had happened after their "date." After she found his tattoo.

Including the day before in his office, this was the third time they'd been hijacked.

"I'm sorry." He bent over at the waist, breathing as if he'd just run a mile.

He tried to explain, but Jackie fell to pieces and melted into tears. Adam tried to console her, but before long she was moving toward him, trying to kiss him, trying to reignite what Ellie had managed to extinguish without even being present. He turned away.

"We're good together, you and me. Don't you see that?" Jackie pleaded.

"Maybe if it were another time, another place." He raked a hand through his hair. *God!* The physical chemistry was there, no doubt, but he couldn't be present—no matter how hard he tried. For that, he was pissed at Ellie. He was pissed at himself for his inability to push Ellie out. What kind of self-antagonistic bullshit was that anyway? "I just . . . can't, Jackie."

"Why?"

He looked at the disappointment in her eyes, in the lines of her face. She almost looked like a forlorn child. Like he'd crushed her.

"I'm sorry," he said, meaning it. "It's not you."

She crossed her arms over her chest, over the sheer black lace as if she'd suddenly regained some sense of modesty. "Then, what? Why?"

"Things with Ellie . . . they're complicated."

The hurt that filled Jackie's eyes transformed almost instantly to anger. She swung her hand, clearly intending to strike Adam's face, but he caught her wrist midair. Things were escalating at an unreasonable pace. Adam started for the front door. From across the room, a vase flew through the air, toward him. It hit the wooden doorframe just as he stepped outside, a gust of wind slapping at his skin. The glass exploded, tiny shards falling to the floor, a few tumbling onto the front step by his feet. The door ajar, he walked to his car, not looking back.

⇥ ⇤

Even though the level of Jackie's rage was admittedly alarming, Adam was guilt-ridden for leading her on.

She continued to call in the days to follow. At first, he tried to reason with her. He apologized and absorbed full blame, but that seemed to only encourage her persistence. It was clear she understood his weakness, and she was smooth in her efforts to attack it. With her, he was on a pedestal. She wasn't shy about her adoration for him.

Let me take care of you. Don't you know how special you are, how long I've waited to find someone like you? Let's go away, just for the weekend, see what happens, give it a chance, she'd said.

Days turned into weeks and his tone became stern, but then she'd cry and he'd feel guilty all over again. Finally, more than a month later, her anger shifted toward Ellie, and her behavior crossed a line he couldn't tolerate.

Everyone knows your wife is crazy. You deserve so much more. She'll never appreciate you the way I do. Never.

At that point, he gave up and simply stopped accepting or returning her calls.

⇥ ⇤

Still, he was plagued with guilt—guilt for leading Jackie on, guilt for betraying Ellie. Even though he'd stopped things before he did something he couldn't take back, he regretted the whole thing entirely. The arms of another woman were never a place he imagined he'd be.

Here he was, months later, and his conscience still wouldn't allow him reprieve. And neither would she.

CHAPTER 43

ELLIE

B y the time Ellie, the baby, and the nurse made it outside, Adam was waiting at the curb.

He drove the car away from the hospital, and one silent mile passed after another. All of the things that weren't being said threatened Ellie's air supply. She cracked her window open.

"Just tell me what to expect." She stared at the blurred landscape. "I need to know . . . if you still want to be with her."

Adam sighed, an agitated sigh. Even without looking at him, Ellie knew he was raking a hand through his hair. "Of course I don't want to be with her. And I never *was* with her. Not really. Not *like that.*"

Ellie's head swiveled on her shoulders, like a stretched rubber band. If he was going to lie, she wasn't going to make it easy. "What do you mean you were never *with* her? She saw your tattoo!"

It was Adam's turn to look alarmed. "How do you know that?"

"What difference does it make? I know! So, since she saw it, well, that can only mean one thing."

"Yah, she saw my tattoo, but . . . " Adam stopped at a red light, turned to look at Ellie. "I couldn't. I mean, we almost did but . . . " He shook his head and looked back at the road. "She wasn't you."

"*Almost?*" she asked.

Adam glanced at her sideways, his expression accusatory and guilt-ridden at the same time. "If you know about the tattoo, then you know she didn't just kiss me on the cheek."

His words were like a punch to the gut. The fact that Jackie's hands were on her husband at all made her dizzy with anger. And jealousy.

"How do I know you aren't lying?" she asked.

"Are you kidding me?"

"We said no more secrets."

"This is not a secret," he said, his teeth clenched.

Ellie's arms were crossed over her chest, her face flushed red.

"We're driving home with a newborn baby, remember," he said, "who isn't mine." The light turned green. The car lurched forward, faster than necessary.

Her body tensed. Ellie the hypocrite. That's what she was. The lump in her throat made it hurt to speak. "You're right."

"I'm sorry," he said, reaching out for her hand. "I shouldn't have said that."

She pulled away, and he put both hands back on the wheel. He cleared his throat, and the silence returned for a moment.

"How'd you know?" he asked. "About the tattoo?"

Ellie huffed. "Bonnie, how else?"

He rolled his eyes.

"You're not just saying nothing happened to make me feel better, right, Adam?" She searched his face for answers. "I don't want you to lie, thinking it will make things better."

Adam shifted in his seat and took control of the wheel with his left hand. He reached out and rested his right palm over Ellie's, above her knee, then threaded their fingers together. "It didn't happen, I swear. No more lies. No more secrets." He picked up her hand and kissed the backside of it. "Okay?"

She managed a half smile, but barely. "Okay."

"So about Ryan—"

"But why does she keep calling you?" Ellie asked, starting to speak at almost the same second he did.

"I don't know," he said.

"You don't *know*?" She raised an eyebrow. Adam glanced at her before returning his attention to the road.

"I told her not to call. That I loved you. She won't listen."

"She called the house."

"What?" Adam's face lengthened in surprise. "When?"

"The night I went into labor. Before you got home. I wondered how she even came across our home number."

Adam released her hand and gripped the wheel with both of his. "We've really made a mess of things," he said, staring straight ahead.

"What are we going to tell everyone about our . . . situation?" Ellie stiffened.

Adam glanced at her, his forehead scrunched up in question. "What situation?"

"You know, the one where I went off and had a baby that isn't yours," Ellie said.

He shook his head. "Don't you know yet that I don't care what everyone else thinks? Not anymore."

"Yeah right." Ellie tried to let out a laugh, but it was filled with resentment and came out sounding like something closer to a snort.

"It's no one's business," he said.

She focused hard on the view out her window, at everything and nothing at the same time.

Adam steered the car into their driveway and stopped. He swiveled his body toward hers and cupped her chin in his hand. "The only thing that matters to me is our family. Mary is a part of that. As far as everyone else is concerned, I don't care. So for now, let's just worry about us, okay?"

Ellie forced a smile, but it all sounded too simple.
Us.
. . . and Jackie.
. . . and Ryan.
Great plan.

CHAPTER 44

ADAM

Adam's phone rang. As he answered and slipped out of the room, he noticed a sideways glance from Ellie.

"Yah, I know it's hard to see in the dark, but what I'm asking is can you do it?" he asked, his frustration building, careful to keep his voice down. "No, she can't know anything. It has to be this way," he said, checking his watch. "We're leaving the house in about an hour for a doctor's appointment."

When he returned to the kitchen, he found Ellie making a bottle for Mary.

"Why do you sneak out of the room just about every time your phone rings lately?" she asked, not making eye contact.

"Just some problems at the office," he said, knowing the excuse was getting old, even to his ear.

"What kind of problems?"

"Top secret ones." He winked, opened the pantry, and popped a cookie into his mouth. He wasn't good at lying. Never had been.

"Top secret, eh?" She met his eyes with a merciless glare that made him squirm inside. "You're James Bond, now?"

"Don't you wish?" He flashed a sarcastic smile.

Ellie dropped a dirty dish into the sink with a clatter. "We said no more secrets, Adam."

Adam crossed the room and stood behind her, wrapping his arms around her waist. "Just trust me on this one, okay?"

"If this is about Jackie—"

"Don't you know it's not about Jackie?" he asked, spinning her around to face him. "I love you, El. Jackie is nothing to me." He tugged at her shirt and lifted it above her belly button. Her stomach was already returning to its normal, flatter shape. He rubbed his thumb over her tattoo. "This is where my heart is. Always has been."

She leaned into him, and he held her tight, but as he looked out the window behind her, he wondered how much longer he could keep this up.

CHAPTER 45

ELLIE

E llie woke to the sound of Mary crying. She forced her left eyelid open a crack, just enough to view the bedside clock—5:56 a.m.

Adam was peaceful beside her, his breath slow and steady. She rolled to her side, pushed the covers from her body, and pulled herself upright. Two weeks after the cesarean, the incision was still sore, but she was finally able to stand without feeling as if her insides were about to tumble to the floor. She shivered, the room cold compared to the warmth of her bed, and reached for a robe draped over a nearby chair. Just as she wrapped herself in it, her cell phone vibrated with an incoming text message. She picked it up from the bedside table and looked at the screen.

Suzanne. She always was an early riser. It was one of the only things they didn't have in common.

Ellie slipped the phone into the pocket of her robe and headed to check on Mary. She reached the nursery and found her daughter fussing as loud as a two-week-old could, her blood-red face scrunched up in frustration. Ellie picked her up and settled into a rocking chair.

Ellie wanted nothing more than to sleep, sleep deprivation the thing she struggled with most as a new mom, all three times. But this time around, when she was asleep, she didn't have to wonder why Jackie kept calling Adam. Or think about all of the phone calls he took in secret.

They vowed to work it out. He claimed to love her, but she couldn't shake the insecurity that gnawed at the back of her mind. She told herself it was just hormones. After all, Adam was finally the doting new father and husband he never was when Tommy and Lizzie were born. But there was something he was hiding from her, she was sure of it.

She even tried to check the call log of Adam's cell phone while he was in the shower last week. But the screen was locked with a password, and none of her guesses matched the magic four-digit code. Heat rose to her cheeks at the memory. Never before had she spied on her husband. Never had she felt the need to.

In an attempt to focus on something else—anything else—Ellie checked Suzanne's text message. She pumped the rocker with her leg, keeping a slow, steady rhythm.

CALL ME!

She pressed Suzanne's number.

"Did you hear yet?" Suzanne asked without so much as a hello.

The question set Ellie's nerves on edge. Her mind jumped back to Adam and Jackie. "Hear what?" she asked, wondering if she really wanted the answer. Her body stiffened, and Mary fussed in response. She repositioned Mary on her lap and tried to relax.

Suzanne sighed, loudly. "I was hoping to get to you first. Oh honey, I'm so sorry . . . "

Mary started crying, and Ellie tried to focus on what Suzanne was saying, missing some of her words and catching others.

" . . . sick . . . "

" . . . the hospital . . . "

" . . . and Bonnie . . . "

" . . . you . . . "

The last part, she heard clearly enough to think she must have misheard. She asked Suzanne to repeat herself and then realized she'd understood just fine the first time.

"She *what?*" Ellie shouted.

Mary began to wail, and Ellie tried to calm her, struggling to remain calm herself, as she listened more carefully to details about how the town gossip was trying to sabotage a life she was just beginning to piece back together.

CHAPTER 46

ADAM

It had been three weeks since Mary was born, and Adam still hadn't returned to work full time. He placed her in the stroller and watched her, amazed, wondering how he could ever love anything more.

"You gonna tell me where we're going yet?" Ellie appeared at their side in the mudroom, holding a bottle and a baby blanket.

"I told you—for a walk." Adam pulled one of Ellie's scarves out of his pocket. "And you'll need this."

She raised her eyebrows. "You're going through my drawers now? Should I be worried?"

He shrugged, a smile stretched across his face. "You should spin around."

"For what?"

"So I can blindfold you."

"You're not serious," Ellie said, her eyebrows still arched.

He nodded.

"No way," she said, shaking her head.

Adam sighed impatiently. "I don't suppose for once in your life you could just follow directions? " He crossed his arms over his chest, feet firmly planted. "Or, we can stand here all day."

Ellie opened her mouth to talk, but no words came out. Clearly, she was still not used his new take-charge attitude. Truthfully, he was only just getting the hang of it himself, but right now—watching Ellie stand speechless—was kind of fun.

Best of all, though, was the relief.

No more sneaking around or whispering on the phone.

Taking advantage of her silence, he spun her around, slid the scarf over her eyes, and knotted it at the back of her head.

She finally found her voice just as he finished. "Adam, really—"

"If you keep talking I'll have to gag you, too."

Shock struck her face instantly. Then a small smile crept across her lips. "If you're trying to turn me on, it's working."

Adam stopped abruptly, thankful that Ellie couldn't see the surprise etched in his expression.

This game *was* fun.

His eyes wandered over her white cotton shirt and floral printed skirt. She'd lost most of the baby weight, but her curves were still accentuated, her nipples poking at the thin material of her sleeveless top. His abdomen tightened in response, enough for him to consider putting this off. Instead, he cleared his throat and placed her hands on the stroller bar. As he leaned in beside her, he inhaled her sweet jasmine lotion.

"Use the stroller as your guide, and I'll help you steer," he said, silently reminding himself to stay focused when his lips brushed against her ear.

He led them out the back door, across a vast span of lawn. The brilliant summer sun was warm on their heads and a subtle breeze came and went every few seconds, bringing with it the scent of freshly cut grass. When they finally reached the far edge of their property, he stopped at the barn and took a moment to gaze at it. Never before had he completed something so significant in such a short period of time.

Shaded by the stroller canopy, lulled by the rocking movement of their walk, Mary had fallen asleep.

"Wait here," he whispered in Ellie's ear. "And don't touch that blindfold yet."

Surprising him with her unquestioning obedience, Ellie stood completely still while he opened the two large entry doors. The rusty hinges had been replaced, gone was the loud protest of screeching that used to greet him on every visit. He flipped on the lights. Though he'd seen it before, it was still enough to take his breath away.

Right, time to do this then.

He returned to Ellie and helped her maneuver the stroller up a gently sloped concrete incline to the inside of the barn. He slipped a finger through the knotted scarf and slid the makeshift blindfold from her face.

Ellie blinked a few times, her eyes adjusting to the light. They widened and filled with tears. She looked around, amazed, her expression even better than he'd hoped for.

As if in a trance, she walked across the wide planked pine floors. Spotting the inscription, she stopped abruptly and bent down to read it. When the cement countertops were poured, Adam had her initials inscribed into the edge of the longest stretch of workspace. She smiled. Still in awe, she moved to the four wall ovens, three refrigerators, and walk-in freezer—all commercial-grade stainless steel. She paused before continuing on, walking past the griddle and a stainless sink big enough to take a bath in. Finally, she stopped in front of the island where a large, rectangular white farmhouse porcelain sink was nestled into an enormous wooden chopping block. It was, without a doubt, the room's focal point.

Her eyes moved to sturdy wooden ceiling beams that showcased the grandeur of an old, strong building. They'd been cleaned up and left exposed. The walls had been painted a creamy tan, and assembled metal shelving was waiting to be filled.

Finally, Ellie's eyes returned to Adam's. "When?" she asked, her voice barely a whisper, as if it was lost in her throat.

"Right after Mary was born. I heard you and Colleen talking at the hospital, and I suppose I thought—"

"You never said anything." Ellie shook her head, her eyes the size of saucers. Adam didn't think he'd ever seen her like this, words out of her reach.

He crossed the room and placed his hands on her hips. "You do want to do it, don't you?"

A smile stretched across her face, and she nodded. "Yeah."

"That's good!" he said, relieved, looking around at the costly transformation, both of them laughing nervously. "Then do it, El." His voice, his eyes, became serious.

Ellie swallowed hard and stared at him, uncertainty blanketing her face.

"It's okay with me, and the kids will be fine, if that's what you're thinking. You'll be right here, only steps from the house."

"I can't believe you did all of this . . . for me."

"I would do anything for you." Adam planted a kiss on her forehead. "I love you."

She swung her arms around his neck and rested her cheek on his shoulder. Adam allowed himself to drift into the comfort of her heart beating against his chest.

It took Ellie a few minutes to recover from her stupefied state, but when she did, they thoroughly checked out the farm kitchen properly, opening every appliance, turning things on and off. When Ellie opened the door to the second refrigerator, she hesitated. She pulled out the sole content—a bottle of champagne—and turned to Adam. He smiled and took two glasses from a cabinet.

"You really are James Bond," she said.

He laughed. "I'm fairly certain you need to be good at sneaking around to qualify as a secret agent. Hiding all of those phone calls from you wasn't easy or fun."

"I'd say you did pretty well. Even though I'm not sure how I didn't find out."

"Careful scheduling, I suppose," he said, pouring a glass and handing it to her. "They even did some of the work in the dark."

Ellie's eyebrow shot up. "The dark?"

"Yah, all the stuff that didn't make noise, like the painting ... things like that. It probably helped, too, that you've been too tired to be as alert as you'd normally be." He raised his glass to her. "Here's to you. Cheers."

She touched her glass to his and took a sip. The refrigerator was behind her. She leaned back, sliding against it, sinking down until she was seated on the floor. Adam picked up the bottle and joined her, setting it on the shiny, varnished pine floor.

"Maybe I should've brought cheese and crackers, too," he said. "James Bond probably would've done that."

She laughed. "I think you did enough."

He watched her eyes scan the room.

"This reminds me of that time when you went out to get caviar and brought me popcorn instead, do you remember that?" she asked.

"You're still not good at pretending," he said, laughing. "The champagne's the real stuff this time. Can't fault me for that." He took a sip.

"I don't fault you for anything," she said quietly, the lines on her face now serious.

"Hey," he said, reaching out, lifting her chin toward him.

"Seventeen years ago, did you ever think we'd be here—where we are now?" she asked.

"I suppose I thought we'd be together. And we are. That's all that matters." He took her hand and dropped a light kiss on the back of it.

Her eyes moved to Mary, still asleep in the stroller, then to the floor, and he knew what she was thinking.

"I noticed when we were at Dr. Van Linden's last week you didn't say anything about me not being the . . . " He cleared his throat. "You didn't mention that I wasn't the father."

"I couldn't."

"When are you going to call Ryan?"

She didn't have to answer, because when she looked up her eyes spoke for her.

"Ellie," Adam said, "we've talked about this."

"He's just so . . . not father material, Adam. I told you the story about the coffee shop."

Adam's eyes dropped before he lifted his glass and drank from it, this time a mouthful rather than a sip. "You *have* to tell him. You know you do. And if you don't do it soon, I will."

CHAPTER 47

ELLIE

"What's up?" Suzanne sounded distracted at the other end of the telephone.

"I need a favor. It's about Ryan," Ellie said, nerves brewing in her stomach.

"Ryan who?"

Ellie could hear papers shuffling in the background.

"Ryan the UPS driver, father-of-my-baby-Ryan."

A sudden silence told her she'd earned Suzanne's full attention.

"Did something happen?"

"Actually, I'm fine with nothing happening. Adam, on the other hand, is insisting I call him. He's threatening to do it himself."

Suzanne sighed. "You know you need to."

Ellie squeezed the bridge of her nose. "Yeah, well, that brings me to the second problem. I accidentally dropped my phone in the toilet and lost all my contact information. I need Ryan's number."

"You're new iPhone?"

"I'm a mother of three with a baby and a new business. Call it a casualty of multitasking."

Suzanne laughed. "Better get to some catering jobs then. That one's gonna cost ya."

"What will it cost me to get Ryan's number?"

"From me?" Suzanne huffed. "As if I carry Ryan's number in my phone! No ma'am. You're all alone on that one."

"Ha-ha," Ellie said sarcastically. "You still see him. Next time he comes in to drop off a package, can you just ask him for me?"

"I can't—"

"Pleeeaaasse?"

"Listen ... no can do. They took Ryan off our route. We have a new guy."

"What? No!"

"What? Yes!" Suzanne mocked Ellie's horror.

"Does he still work for UPS?"

"How am *I* supposed to know?"

"Perfect," Ellie said, wondering if maybe it *was* kind of perfect.

"Maybe you could visit the coffee shop and look for some of his other girlfriends."

"Very funny."

"You do know where he lives."

"Even less funny."

She hung up the phone and tried to convince herself she tried, the effort to contact Ryan good enough.

CHAPTER 48

ADAM

A dam tapped at his keyboard, paused, and then deleted the entire paragraph he'd just finished typing. It was his first day back at work in more than a month. He couldn't focus, his thoughts drifting back to Ellie. It had been a little less than a week since she started working in the farm kitchen. She seemed so happy, and that made him happy. But their newfound happiness was coupled with a sadness that filled him with angst.

Mary. It was so complicated, the way he felt about her.

And the "other father."

He wondered if Ellie had *really* tried to contact Ryan yet, like she said she had. It scared him to death, all of it, thoughts swirling around in his head, making him crazy.

He woke up, just last night, his shirt soaked with sweat after another nightmare. The father—this Ryan—actually stole Mary. Took off to another state or another country. Who could tell, because they never could find them, even after years of searching? A few days ago he dreamt the father demanded money from them. They were stuck in endless years of court proceedings. Last week, he woke up with a vision of an older, teenage Mary. Her nails were painted black, black lipstick and no smile, her body pierced in every unimaginable place. She never spoke except to curse, and she rarely came out of her room except to jump into a battered car with the next random boy.

The unknown—it was killing him. He'd considered telling Ellie, but she had enough to deal with. And as much as he worried about Mary, no matter how much love and affection he lavished on her, deep down he felt he had no right to govern her.

The one thing he did know—that he wasn't her father—was a fact wedged at the center of his heart.

He pulled at the tie knotted around his neck and considered taking an early lunch, desperate for fresh air. But before he had a chance to stand, his phone rang.

Sam.

A few minutes later, with board-related hospital issues out of the way, Adam was about to hang up, but Sam fell silent on the other end of the phone.

"Sam?" Adam asked.

"I want you to know how sorry I am about this thing with Bonnie," Sam said. "I've talked with Tom, and we're going to ask her to resign from the board."

Adam's cheeks flushed, his mind immediately on her knowledge of his tattoo—and worse, how she came to learn about it.

"Sam, I'm . . . " He was trying to decide how to respond, embarrassed, his personal life tangled with hospital business, but Sam continued.

"It's reprehensible for a board member of ours to take someone's illness and turn it into a personal agenda."

"Illness?" Adam asked, scrunching his forehead, trying and failing to piece their conversation together.

"We all know how Bonnie can be, but this time she's gone too far," Sam continued as if he didn't hear Adam's question.

Adam noticed an unusual tone in Sam's voice. Anger? Alarm?

"How's Ellie holding up by the way?" Sam asked.

"Ellie?" Adam, confused at the change of topic, wondered if he'd missed part of what Sam was saying in his attempt to understand what they were talking about in the first place.

"I hope this didn't hurt her new business," Sam added.

"Sam, forgive me, but *what* are you talking about?"

CHAPTER 49
ELLIE

E llie stood in the farm kitchen washing tomatoes and moving her hips to the tune of Madonna, the eighties channel playing through the sound system Adam had installed.

True to his word, Adam arrived at lunchtime—early, to her surprise. As soon as he appeared in the doorway, her eyes landed on him, drinking in the features that first attracted her to him two decades ago—his dark hair neatly combed away from his clean-shaved face, bright blue eyes shining above a blue silk tie that hung loosely around his neck, his top shirt button undone. It was the first time he'd worn a suit in ages. He looked good. Better than good.

He strode through the room, straight toward Ellie, and bent down, placing a soft kiss on her cheek. When he pulled away, she grabbed his tie and reeled him back for a deeper kiss.

"Done for the day?" she asked, her finger still looped around the partially undone tie.

"I wish," he said, raking a hand through his hair.

She slid an arm around his waist. "We could both play hooky this afternoon?" She flashed a mischievous grin, but Adam pecked her on the cheek and took a step back.

Her body stung with rejection. She told herself not to be silly.

Adam moved toward the baby swing a few feet away. Ellie watched him kiss the top of Mary's soft head. She smiled, amazed at the depth of his love for a child he didn't father. At the same time, guilt coursed through her veins.

"There's something we need to talk about," he said, placing his keys and phone on the countertop. "Be back in a sec."

He disappeared around the corner toward a private area in the back of the barn, and she was instantly filled with a sense of dread, her body stiff.

Talk about what?

She tried to redirect her attention back to the cutting board in front of her when Adam's cell phone buzzed against the countertop. She glanced at the screen: *Jackie.*

She froze. Her hand, gripping a chopping knife, was suspended in mid-air above a head of cabbage. Angry, she considered bringing the knife down, square on top of the phone. It stopped moving, the call sent to voice mail.

Just then, Bonnie Singleton walked in through the opened door, huffing for air and pausing in her usual dramatic way.

Great.

Ellie swiftly lowered the knife, severing the cabbage in half. She forced a smile.

"Ellie dear, so nice to see you. I heard you had a great little thing goin' on over here, and I just had to come an' see for myself. Heard it was all because of my brilliant plan to have you host a little ol' dinner for the hospital ball. Who'd have known you'd end up with all this because of me?"

Yeah, right.

Her plump cheeks were rosy, her lipstick-lined mouth pulled upward into a broad, smug smile. Ellie thought about slapping it off, especially after she tried to sabotage her.

Adam emerged from the back and paused mid-step. A flash of irritation crossed his face.

"Bonnie," he said, "what a surprise. Come to order some of Ellie's delicious food?" He moved to Ellie's side and slipped a hand around her waist.

The protective gesture warmed Ellie, made her smile.

"Well hello, Adam," Bonnie said, making a tisk-tisk sound. "I missed you at the last hospital board meetin'. I wanted to thank you again for being a bachelor for us. Who knew you had such a naughty side?" She winked. "You're quite a mysterious man."

Ellie's body tensed, and Adam's hand tightened around her waist.

"Actually, Bonnie," he said, "what you see is pretty much what you get. On the other hand, your friend Jackie has a tiny bit of Jekyll-and-Hyde syndrome going on, and"—he pointed a finger in her direction—"I'd be willing to bet you do, too."

Bonnie's face hardened, like stone, her fake smile stuck in place.

"I'll tell you what," Adam said, picking up a box of scones Ellie made yesterday and walking toward Bonnie. He shoved it gently toward her chest until she was forced to place her hands under the package. "Take these as a parting gift. You can put them out at your store and share them with your customers. While you're at it, you could invite Jackie over and share one with her, remind her that I'm good at keeping my promises. I just told her yesterday that if she called me again I'd contact an attorney and have harassment charges filed."

Wide-eyed, Ellie dropped the knife in her hand, nearly cutting herself. It clattered against the counter. Bonnie stood holding the box of scones, still as a tree trunk, eyes threatening to pop out of her head.

"I could do the same for you if you'd like to keep interfering with our personal lives," Adam continued. Mary began to fuss, and Adam picked her up. "By the way, have you met our new daughter, Mary? I suppose your congratulations card must still be in the mail, because we haven't received it yet." He shushed her before turning back toward Bonnie, as if he'd forgotten one last thing. "Oh, and maybe you ought to take some antacids before eating those scones. After all, you never know." He winked. "Ellie may've made that particular box just for you." His lips curled into an uncharacteristically sarcastic smile.

Ellie stood, frozen in disbelief.

Bonnie looked on, her face beet red. She huffed, and snorted, and stomped out of the farm kitchen. Glass jars nearest the entrance rattled against metal shelves as she went.

"Wow." Ellie stared at Adam, overcome with shock and admiration. "I can't believe you just did that."

"I should've done it a long time ago." He glared at the door as if to silently challenge Bonnie to return through it. When she didn't, Adam settled Mary into her swing with a pacifier and a small purple plush toy.

He stood for a few seconds, staring out the window, his back to Ellie.

"Anyway, that's what I wanted to talk about," he said. "Why didn't you tell me?"

She knew what he was referring to. Of course she knew. It was obvious just now in his go-round with Bonnie.

Suzanne called to tell Ellie about her Judas a few weeks ago. At first, she was alarmed, not at the treachery itself, but at the insinuation that accompanied it. But once she'd calmed down, she was able to rationalize things. Bonnie wasn't exactly the most credible person in town. She was one of those people you had to deal with, even if you didn't want to. And she was on the hospital board with Adam, so there was bound to be a certain level of social interaction.

The bottom line, Ellie had decided, was that she refused to be pushed around by a nervy town crier who owned a dress shop but desperately needed a lesson in style and makeup application.

Besides, her business hadn't been affected, and she didn't want to bother Adam with anything that would make their life any more complicated and stressful than it already was.

The only questions now were what exactly did Adam *think* he knew, and how did he learn about any of it in the first place?

CHAPTER 50

ADAM

"Tell you what?" Ellie asked.

He turned to face her. Disbelief, anger, and a fresh sense of betrayal rose from the pit of his stomach. "No more secrets. That's what we said. I thought we were past this."

"Past this?" she asked. "Your girlfriend was just calling you, by the way. When you stepped into the back." Ellie slammed her palms on top of the counter and leaned against it.

"Don't deflect," Adam said, his eyes narrowing on her.

"It's Bonnie," Ellie said. "No one takes her seriously."

"The woman tried to ruin your new career. She claimed the food at your dinner party made people sick. Sick enough to be in the hospital!"

That's what Sam had been going on about. Right after Ellie's dinner at Tom and Kathy's house, there was an outbreak of a seriously painful stomach virus. Kathy was the first to get sick. Tom took her to the emergency room, and they bumped into Bonnie, who happened to have just finished with a fundraising meeting upstairs. The next day she called to check on Kathy and started a rumor that the sickness had begun because of a "rancid" ingredient Ellie had used in the preparation of dinner that night.

Of course, Tom and Kathy knew Bonnie too well to get caught up in her gossip. They also knew Ellie too well to believe it. But within a couple of days, Bonnie had broadcast the news to everyone who'd walked into her shop.

"I'm on the hospital board for Christ's sake. You don't suppose it might be good for me to hear this from you instead of from Sam?" Adam finished.

Ellie shot up an eyebrow. "Is that what this is about? Your pride is hurt again? Or is it your public image?"

"We're supposed to be a team," he said, practically shouting.

"This is a goddamn rollercoaster ride, Adam," she said, massaging her temples.

Adam walked toward her, swiftly closing the gap between them. Once he was directly in front of her, his hand moved to the back of her head, his fingers threading a fistful of hair into his palm. He pulled her into his arms with a force that made her gasp in surprise. Full of frustration, he held her there and stared into her eyes—only inches away from his—searching for a way to make her understand.

Ellie was totally still, her eyes trying to communicate just as silently as his, only he didn't know what they were saying. Finally, her eyelids began to flutter, and she attempted to move toward him. But he pulled at the back of her hair, keeping her at a distance. Her eyes popped open and revealed an overwhelming sadness that made Adam's heart ache under his chest.

Finally, he pushed his lips to hers—hard and passionate—his hand still grasping her hair, holding her tight. At first, her body was stiff. He could tell she was startled. Maybe even confused. But she reciprocated. Eventually, their kisses became soft, tender, but he wasn't ready to let go. He pressed into her again, his mouth assaulting hers, desperate to show his strength, his love, his commitment. All of the things he couldn't seem to say well enough for her to understand.

When he finally released her, Ellie swayed on her feet.

"Why didn't you tell me?" he asked again.

"You don't normally do well with confrontation," she said, raising a hand to her lips, now swollen, a brilliant red. "Although after your showdown with Bonnie this morning—and me just now—I'm beginning to wonder."

"Call this the new and improved version of your husband," Adam said, trying to lighten the mood, wondering if he'd come on *too* strong.

Ellie rested a shaky hand on the counter. "I just . . . didn't want to bother you. There's so much other stuff going on and—"

"This may be a rollercoaster, El, but it's our rollercoaster." Adam placed his left hand over hers on the counter and stroked her cheek with his right thumb. "If you're hurting or unhappy, I want to know. I want to help. I promise to be there for you. But I need you to trust me enough to let me in."

CHAPTER 51
ELLIE

An orange glow from the late afternoon sun filtered in through transom windows on the west side of the farm kitchen. Mary had been fed and changed numerous times, and Ellie had managed to fill two private catering orders in spite of the drama brought on by Bonnie and Adam a couple of hours ago.

She pulled a chocolate cake she baked yesterday from the freezer and placed it on the counter. Mary cooed at her from a baby swing while she dipped a spatula in a fresh batch of cream cheese icing, gliding it easily over the cake, lost in the mindless motion.

A rumbling noise outside forced her to look up. In her peripheral vision, a glimpse of a shadow moved against sunlight streaming in through the door. Her hand stopped, mid stroke, her heartbeat doing the same.

There, entering the farm kitchen, pushing a dolly stacked with boxes, was Ryan, wearing a brown UPS uniform.

"Oh hey," he said, flashing his infamous white smile. The space behind his eyes, though, still looked blank, just as she'd remembered.

"Hey," she said in return, trying to recover from the shock of seeing him unexpectedly.

He stopped. The dolly and boxes stood in front of him. "Where do you want me to put these?"

"Oh . . . um . . . right over here." She dropped the spatula and ambled toward the walk-in freezers on the wall to her left, nearly tripping over her own two feet on the way.

Ryan finished transferring the boxes and glanced up with another smile. Mary made a loud cooing sound and caught his attention.

"Heyyy, you had the baby," he said, nodding his head in that same absentminded way he had at the coffee shop.

Ellie wondered fleetingly if he'd lost too many brain cells over the years. Maybe he did too many drugs. A brief wave of panic washed over her, bringing with it a vision of an older Mary, carrying the same vacant expression, wondering if she could've inherited some of his degeneration. Ellie shook her head, trying to rid herself of the thought.

Focus.

You have to tell him.

"Ryan, about the baby . . . " Nervous, Ellie wiped her hands against her apron.

"She's cute," he said. "Congratulations on that, dude."

"Thanks, dude," Ellie said, raising her eyebrows and forcing a smile. She tried to think of a way to relate to him, to speak his language. "I think she may have inherited that cuteness from her father, actually," she said, recalling Ryan's fondness for flattery.

"Uh-huh." Ryan nodded methodically, a smile still settled on his face.

Ellie rifled through the drawers and pulled out a large metal spatula. "See?" She held it up in front of his face. "Cute like her dad."

Ryan's eyebrows and forehead crinkled. Then his smile slowly faded, replaced by a puckered look of confusion.

"She's yours, Ryan. That's what I wanted to tell you that day in the coffee shop." She lowered the spatula. "I just haven't been able to figure out how to say it."

He flinched, as if someone had just slapped him across the face. Then he frowned.

"Dude, *that*"—he pointed at Mary, suddenly looking repulsed—"*that* is not *my* baby."

Ellie sighed and rested her hand on the countertop, leaning on it for support.

"Look Ryan, I'm not asking you for anything. That's not what this is about. I just thought you should know. I'll raise the baby, and you don't need to be involved."

Ryan took two steps back and tripped over the dolly he used to deliver the boxes. He stumbled, then recovered, becoming steady on his feet again just as he was about to fall to the floor.

"You're crazy, lady. I don't know what kind of sick joke this is, but that's not my baby!"

"Okay, so I *imagined* that night. You know, the one that happened last December?" Ellie's patience was wearing thin.

"You mean the night when you came onto me at the bar? And then when I took you home—like you *asked* me to—you passed out on me? *That* night?"

"Wait," Ellie shook her head. "What?" She blinked and stared at Ryan, her eyes wide with disbelief. "You mean we didn't . . . ? This isn't . . . ?"

Ryan shook his head furiously. "No dude!" He said, his eyes wide, too, but with fear. "No way!"

"Then how did I end up in your bed?" Ellie crossed her arms.

"What was I supposed to do with you?" he asked. Then his eyes lit up with a thought, and he held a finger to his chest. "*I* was a nice guy." He nodded, pleased with himself, and smiled again. "I even gave you the extra blankets."

How chivalrous.

"*Nothing* happened?" Ellie asked. "Nothing at all?" The conversation between them seemed to have decelerated to slow motion. Everything around her—the sound of Ryan's voice, the echo of hers, every physical movement between them—was sluggish and magnified, as if they were in a tunnel.

"Nothing," Ryan insisted. "Honestly, I spent some time wishing it had." He smiled. "I mean, who doesn't want to be with this?" He pointed to his chest again. "And dude, I use protection anyway. You should, too." He shook his head and exhaled, long and slow, leaning on the dolly that was now in front of him.

Ellie stood completely still for a long moment, allowing it to sink in. She thought about waking up in Ryan's bed, fully clothed except for her panties on the bathroom floor. She thought about finding Ryan asleep on the other side of the bed, not curled around her, not even partially in her space. No wonder she couldn't remember. And Adam had only moved out the month before. Mary, born earlier than expected.

Her shoulders and her chest felt lighter. Her head felt clearer.
Adam.
The baby is Adam's!

She couldn't decide if she should laugh or cry. Her chest wanted to open up so her heart could happily float away. She hopped the few steps it took to reach Ryan and grabbed onto his cheeks with both of her hands. Without thinking, she planted a huge kiss smack in the middle of his lips. When she pulled away, he looked like he might pass out.

"Thank you for not having sex with me!" she said, a smile digging high into her cheeks.

CHAPTER 52

ADAM

At exactly 5:30 p.m., Adam pulled into the garage and parked the car. He collected the papers from the passenger seat and shoved them into a plastic grocery bag.

"Hey," he said, walking into the kitchen. He stopped to plant a kiss on Ellie's forehead before setting the groceries on the counter.

"You're early," she said.

"New and improved, remember?" He winked, immediately regretting the comment. The nervous edge to her voice made him wonder if she was upset with him for coming on so strong earlier at the farm kitchen.

Tommy and Lizzie were at the table, eating chicken fingers and fries. He kissed each of them hello and popped a bite from Tommy's plate into his mouth.

"Why are the kids eating already?"

"I have a special dinner for us tonight."

"Oh?" He raised an eyebrow.

"Lasagna," she said, a coy look settled on her face.

Adam smiled. "My favorite."

"I know," she said, meeting his eyes, just for a moment. "The kids won't eat it, so I thought I'd get their dinner out of the way. It's

cooking in the farm kitchen." In the middle of unloading the groceries, Ellie plucked the papers from the plastic bag. "What's this?"

"Why didn't you make the lasagna in here?" Adam asked, ig-
noring her question and pouring a glass of lemonade.

Ellie scanned the papers. "I already had the ingredients out
there."

A knowing smile spread across Adam's face, his pride in finishing the farm kitchen as obvious as her love for it. She'd been cooking more and more out there rather than in the house, even when
she was only making dinner for the four of them. She beamed
whenever she spoke about it. Just last night she told him she would
live in there if she could.

"Adam?" she asked, reading the papers. Really reading them.

"Mmm," he said, finishing his glass of lemonade.

Ellie looked up, her face struck with surprise.

He shrugged. "I wasn't kidding." True to his word, Adam had
met with his attorney after lunch and filed harassment charges
against Jackie. "That last phone call earlier today was about
enough."

CHAPTER 53

ELLIE

Ellie half walked, half skipped the two steps it took her to reach Adam and flung her arms around his neck. She smiled and pulled him close for a kiss, soft, intimate, sexy. Lizzie squealed in protest from the table, no doubt hiding her eyes beneath her tiny pudgy hands, but Ellie didn't care. Adam wasn't just avoiding Jackie, he was pushing back hard. She couldn't help being swept up in the chivalry of it all.

She used to count on Adam to be late. That night, she sent him to the store for stuff she didn't really need just to keep him away from the house a little longer so she could execute her plan, and he was still early. She was practically bursting at the seams. She wanted so badly to tell him the news about Mary, but she'd planned the night too carefully to mess it up.

Slowly, she released him. He reached out for her playfully, his eyes locked on hers, but she just smiled as she backed away. She finished the dishes and cleaned up after the kids, staying busy, silently reminding herself to stay on task.

Two hours later, the kids were bathed, dressed in their pajamas, and Lizzie was put into bed—for the third time. Ellie slipped into Tommy's room and found him already asleep. On her way back down the hall, she bumped into Adam. Or, rather, he bumped into her—on purpose.

"Go take a shower," she said.

"You trying to get rid of me?"

"'Course not." She pulled at the blue silk tie, still loose around Adam's neck. "Why aren't you out of this thing yet, anyway?"

"I suppose you could help with that," he said, pulling closer. His lips met hers, his kiss making her dizzy.

Stay focused.

She pulled away. "Meet you downstairs," she said, untangling herself from his hands.

"Have I told you you're getting boring in your old age?" he asked.

She started toward the staircase. "Hardly." She turned to wink at him, but kept going before she could change her mind.

She moved the lasagna, salad, and bread into the dining room. She slipped off her apron and smoothed down the fabric of a low-cut black dress. She crossed the room, acutely aware of the cotton brushing against her skin, and lowered the lights. Then she set a match to two candles.

A minute later, Adam appeared in the doorway. "Wow," he said. "What's the special occasion?" Candlelight danced on his face. Ellie wanted to reach out and touch it. Instead, she smiled and motioned for him to take a seat.

He did.

"You got the good stuff out," Adam said, plucking the bottle of vintage red wine from the center of the table. He uncorked it, poured two glasses, and held one out for Ellie. When she tried to take it, his grasp remained on the glass a few seconds longer than necessary. His eyes held hers, a cryptic trance, until she finally forced herself to look away. Heat prickled up her neck, and her heart skipped.

They remained silent as Ellie dished out the food. Adam glanced at her in between every bite, clearly suspicious. She was surprised at his ability to play this game without pressing her for more information, the tension between them palpable.

Finally, Ellie was the one who couldn't stand it any longer. "I spoke to Ryan today."

Adam's hand was midair, a fork full of lasagna on its way to his mouth. He froze, and the fork came down onto his plate with a clank.

She flinched. *Maybe not the best way to have broached the subject.*

He didn't speak. Tension visibly wound through his body like a balloon filling with water.

This wasn't her intent. Her mind scrambled for what to do next.

She walked to the other side of the table and took a seat on his lap. Lifting his wine glass, she inhaled the dry, peppery aroma. Then she ran her finger around the edge, dipped it into the red liquid, and pressed her finger to Adam's lips before leaning in for a kiss. He was receptive, but his posture remained defensive. She pulled away and stared into his eyes, blue and strong. She still couldn't imagine not wanting to see them every day.

"It seems I've made a mistake," she said. "Nothing physical ever happened between me and Ryan. Mary is yours."

Adam's forehead wrinkled in confusion. His eyes narrowed. "What?"

"I know." She ran her fingers through the hair above his right ear. "I couldn't believe it either. Apparently I was wasted, and Ryan gave me a place to sober up. That's it. Nothing more."

Adam studied her, his expression doubtful. "Ellie . . . " He gently pushed her off of his lap, so she was standing. "I know you don't want to tell him but—"

"Adam, I told him. I saw him today."

"We said no more secrets. No more lies."

He doesn't believe me? This, she wasn't expecting. This was what their relationship had come to—one where Adam questioned her sincerity? Panic bubbled at her core, but she pushed it down.

"I'm not lying! He showed up at the farm kitchen with UPS packages. I told him. And it's true."

She recounted the details of her conversation with Ryan, and Adam stared at his food. He didn't move for what felt like an eternity while Ellie stood, waiting. Remembering the slow-motion feeling of earlier today, she remained quiet, allowing him to process the information. When he finally looked up, candlelight reflected against tears swelling in his eyes.

"That night at the hospital . . . I remember thinking Mary was too big to be a preemie. Dr. Van Linden was telling me something when I mentioned her weight, but I wasn't listening." He looked at Ellie, his expression hopeful.

She smiled and nodded.

Adam's face lengthened again. "But are you sure, El, because I couldn't handle . . . "

She nodded, fighting back her own tears. "She's yours Adam."

Adam stood, removed the wine glass from her hand, and set it down. He cupped her face in his hands and moved his thumb over her cheekbone, his fingers in her hair. "I love you, Ellen Thomas." He kissed her until all that was left of her was a pile of nerves. Finally, he released her. Then he bent down, slipped an arm under her knees, and lifted her off her feet. She squealed, surprised. Adam maneuvered his way out of the dining room. He carried her up the stairs and deposited her onto their bed. In an instant, he was above her, hovering, his eyes piercing her.

They both paused, staring at each other. The intense intimacy radiating between them was something Ellie had never felt before. Not like this. Not in the beginning. Not even after almost twenty years. Adam was still Adam, and she was still Ellie. They were different, yet they were the same. She realized she'd never loved him or cherished what they had together more than she did at that moment.

She reached up and unbuttoned his striped cotton shirt. His hands moved under her dress, along the smooth skin of her legs. He pressed into her, and she pulled at the button on his jeans and then . . .

Mary began to wail.

They both fell onto the bed, each of them only half undressed, breathless.

"Your turn," they both said in unison.

PART VII

Till Death Do Us Part

EPILOGUE

The September sky is blue, dotted with puffy white clouds, much like the day Adam and I were married nineteen years ago. I came to the farm kitchen, to verify that every last bit of food made its way to the main house. Of course, I already knew it had. Maybe I just wanted quiet, in my favorite place, time to reflect on these last two years.

A small office, storage room, bathroom, and play area for Mary were tucked at the back of the barn. That's where I stand now, staring at an eight-foot-tall mirror propped up against a wall, checking my reflection one last time—my hair is pulled up loosely on top of my head, relaxed curls spilling out around my neck and shoulders, just above the v-shaped neckline of my white dress. The soft, cotton material hugs my upper body like a glove, gathers together at the waistline, floats dreamily to my feet. Painted toes peek up at me from gold beaded sandals. Lost in thought, I finger the gold cuff bracelet on my right wrist. Adam gave it to me last night. An anniversary present. The things we've been though, where we're at now, it's almost too much to process today. I take a deep breath, filling my lungs, my chest, with oxygen, with pride, with love.

A clock ticks on the wall, against the silence, reminding me to keep moving. As I step out of the barn, a warm breeze pushes through the air, blowing against my dress, causing the bottom hem to soar this way and that. I pass by Tommy and Bobby playing catch with a baseball, their unrestrained laughter echoing through our yard.

I enter the house through the kitchen and bend down, dropping a kiss on Mary's head where she's seated in a highchair, eating dry bits of cereal strewn across a tray, a snack I hope will keep her occupied a while longer. Chasing her around these days is tiring, even when there's nothing else going on. And today there's a lot going on.

Suzanne is at the stove, stirring a pot of marinara. "Better steer clear of me in that white number you're wearing," she says, glancing up with a smile. "You look beautiful by the way."

"Thanks," I say, meeting her eyes, smiling.

Colleen is slicing cheese at the counter. She stops and takes a sip of her wine. "You do. And you really didn't need to prepare the food today, Ellie. I tried to tell you we'd take care of it."

"Adam loves my cooking. I couldn't have anyone else take over today." I wave my hand dismissively. "Besides, I did most of it ahead of time, and with all the food coming from you and John it was easy. Thanks again by the way, even though you really didn't have to do that."

"Are you kidding?" Colleen says, "business has exploded since you started catering—in a little more than a year we've almost tripled our numbers."

I glance at a bulletin board on the wall, overflowing with messages, each a potential catering job. It feels good to do something productive, other than housework, other than the kids. This last year, I've often found myself overwhelmed with gratitude that I was able to find not just one, but two careers I love.

I blink back the tears threatening to ruin my mascara and wonder if I should've purchased an entire set of waterproof makeup just for today. At the sink, I busy myself by filling a pot of water. The windows are partially opened. I glance out at the backyard, where Adam is talking to Sam, Tom, John, and Dan. He looks good, in a white linen shirt and tan pants.

Lizzie is running through the lawn, screaming with delight. Buster is barking at nothing in particular. Or maybe at Dr. Van Linden, who just arrived. He walks toward Adam, a bottle of wine in his hand.

Further in the distance, Cindy and Kathy are sipping from wine glasses, talking, thoughtful expressions stamped on their faces. Then there's Tommy and Bobby, playing catch. They've become a big part of our lives, Adam somehow discovering an inner peace through Bobby's journey.

Water spills over the edge of the pot, onto my arm, forcing my attention back to the kitchen. I shut off the faucet and reach for a towel.

Then the front door slams shut, and I jump, distracted. Young footsteps gallop noisily through the house until a three-foot, rosy-cheeked girl wearing pigtails stops at my feet. A box, neatly wrapped in white paper, is in her hand.

"This is for you," Mia says, holding it out toward me.

"For me?" I hold a hand to my chest, theatrically, making her smile.

She nods enthusiastically, her yellow pigtails bouncing up and down. Her unchecked joy, her sweet expression, is enough to melt my heart.

"Why thank you," I say, bending down to accept the package. I lean in, toward Mia's ear, and whisper, "Don't tell, but I think Lizzie's outside looking for someone to play with."

Mia scampers away just as Toni and Marc walk into the kitchen. Toni, looking tired, immediately pulls a wine glass from the cabinet.

"How are you holding up?" I ask.

"I forgot what five was like." Toni offers a smile, pouring herself a glass of wine.

"Yeah, but she's great," Marc says, winking at Toni. He waves hello to Suzanne and Colleen then heads outside to greet Adam. I smile, relieved to see the sparkle back in his eyes.

Toni slides onto a barstool and takes a sip of wine. She looks out the window, watching Bobby and Tommy, who have moved onto a soccer ball. "We owe it all to Bobby, you know," she says, motioning toward the window. "To Cindy and Dan. For teaching us that love is so much more than . . . than what we thought it was."

I glance at the boys then back at Toni and nod in agreement.

"Not that anyone could ever replace John—that could never happen—but I thank God every day that we had the courage to adopt Mia," Toni says.

"I'm sure she does, too," I say, smiling. "No doubt."

An hour later, I'm standing at the back of the house, chest expanded, heart pounding. I'm staring at my family. They're standing near the arbor toward the edge of our lawn. Adam is holding Mary in his arms. She's wearing a lilac-colored silk gown, slipped on at the last minute in an effort to keep it clean. She's surprisingly still, not yet wriggling to get down. Lizzie, in a matching dress—a perfect princess dress according to her—is holding a basket of fresh flowers. Earlier today, Cindy borrowed some of the flowers and weaved them into a golden braid on top of Lizzie's head. Tommy, in khakis and a white button-down shirt, looks like a miniature version of his father. To me, they all look like the perfect definition of love.

Our friends, seated on white, wooden folding chairs, are smiling, the sun warming the crowns of their heads. But the emotion I feel is so much more than the widest smile, hotter than the sun. I look up at the sky, sure that my dad is looking down on me.

The sweet sound of "You Are So Beautiful" pours from speakers Tom set up on the patio earlier today.

Sam is by my side. He takes my arm in his. "You ready?" he asks.

I nod, and we begin to walk together, toward Adam, toward the renewal of our vows, the continuation of a love that has always been a part of the fabric of my being, the other half of my heart.

READING GROUP GUIDE

Discussion Questions

1. Would you say that seeing both Adam and Ellie's points of view gave you the experience of being a friend to both of the main characters? Were you personally invested in one character's story over the other or were you equally invested in both?

2. Since you get to know Adam and Ellie at their worst, do you find this makes them more or less sympathetic when you see them at their best? Discuss the moment you understood Adam's motivation and Ellie's motivation?

3. To some degree, everyone puts on a public face. Do you think that seeing inside Adam and Ellie's marriage gave you a new understanding of what other people might be going through in their relationships?

4. Would you say that Ellie's experience with motherhood is true to life? There is a scene where she gives Adam caretaking advice that will (and does) backfire on him. Could you relate to this impulse?

5. Bonnie Singleton is one of the most vivid side characters. Do you know a Bonnie Singleton? Was it satisfying to see her comeuppance? Do you think it will make a difference in the end? Will Bonnie strike back or move on to weaker prey?

6. After Jackie and Adam's first date, did you think they would make a go of it? Were you drawn to her girl-next-door charm? Was there ever a moment where you were rooting for Jackie and Adam? Why or why not?

7. Adam and Ellie live in an insular community that they feel oppressed by. However, this same community also contains their support system. How do Adam and Ellie reconcile that conflict? What does their story say about friendship, community, and keeping up appearances?

8. Adam and Ellie's backstory is told throughout the book in flashback. How does this information change your perception of the characters and their decisions at each new revelation? To what degree are their choices informed by their pasts?

9. Can you relate to Ellie's hesitation to tell Adam about her pregnancy? Was her fear of the consequences of telling the truth understandable? Did you agree with Ellie that there was never a good time to tell him?

10. What do you think about Adam's journey to heal his old wounds? Does this explain how he can forgive Ellie and agree to raise her child as his own?

11. How do you think things will work out for Adam and Ellie moving forward? Why and how will things be different for them? Where will they be in five years? In ten years? In twenty? Will these problems resurface or have they made them stronger?

12. If Olson were to write a sequel to their story, would you read it? Do you want to know more about these characters? Would you be interested in seeing what choices they make down the road?

13. "The Day You Left" can easily refer to several different people and situations throughout the storyline. Can you name them? Which one do you think Olson was referring to when she titled the book?